ENTANGLEMENT

A Hollywood Lights Novel

The Hollywood Lights Series
Book 1

KATIE ROSE PRYAL

Blue Osprey Books

Copyright © 2026 by Katie Rose Pryal and Pryal Consulting, Inc.

All rights reserved.

Pryal, Katie Rose Guest 1976-.

Entanglement : A Novel / Katie Rose Pryal.

ISBN Paper: 978-1-947834-80-4

ISBN Ebook: 978-1-947834-81-1

1. California—Fiction. 2. Friendship—Fiction. 3. Love—Fiction. I. Title

813'.6—dc23

Updated Blue Osprey Books Edition, 2026
First Blue Crow Books Edition, 2017
First published by Velvet Morning Press, 2015

Blue Osprey Books

Published by Blue Osprey Books,
a division of Pryal Consulting, Inc.
Chapel Hill, NC
blueospreybooks.com

Also by Katie Rose Pryal

NOVELS

Entanglement

Chasing Chaos

Fallout Girl

Take Your Charming Somewhere Else

NONFICTION

Life of the Mind Interrupted: Essays on Mental Health and Disability in Higher Education

The Freelance Academic: Transform Your Creative Life and Career

Even If You're Broken: Bodies, Boundaries, and Mental Health

A Light in the Tower: A New Reckoning with Mental Health in Higher Education

Your Kid Belongs Here: Parenting Neurodiverse Children

Praise for the Hollywood Lights Series

Entanglement is an evocative story of enduring friendship, rivalry, and the ties that bind. A heartfelt, fabulous novel!

> Bestselling author Diane Haeger for *Booktrib* Magazine

"*Entanglement* is a rich romance that had me hooked until the last page. Pryal's characters sparkle with charm and wit—I devoured the whole series!"

> Lucy Day, award-winning author of *My Star-Crossed Summer*

Women and men, love and obsession, need and want: *Entanglement* has it all!

> *USA Today* bestselling author Ann Garvin

Equal parts heartbreaking and heartening, *Entanglement* shines a light on the interior lives of two flawed and fascinating women.

> *Washington Post* bestselling author Camille Pagán

Poignant and thoroughly entertaining, *Love and Entropy* is a novella you won't be able to walk away from and you'll think about long after the last page. Fantastic read!

> *New York Times* bestselling author Kristy Woodson Harvey

Love and Entropy is utterly captivating ... Pryal writes with a rare understanding about the complexity of new adulthood and what it means to be a true friend.

In *Chasing Chaos*, Pryal pierces L.A.'s film industry veneer to find complex and relatable characters and then winches the ties between them, pulling the reader right into the fray. The result is as psychologically astute as it is engaging.

As glamorous and mercurial as Hollywood itself, *Chasing Chaos* is a novel that glitters.

In *How to Stay*, engaging characters lead the reader through a poignant and layered narrative about the universal desire for something so elusive—a safe place to fall.

How To Stay is an intelligent romance. The central tension isn't whether the girl will get the guy, it's whether she will let herself–something all readers can relate to and enjoy.

Modern, fresh, and entirely credible, *Fallout Girl* is a love story wrapped inside a heart-rending struggle for personal freedom.

For Michael, who believed in me

Author's Note

Content Warning

Some people, like me, need content warnings because they allow us to fully engage with and appreciate our world, including books.

This book contains a mention of sexual violence against a teenage girl, an on-page physical assault against an adult woman, and flashbacks to verbal abuse of children by their parents.

Greta's Undiagnosed Autism

Greta Donovan, the main character of this book, has undiagnosed autism.

Because her autism is undiagnosed, the word "autism" does not appear on the page. As an autistic author, I write Greta's story by drawing from my own experiences as an autistic person who went undiagnosed throughout childhood and much of her adult life.

Please note: even when a character's disability is undiagnosed and not mentioned on the page, writers still have a responsibility to portray the character and their disability with accuracy and respect.

Chapter One

GRETA

One Year Ago

When Greta Donovan turned her 1985 Ford Ranger into her parents' driveway, anger consumed her. Anger at her father, Jim, for being such an asshole, and at her mother, Beatrice, for letting him. It didn't matter that her mother was stuck in a hospice bed with an IV in her arm. At that moment, Greta hated her mother as much as she hated her father.

Most of all, she hated herself for feeling that way, knowing how close her mom was to dying.

She pulled to a stop in front of her parents' three-story Victorian.

"What a beautiful house." Sitting in the passenger seat, Daphne Saito, her best friend, sounded awestruck. "Look at those balusters on the porch. This place must be a hundred years old."

"Ninety-three," snapped Greta.

Daphne had once said that she could tell when Greta was upset: *You start spitting out numbers.*

Daphne was right. Numbers were easy. Predictable.

Right now, Greta was distraught. She didn't want to be here, and she didn't want Daphne here, either. Daphne was the best thing in her life. Inside that house was the worst.

"Why are we just sitting here?" Daphne asked.

"I'm deciding how badly I want my grandmother's furniture."

"Of course you want it! It's all you've talked about since you said you'd move in with me."

It was late May, the summer before their final year of college. Greta had to be out of her dorm in two days. Sutton, Daphne's now ex-boyfriend, was off to Wharton, so Daphne had asked Greta to move into her apartment. Now they were outside of Greta's family home to get the furniture her mother had said she could have, that Beatrice Donovan's own mother had received as a wedding gift when she was Greta's age.

Greta pointed at the two vehicles parked in the driveway. "The Porsche belongs to my father. He may or may not know we're coming, since the only person I informed was my mother. He's not pleasant when he's surprised. The Alfa Romeo piece of shit belongs to Anna, his research assistant girlfriend, who also has terrible automotive judgment."

"Excellent! You have two very good reasons to hate her."

"That's it," Greta said. "We're out of here." She stepped on the clutch and slipped the gearshift into reverse.

"No, Greta," Daphne said, touching Greta's arm. "Don't run away."

Greta turned off the engine and set the brake with an angry stomp.

Daphne got out of the car and waited. She was, as always, Greta's strongest supporter.

They stood side by side, facing the front porch.

"Greta," Daphne said. "Start walking."

She shook her head. She really didn't want to go inside. Forget the people—the memories alone were enough to frighten her.

Daphne held up her hand as Greta was about to speak. "Whatever is in there will not freak me out."

"How do you know?" She was afraid that after Daphne met her messed-up family, she wouldn't want to be her friend anymore. And at this point, Daphne was the only person who cared about her. Well, her mother cared, but her mother was nearly a nonentity.

This was Greta's problem with Beatrice. She was weak. Even when her mother had been healthy, Beatrice couldn't protect Greta from her father's cruelty.

Plus, if Beatrice had been stronger, she would never have let Jim steal her graduate school research, and Greta wouldn't have the burden of finishing it for her and exposing her father for the fraud that he is. Not that Beatrice ever asked her to. But Greta couldn't stand letting her father get away with stealing her mother's work.

"Because I never, ever freak out," Daphne said.

Daphne took Greta's hand and led her up the porch steps, then she rang the bell.

The door opened immediately. Her father must have heard her pull up and waited by the door. Greta's old pickup wasn't exactly quiet.

Greta watched Daphne assess her father: Dr. Jim Donovan. Decorated professor of physics and inductee of the National Academy of Sciences. Tall, six-foot-five, towering over both of them, even Greta herself, and she was six feet tall. His hair was reddish-brown, like hers, but speckled with silver. His jaw was strong and stubborn, and he was handsome. Greta wished she'd inherited at least some of her parents' beauty. But instead, she was a funny mix of both.

When his dark brown eyes fell upon her, they narrowed. Greta gritted her teeth and stood taller. She would not let him intimidate her.

"Did Mom tell you I was coming?" she asked. She made no move to enter the house, and her father made no gesture to welcome them in.

"She mentioned it last night, but she didn't say when. In the future, please call before coming over."

Greta stared at her father, a silent stalemate.

Daphne cleared her throat, which caught Greta's attention, and Greta took the cue. "Dad, this is Daphne."

Daphne held out her hand, forcing politeness upon her father. Greta wondered for a moment whether he would refuse to shake it. He was such a dick.

"Professor Donovan," Daphne said. "It's nice to finally meet you." As Daphne shook her father's hand, she met his eyes directly, like she was daring him to be rude to her, too.

"You're the one with the apartment." His tone sounded like an accusation.

"That's right." Daphne gave him the smile she used—with great effectiveness—on every difficult professor. Greta almost snorted. Her father, like all self-centered, decorated academics at Cameron University, had a weakness for gorgeous students.

After all, one was in the house right now.

For a moment, her father paused, open-mouthed, stunned by Daphne.

Squeezing her lips together, Greta suppressed a laugh. Finally, she interrupted the moment. "I'm going to talk with Mom," she told him. "We won't be here long."

"Fine." Jim snapped back to reality and stalked into the kitchen.

Daphne rolled her eyes and gave Greta a reassuring smile.

For not the first time, Greta wished she had Daphne's bravery. Daphne wasn't intimidated by Jim Donovan because Daphne wasn't intimidated by anyone.

The interior of her parents' house was as objectively magnificent as the exterior—heart-pine floors, tall moldings painted glossy white, and a grand curved staircase leading to the second floor, its dark handrail gleaming.

Voices echoed from the kitchen, a man's—Jim's—and a woman's.

Daphne nodded toward the voices. "That must be Anna from Argentina. With the terrible automotive judgment."

"Honestly," Greta said. "An Alfa Romeo?" She clomped up the stairs, making no effort to quiet her footsteps. "The perfect look-at-me car for a damsel in distress. Gross."

Greta knew why Daphne was sympathetic to Greta's situation. Daphne's own father was also a bully, and her mother, although not sick like Greta's mom, was similarly unable to stand up to her husband, even at those moments when a mother should.

Like Greta, Daphne had been hurt by her father. Deeply.

Perhaps she and Daphne were trauma-bonded, but she didn't care. Daphne understood her better than anyone on earth. Daphne didn't ask for deep explanations that Greta wouldn't be able to give. Such as proof that growing up with a family that could have given her anything—they were certainly wealthy enough—actually gave her so little.

At the top of the stairs, they entered a light-filled room. In a hospital bed, her mother, a frail woman with thin blond hair, lay with her eyes closed. Her mother's hair had only recently started regrowing after she stopped her cancer treatments. An IV drip hung from an electronic dosing machine that beeped every few seconds.

"Mom," Greta said.

Beatrice Donovan's eyes opened, and Greta met bright green eyes that matched her own, the only resemblance between her and her mother.

Greta introduced Daphne, and Beatrice smiled, holding out her hand.

Stepping forward, Daphne squeezed it in greeting. "It's so lovely to finally meet you."

"We're here to pick up Nana's furniture," Greta said. "Thanks for letting me have it."

"It's always been yours." Beatrice smiled, gesturing at a Queen Anne loveseat pulled close to the bed for visitors.

Not that Beatrice got many of those.

After a long pause, Greta asked, "How are you feeling?"

"The hospice drugs are fabulous." Beatrice pointed at the IV. "Now that I've given up on the chemo, it's pretty smooth sailing." Beatrice turned to Daphne. "I have terminal leukemia. I might die in six weeks, or I might die in a year. But I'm not going to get better. I figure we might all be honest about it."

Greta blushed furiously, glancing at Daphne. Talking about death so frankly would definitely freak out most people. But not Daphne. Of course not. Instead, Daphne put her hand on top of Greta's and squeezed.

Beatrice looked at Greta intently. "Have you had a chance to read the notebooks?"

She shook her head.

To Daphne, Beatrice said, "I gave Greta my grad school notebooks. She doesn't want to read them because she's afraid that she won't understand my research."

Daphne and Beatrice laughed as though the notion were

preposterous. But Greta had a plan. She needed more than an undergraduate degree in physics to take down one of the most towering minds in the field.

"Read them soon," Beatrice said. "I'm interested to know what you think about my work."

"I'll read them." Greta cleared her throat. "Anna's downstairs."

"I know."

"And it doesn't bother you?" Greta tried to keep the annoyance from her voice, but failed.

"I don't think any woman actually *wants* her husband's trampy graduate student eating off of her fine china. But short of breaking it all, there's not much I can do about it."

"You could tell her to go."

"Only if she comes up here." Beatrice's eyes narrowed. "Which she does not."

For the first time in a while, Greta recognized toughness in Beatrice. Anna stayed downstairs because she was terrified of a bedridden woman. And she should be.

"What do you two have planned for after graduation?" Beatrice asked.

"I'm moving to Los Angeles," Daphne said. "I'm trying to convince Greta to come with me."

Greta rolled her eyes.

"You should go," Beatrice said, with more force than seemed possible given her slender frame.

"Why?" Greta asked, sounding incredulous.

"Because I love you. And this seems like a path that will change you in unpredictable ways. I took a path like that once, and I've never regretted it."

"Great! It's settled then," Daphne said. "One more year at Cameron and it's off to Hollywood!"

"Hardly," Greta muttered.

Beatrice smiled. "The furniture is still in your room, all ready for you. I know you don't want to stay in this house any longer than necessary."

Greta stood, and Daphne did the same.

"Remember I love you," Beatrice said, her smile fading.

"I love you too." Greta turned to leave the room. Then she paused and ran to her mother's bedside, embracing her. She had a horrible feeling that she would never see her again.

Beatrice wrapped her frail arms around Greta. "Goodbye," Beatrice said, kissing Greta's forehead.

In the hall, Greta wiped away tears. Daphne remained silent, thankfully. "This way," she said, leading Daphne into the bedroom next door, bare of decoration, the full bed stripped of linens. "This was my room."

"Where's all your stuff?" Daphne asked.

"When I came home for Thanksgiving my first year, everything was gone. I didn't ask. I'd brought the important things with me to college. Who cares about back issues of *Scientific American*?"

Greta was trying to sound brave, but when she'd come home for break to find her room bare of any trace of herself, she'd walked out the front door and into the wooded yard and sobbed. How could her father hate her so much that he wanted to erase her from his house?

"Let's move the desk first," Daphne said. "It looks easiest."

They lifted the desk, heavier than it appeared, and started down the stairs. In the foyer, they set it down and rested for a moment.

"Hola, Greta." Anna stood in the kitchen doorway, her thick blonde hair pulled into a ponytail.

She looked no more than thirty years old. Her nose was slender and straight, her eyebrows perfect blonde wings above her blue eyes.

"Oh—" Anna said, walking into the foyer. "It's the furniture from the bedroom upstairs, no?"

"The furniture from my bedroom, yes," Greta said.

"It is so, so beautiful. Look at those delicate inlays. I just love Art Deco. Don't you?"

"Not really."

Greta didn't give a fig about Art Deco. She valued craftsmanship, not stylishness.

The inlays Anna admired radiated from the center of the drawer in an oval, a sunburst of delicate pale wood. Each tiny piece had been hand-chiseled, hand-sanded, hand-glued, then rubbed with wax until it gleamed—nearly a century ago, for Greta's grandmother.

As they walked back up the stairs, Greta felt a familiar churning in her gut. Things were about to go badly.

"Prepare yourself," Greta said. "My dad's going to be waiting for us."

Daphne nodded gravely. "Anna wants the fancy furniture to go with her fancy nose job?"

Greta nodded. "That's my guess. I'm going to have to bargain away something to keep this stuff. Just let it go, okay?"

Putting her hands on her hips, Daphne stared out the window. Greta knew the expression on her friend's face. She was trying to figure out how to say something in a way that Greta would believe.

"Your father is afraid of you. Do you know that?"

Greta snorted and shook her head. "That's preposterous."

"Think, Greta. He's like the Wizard of Oz, and you see behind the curtain. He's a coward, an adulterer. A thief. Most people can't see it. And the rest are too scared to say it." Daphne rested her hands on Greta's shoulders. "But see through him. And you aren't afraid of him."

Greta wasn't so sure about the second part. She was always afraid of her father, right?

Wasn't she?

No. She was no longer afraid. Nevertheless, standing up to him was pointless. "What's the point, Daph? We'd fight, he'd throw me out, and we'd be right back to where we are right now. Powerless in his flying-monkey kingdom."

Daphne nodded. "Fair enough."

But Greta had a sense that Daphne wasn't satisfied with Greta's answer.

They tackled the dresser next, setting the six drawers on the floor to lighten it. As they wrestled it down the stairs, Greta walked backward and bore most of the weight.

When they set down the dresser, her father was waiting by the front door. Anna watched from the kitchen.

"Why are you taking that furniture?" her father asked.

"Mom said it was mine, from Nana."

"Don't you think you should have asked me before dragging it down the stairs?"

Greta glared at him. It didn't matter that she'd announced when they'd first arrived that she was here for the furniture. He changed the narrative to suit his purposes.

And now, once again, she would have to give up something of herself to satisfy him. To barter. Her father always used money and precious things to control her. His controlling nature was why she'd bought her own car. She battled for every bit of independence she could get.

He crossed his arms. "It's in my house, so it belongs to me, and I say whether it stays or goes."

When Greta glanced at Daphne, Daphne nodded, a gesture to convey two things: First, that her was indeed an asshole, and second, that whatever Greta chose to do, Daphne would support her.

Jim put his hand on the desktop. "I will not allow you to take this furniture."

Greta knew that Anna had changed her father's mind about the furniture. Until Greta arrived today, it was beneath his notice. Now, it had power.

"Unless," her father said, "you apply to and enroll in the doctoral program in physics here at Cameron. No flitting off to MIT or Stanford."

And here was the bargain. Control, like always. She simply stared at him, waiting for more. There was always more.

He said, "I only want what's best for you. Cameron is the right fit."

And there it was. How he justified his behavior. In his twisted logic, it was always for her benefit.

She almost snorted. He was so arrogant. But she didn't want to study in her father's program. Her plan—exposing him—would never work if he were looking over her shoulder.

She glanced at the furniture, which somehow appeared dirty in the foyer light.

"No," Greta said. "I'm leaving now, and I'm not coming back. Ever."

"Then the furniture stays."

She ignored him. His manipulation didn't work on her, not

anymore. "Remember, Mom doesn't want lilies at the funeral. She says they're too depressing."

Anna lowered her eyes when Greta said the word *funeral*.

Her father's face dropped. "I...I am aware of that." If she didn't know him better, she'd swear he looked sorrowful.

Pulling the long, narrow drawer from the desk, the one with the inlays that Anna had admired, Greta held the drawer close. She ran her thumb over the inlays, bidding them goodbye.

Then, she threw the drawer on the floor with all her strength, smashing the dovetails to pieces, splitting the sunburst in half.

She stalked from the house, and Daphne followed on her heels.

In the truck, Greta's hands shook so violently she couldn't insert the key in the ignition. Daphne took the keys and did it for her.

"I'm never coming back here again," Greta said.

"I know." Daphne's voice was soothing.

"It doesn't mean I don't love my mom."

"I know. And your mom knows it, too. That's why she said goodbye."

Chapter Two

GRETA

July 1999

On a blistering Saturday in early July, Greta turned her pickup truck down an alley just off of Melrose, an interminable concrete strip lined with two-meter-tall iron gates and faceless garage doors. At the correct address, she spied the open back door to the duplex through a metal gate. Rolling down her window, she called out, "Daph! Open up!"

After the gate clanked open, she pulled into the carport next to Daphne's Honda Civic. Daphne had moved out to L.A. one month earlier, right after college graduation, and stayed with a friend from college while searching for an apartment for them. Two days ago, as soon as Daphne told her she'd found a place, Greta packed her truck and left.

Breathing a sigh of relief, Greta was grateful that the long drive was finished and that a continent now lay between her and her father. She was leaving all of her ghosts behind.

Even the living ones. Her mother still held on, despite the doctor's predictions. They'd spoken on the phone, but Greta had never gone home again after that awful day when she'd finally stood up to her father.

She tucked her chin-length, curly red hair behind her ears and plucked her sweaty tank top from her belly. Her truck's air conditioning had conked out at the California state line, and in summer, the heat of the desert was severe.

"Greta!" Daphne ran through the open door, skipped down the steps, and jumped into a hug. As they embraced, Greta became self-conscious about what she called her *chronic outsizedness*. Greta considered herself an anomaly: nearly six-feet-one and not in the small-boned way that would let her pass for willowy. *My body is positively Euclidean*, she used to say in college, gesturing to the sharpness of her elbows and hips, the squareness of her shoulders.

Daphne told her to knock it off because she was beautiful. Daphne was lying, but Greta appreciated the effort.

"I knew you'd be early," Daphne said. "You're always early."

"I'm only half an hour early. Besides, that's better than always being—"

"I am *not* always late." She set her hands on her hips. "I always arrive just in time."

Greta suppressed a laugh. "You arrived just in time to prevent me from getting heat stroke."

Daphne rolled her eyes and hooked her arm through Greta's, leading her to their apartment door.

Assessing her surroundings, Greta strolled through their new, very empty apartment, located in the back half of the duplex. "You should have the southern bedroom." A privacy fence blocked the light in the northern one. Daphne, like a plant, needed sunlight to thrive, but Greta herself couldn't care less.

When Greta entered the bathroom, the toilet was running. She imagined a water bill here would be large, given Los Angeles's endless water shortages. She lifted the lid from the tank.

"Anything interesting in there?" Daphne asked with a laugh.

Greta nodded at the running water. "There are mineral deposits caked on the valve flapper, breaking the seal. A six-dollar repair."

"I was hoping someone left behind their pot stash."

Greta flipped the ceramic lid over to peek at the bottom, then looked closely into the tank. "Nope. We'll have to ask your boyfriend to buy some for us."

"What boyfriend?"

"Whichever one sells pot?"

Daphne waited until Greta lowered the lid back onto the toilet, then punched her on the arm.

The interior walls were painted an uninspired chalky white, and the hardwood floors were dull with age. But they were clean.

"Well? Do you like it?" Daphne gestured to the space.

Greta nodded. No bugs, no leaks (except the running toilet), no funny smells. Greta's standards weren't low, but she often had to make the best of things. In that, she and Daphne were a lot alike.

"I'm so happy you're here," Daphne said, her brown eyes warm.

The words made Greta feel welcomed, wanted, accepted. Loved. Things she'd rarely felt in her life, but that Daphne always made her feel.

Back out in the carport, Daphne looked in the bed of Greta's truck, aghast. "Is this all you brought?"

"We've lived together for a year. This is all I have. My dad threw out the rest. You know that."

"It just looks like so little."

Greta shrugged. At least she was able to take off for L.A. without feeling like she'd left behind anything important. Except for the one thing she chose not to think about—her dying mother.

"I hate him," Daphne said quietly. "But don't worry, I have enough crap for both of us. Except for furniture. We'll need to track down some of that."

"Some ugly furniture," Greta said.

Daphne nodded in agreement. "Truly hideous."

After Greta destroyed her grandmother's desk because her father tried to manipulate her with it, they made a vow that no furniture they owned would ever be beautiful.

Daphne helped her carry in her two boxes of books—an eclectic mix—books by Penrose and Hawking and Einstein that had been her mother's, and Greta's physics textbooks from college.

They carried in two suitcases of Greta's clothes and one duffel bag full of Greta's beloved shoes, her only vanity.

Finally, Greta pulled the box of her mother's graduate school notebooks from the passenger seat. Greta still hadn't opened the notebooks, but she knew what they contained because her mother often talked about them, chiding her to read them, daring her to understand the complex theorems inside.

In the north-facing bedroom, Greta set the box of notebooks on the closet floor and pushed it back against the wall.

In Greta's sophomore year, when her mother first gave her the notebooks, they felt like an incredible gift. Later, once Greta returned to school, the notebooks felt like an incredible burden, too. She stashed them in the back of her dorm room closet and formed her plan to avenge her mother.

Jim always acknowledged that Beatrice had been the most brilliant student in their doctoral program at MIT. But Beatrice had dropped out just before finishing her degree. Then, a few years later, Greta's father published a paper on a new elementary particle and began to rise through the ranks of the scientific community. But Greta wasn't proud of her father's success. No. Greta knew, without any doubt, that her mother's name should have been listed as an equal co-author on her father's work.

Now, she'd graduated with her undergraduate degree in physics, but she still didn't feel ready. She would get one chance to bring down the illustrious Professor Jim Donovan. She needed a doctoral degree, or no one would take her seriously.

A familiar fear ate at her now. Should she have applied to graduate schools instead of moving cross-country on a whim? Greta didn't do whims. She liked plans, and right now she had no plan for her future at all.

She didn't tell Daphne about how unsure she felt about the move. She was here—for now, at least. Besides, the application cycle for graduate school would take another year. She could get some distance from her family and her father's reputation before applying. She'd have to leave Daphne behind, too, which seemed unimaginable. She couldn't share her worries with Daphne. Her leaving would break Daphne's heart as much as her own.

"That's the last of it." Daphne's voice broke into her thoughts. Standing in the doorway of Greta's bedroom, Daphne jangled Greta's car keys in her hand.

Suppressing feelings of guilt at keeping a secret from Daphne for the first time since they'd met, Greta followed her into the sunlight.

"Fair warning," Daphne said as Greta followed her to their landlord's door to sign the lease. "Our landlord is creepy."

"Creepy how?"

"He's xenophobic, pushy, and nosy."

Greta shrugged. "He sounds like a landlord." She paused. "And my dad."

"At least he gave us a break in the rent," Daphne said. "And I also bargained us the back patio and carport, and a six-month lease to give us more flexibility."

"Is it possible you're being too hard on him?"

Daphne threw Greta a glance. "I'll let you decide." Then she knocked on the front door of the duplex.

"Hello, hello!" The man who answered was about five-feet-six, with dark hair and a permanent tan. Opening the door wide, he nodded at Daphne and then introduced himself to Greta. "I am Marcellus Skiadas."

"Thank you for renting us the apartment," Greta said.

"Of course! Anything for Daphne."

Greta eyed Daphne, who had clearly made judicious use of her charm on this man.

"Are you American?" Marcellus asked Greta.

Startled by the question, Greta nodded slowly. "Yes. And you're from Greece?"

"No," Marcellus said.

"Cyprus, then?"

"Yes! A smart girl." Turning, he led them into his home.

Greta smiled stiffly. Greta's father used to call her *smart girl* as though the phrase were oxymoronic.

But no. Marcellus wasn't her father. He seemed to be a cheerful older man who was a little too nosy, like Daphne said.

After inviting them to sit at his kitchen table, Marcellus pulled out two copies of the lease.

Greta read every word of it. Daphne had already signed her legal name, *Akane Saito*, on both copies.

Daphne had changed her name in high school after her father had harmed her deeply. For Daphne, her new name represented rebirth. And freedom from her father's tyranny.

They might not look like a matching pair on the outside, but she and Daphne were much alike on the inside.

Greta signed her name next to Daphne's in a boxy scrawl.

Marcellus took one copy of the papers and pushed the other to Daphne. "I expect no problems from you. You are sensible girls." Marcellus shook his head. "The last girls I rented to were always making strange noises late at night."

"There won't be any problems," Daphne said. "I promise."

IT WAS A SHORT DRIVE TO THE APARTMENT WHERE DAPHNE HAD BEEN subletting a room. Once there, Greta stood in the doorway of Daphne's bedroom, taking in the chaos. "I don't think you bought enough laundry baskets." Greta nudged a pile of clothing with her toe. More piles lined an entire wall of the room. Against another wall was a folding table with Daphne's laptop and scattered papers, and against the window was a full-sized bed.

"We can also use pillowcases. Plus, the bed isn't mine, so we don't have to move that. That's good, right?"

"It's good not to have to move a bed," Greta said. "It is not good to *have* no bed."

"Right. Bummer. But we'll make do!" Daphne stepped into the room, laundry basket in hand, and began heaping things into it.

Smiling, Greta followed with another basket. Daphne was right. They always made do.

After an hour, they finished loading Daphne's things in the truck, then started the half-mile drive back to their new home.

When they were almost home, Greta pulled over. On the curb was a cane-bottomed armchair with a sign that read "Free to Good Home." When Greta inspected the chair, she noticed that a front leg had split.

"It's totally broken, Greta," Daphne said, bending down to survey the damage.

"I'm more worried about whether we qualify as a *good home*."

Daphne looked indignant. "We would take excellent care of this chair."

"Is it ugly enough, though?"

Daphne tapped her lip. "I think those are cherubs carved onto the back."

Greta leaned in to examine the hideous baby angels. "Excellent. Plus, it's made of solid walnut, which means I can repair it." She loaded the chair into the truck bed alongside Daphne's things.

Back at the duplex, they unloaded quickly. Once everything was inside, Greta did a quick survey of their things: they had one lamp, one folding table Daphne used as a desk, Daphne's well-worn desk chair that used to belong to her boss, and the broken, cane-bottomed armchair. They did not have a sofa, a coffee table, a kitchen table or chairs, dishes, utensils, or beds.

"Come here!" Daphne called from her room. As Greta entered, Daphne shook out her bright yellow comforter and laid it on the floor. She picked up her two pillows and dropped them onto the comforter. Then Daphne lay on her back, arms spread wide. On the yellow bedspread, her black hair shone like the center of a sunflower.

"We'll sleep here for now," Daphne said. "Who needs a bed?"

Greta cracked a smile. Maybe things would be all right after all.

———

AT EIGHT A.M. ON MONDAY, WHEN DAPHNE'S ALARM CHIMED, GRETA was already awake, body stiff. Sleeping on the floor was all right in theory, but in reality, it kind of sucked. She shook Daphne's arm to make sure she woke and then headed to the shower.

A few moments later, Greta heard the sink turn on. "Hey," Daphne said, sounding sleepy.

"Hey." Greta opened the shower curtain a bit so they could talk. "When do we need to leave by?"

"Nine, if we want a coffee stop."

They always wanted a coffee stop.

Today, Daphne was bringing Greta to work with her. Before Daphne moved to L.A., she'd landed her job, so she'd been working for a month already. Her boss was a low-level producer, and his office was in Venice Beach, far from the Universal lot in North Hollywood where his corporate overlords worked. The neighborhood was up-

and-coming at best, Daphne told her, but the office was only two blocks from the ocean, which Greta was looking forward to seeing. She loved the ocean.

"Today, we will find you a job." Daphne sounded confident.

"Probably not," Greta replied. "But that's all right. I have enough money saved to pay rent and buy food for three months. Four, if I'm really careful."

"Or, if you let me pay a larger portion of the rent, even longer than that."

Greta clenched her jaw. She knew Daphne didn't mean any harm by offering to pay Greta's fair share. Daphne would never attach strings to a favor. But the visceral response was hard to overcome, a rejection of anything that could be used to control her. Gifts. Money. She couldn't bear it after a lifetime with her father.

"Daphne," Greta said. "I can pay my way."

Meeting Greta's eyes, Daphne said, "Of course you can. But Greta—someday you'll realize that a person might want to help you just because they love you. And you should let them."

As Greta rinsed the conditioner from her hair, Daphne's words echoed in her mind.

After showering, Daphne dressed in a knee-length red skirt, a black blouse with a ruffled neckline, and black leather boots. Her appearance was flawless.

Greta put on her uniform: jeans—men's Levi's 501s—and zip-up ankle boots. Her black tank top revealed her slender but muscular arms.

"Do I look okay?" Greta gestured at herself, feeling the familiar uncertainty about her appearance. "I brought a sweater to throw on in case I need to look nicer."

"You look perfect," Daphne said.

And Greta could tell Daphne meant it.

———

Greta first met Daphne back at Cameron University during summer school after their first year of college. It was a sweltering North Carolina day in June, ninety-five degrees easy, driving summer school students to the college pool. Greta wished the pool were less crowded because she didn't come to play. She came for her daily workout. The Cameron pool was an old rectangle, with a single lane rope running down the middle. On one half of the pool, professors played with their kids, and college students cooled off. The other half was for lap swimming.

Kicking off her flip-flops on the pool deck, she dropped her towel on top, then stripped off her t-shirt and shorts, revealing the one-piece suit underneath. She pulled on her swim cap and goggles, then dove into the pool, flying above the words painted on the deck that proclaimed *No Diving*.

As she swam, falling into the soothing rhythm, a familiar sight caught her eye—a bright yellow umbrella set up next to the pool, glowing like a second sun. It was impossible to miss, even during the brief moments she turned to the side to breathe. She'd seen it at the pool frequently that summer.

Forty-five minutes later, Greta finished and climbed from the pool. As she dried with her towel, a strange girl stepped into her line of sight.

"How far did you swim today?" The girl was Asian and absolutely stunning. Greta felt the strange need to step back, but stopped herself because she knew it would be weird. She did a lot of things that other people thought were weird.

"Thirty-two hundred yards."

"Two whole miles?" the girl said, seeming amazed.

Greta replied, "Two miles is three thousand, five hundred, and twenty yards."

Chewing on her thumbnail, the new girl examined Greta so closely she started to fidget.

"My name is Daphne." The girl held out her hand. After a moment, Greta shook it. The girl continued, "I'm an English major. What's yours?"

"Physics." As though there were ever any doubt. Her father only agreed to cover her tuition if he chose her major, and she attended Cameron. Her residual anger toward him must have shown on her face.

"Do you not like physics?"

Greta shook her head. "That's not it. I was accepted to Princeton, a much better program, but my father insisted I attend Cameron because my tuition is free. He's a professor here." She stabbed the toe of her flip-flop into the pool deck. "I really wanted to go to Princeton." Her father refused to pay for Princeton, of course, and his name was on her financial aid application—along with his salary, which bumped her out of the running for any need-based scholarships. Even if she got a merit scholarship, she'd be on her own for all other expenses. So she caved to him, like she always did.

Greta noticed the other girl staring at her, as though she were a mystery that needed solving. It made her skin crawl. "I...it was nice to meet you." She turned quickly to go.

"Wait," the girl called out. "Do you want to sit?" She pointed at the yellow umbrella, casting cool shade on two pool loungers. "I don't like to get too much sun."

Greta gestured at her pale, freckled skin. "Me neither." After a long hesitation, Greta agreed. She didn't have many friends.

Lie. She didn't have any friends. Daphne drew her somehow, like they already knew each other and could skip the pleasantries.

Greta hated pleasantries.

As they lounged in the chairs, Daphne told Greta she grew up near the beach.

"No one at Cameron knows where I really come from," Daphne told her. She gestured at the umbrella. "I know I should get over it, but the sun-avoidance is a holdover from my parents' prejudices about skin color."

Greta raised her eyebrows.

"I'm the oldest of four daughters, and my skin is the darkest. My father never lets me forget it." Daphne laughed, but there was bitterness underneath. "When I would stay out in the sun too long, he'd say I looked like a peasant. Meanwhile, I spent my entire childhood changing sheets in my family's run-down motel. He literally treated me like a peasant."

"Why are you telling me this?"

Daphne tilted her head. "I have a feeling."

Greta drew her brows together. "That's not a good enough reason to trust someone."

"Are you going to tell anyone?"

Greta shook her head. "Of course not." Greta nodded at Sutton, Daphne's boyfriend, who was talking to the lifeguard. "Even he doesn't know?"

"Especially not him," Daphne said.

Greta wanted to ask why not, but she didn't know how. She could tell the topic was sensitive. Instead, she said, "I love swimming in the ocean."

"I like it too," Daphne replied. "You'd think it might get old after living there your whole life, but it doesn't. Every time it's a little bit scary because the ocean is so big. The water connects to everything, every part of the world." She laughed. "You could say that the scope of it is overwhelming. But at the same time, that overwhelmingness is exactly what comforts me."

Greta was startled by Daphne's words because she felt the exact same way. About the oceans. About the entire cosmos.

After that day, they became close friends and then roommates. Daphne taught Greta how to style her hair properly so her curls would look pretty. She helped Greta buy clothes she actually liked and that looked good on her.

She also insisted that Greta was beautiful, which Greta appreciated even if she didn't believe it.

And as Greta got to know Daphne and learned of the horrible things she'd endured as a child, Greta taught Daphne that she was more than a pretty girl who was empty inside, having been sucked dry by the burdens of her family.

Now, years later, in another city across a continent, they were still keeping each other steady. Greta was honest enough with herself to know that she came to Los Angeles in part because she didn't know how to live in a world without Daphne. Daphne was her family. Her only family.

Chapter Three

GRETA

After they were ready to go, Greta folded herself into the passenger seat of Daphne's Honda Civic, and they sped south toward the Santa Monica Freeway. Daphne explained directions to Greta as she drove, how the freeway would take them west to Venice Beach.

"Are you sure it's okay to bring me to work with you?" Greta asked.

"Of course! I'm the best production assistant he's ever had, so he keeps me happy."

Greta glanced at Daphne. "And just how serious is his crush on you?"

Daphne laughed. "Maybe an eight out of ten?"

Greta snorted. "And now we get to the real reason."

Faking insult, Daphne said, "I really am the best production assistant."

"Of course you are. Is that why you get to roll in at ten a.m.?"

Acting affronted, Daphne said, "My work hours are ten to seven, thank you very much."

"But why?"

"Marco likes to say that because he made it big, he never has to sit in traffic again."

"But I thought he mostly did small stuff."

"In L.A., sweetie, *making it big* is relative. He created a couple of really successful television series in the late eighties. Sure, now he only works on made-for-TV movies and low-budget stuff like that. But I'm not complaining." She gestured out the window. "We're not sitting in a freeway parking lot, are we?"

No, they weren't. Daphne was speeding along like she always did, pushing ninety.

"But he also owns a restaurant, right?" Greta asked.

"It's kind of a scam," Daphne said. "Universal pays my salary, but he also has a second, quote-unquote production assistant, Olivia. You'll meet her today. Her entire job is handling the restaurant."

"And no one notices?"

"We're far from the main Universal offices, and he's a small fish. A king of his own little kingdom."

"The worst kind," Greta muttered. Her father was the same, with the entire Cameron physics department under his command.

"You'll get to see Rivet soon. It's actually amazing."

Rivet—Marco's restaurant. Like Greta would ever be able to afford it. "I wish I already had a job," she said, fussing with the strap of her bag. "I should have applied months ago, like you did."

"Months ago, you were still lying to yourself that you weren't coming with me."

Greta rolled her eyes. Daphne was right, of course. But she also knew Daphne was sympathetic. Neither of them enjoyed instability. Or relying on others.

"Maybe a lab tech job at one of the universities?" Daphne suggested.

"They won't hire someone with only a bachelor's degree."

Daphne pointed to the back seat, where a folded newspaper lay. "That's the *L.A. Weekly.* Job listings are in the back."

Greta immediately snatched it and started reading.

The job ads were sorted by area of work—acting and modeling were listed first, but most of those ads said something like, *Models Wanted. Female. Some nude work.*

No thank you.

Then there were the professional listings, but most of those were sales jobs, and Greta was not a salesperson. A job where she would have to pressure a stranger to buy something they didn't need or want seemed more demeaning than *some nude work.* But because she was practical, she circled a few that said no experience necessary, or NEN.

After the professional jobs was a section called *Technical.* Greta wasn't sure what technical jobs were, since construction and other trades had their own section. The first ad under technical read: *Prod Ltg. FT tech hand. Live & film/vid. NEN. Venice.*

As they were pulling into a parking space, Greta asked, "Hey, what does this mean?" She pointed to the ad.

After she put the car in park, Daphne looked at the paper. "Production Lighting," she said. "That's a tech company."

"Yeah, but what's a tech company?"

"There are a lot of companies around here that support the industry," Daphne said.

"And this one does lighting?"

"Right. It's cheaper for smaller productions to hire subs than to stock their own gear. Lighting, audio, even camera gear. We let the contractors deal with the unions." Daphne studied the ad. "I wonder which shop this is. We use a lot of contractors on our small projects." She laughed. "And ours are all small projects. I probably know these people. They're located just south of here, closer to the airport."

"I think I'll call them," Greta said.

Daphne pinched her face with distaste. "Do you really want to do tech work? It's a lot of heavy gear and late hours."

Greta said, "I like circuits. It seems like there'd be a lot of circuits."

The girls cracked up at Greta's imitation of herself from years before.

The summer they first met, Daphne complained that an outlet in her apartment wasn't working. Greta was more than happy to fix it.

"It's this one here." Daphne pointed to the outlet next to her sofa. "Right where I write on my laptop. And I can't plug in!" She sounded very put out.

"Have you checked the fuse?" Greta asked, starting to troubleshoot.

"Yes."

Greta cocked an eyebrow. She didn't believe that Daphne had ever opened her fuse box.

"Well, Sutton checked the fuse, and he swears that's not the problem. He even took off the outlet cover thing and looked at the wires to make sure they're all connected."

Greta snorted. "Don't tell Sutton I told you this, but you can't see if the wires are connected if you only remove the cover plate."

Daphne sighed. "I'll get you a screwdriver. The fuse box is in the kitchen."

After Greta pulled the fuse to disconnect the circuit, Daphne stood over her while she worked. She removed the outlet from the wall, located the corroded wire, and reconnected it after stripping some insulation with her Leatherman tool.

"How do you know how to do this?" Daphne asked.

"I really like circuits." As Greta reinstalled the outlet, she became aware of the silence in the room. When she glanced at Daphne, her friend's face was blank, but Greta could see the laughter in her eyes. The laughter wasn't cruel, though.

At the time, even Greta knew she'd sounded weird. She was pretty normal compared to the other physics majors, but that wasn't saying much.

From that day on, she let Daphne guide her a bit. Daphne helped her learn what to share and what to keep to herself—without selling herself out. Daphne showed her which clothes looked better on her tall frame and which ones didn't. With Daphne, she discovered she loved shoes. Daphne pointed out her strengths, such as her arms and shoulders shaped by swimming and her long legs. So, she wore shirts that bared her arms and jeans that highlighted her legs, hoping to distract people from her otherwise mediocre appearance.

But Daphne insisted that nothing about her appearance was mediocre. She constantly called her *striking*. But that word bothered her. *Striking* seemed like a liability; she never wanted to be the center of attention.

On the sidewalk in Venice Beach, the cool morning was starting to give way to the heat of the day. She asked Daphne, "Can I use your cell phone? I'll call and see if the job is still open."

After Daphne handed over her phone, Greta dialed the number listed in the ad.

"Pac Lighting," a man answered.

"My name is Greta Donovan. You have a job listing in the *LA Weekly*."

There was a long pause. "I do."

"Oh, um." Greta wanted to throw the phone—of course the guy knew the company had a job listing. She hated talking to new people when she couldn't see their facial expressions to help interpret their words. And then she realized what he'd said exactly—*I do*. She was talking to the boss.

Now she really wanted to throw the phone. Or at least hang up and start over with another company.

But no. She really needed a job. "Can I come over and apply?"

"Sure," the man said. "I have time now."

Although the man's voice sounded young, it was strangely soothing to her, as if he were used to dealing with surprises and they didn't faze him. He definitely didn't seem to mind her awkwardness on the phone.

"Great, thank you. Um. I'm new to town?"

"No problem." Now she could hear a smile in his voice, but it was kind. He gave her careful directions to his office.

Maybe she was getting better at reading people on the phone after all.

Once she hung up, she handed the cell phone to Daphne in exchange for the car keys.

Daphne pointed to the narrow building she'd parked in front of. "This is where I work. When you're done, come back here and tell me all about it."

———

GRETA PARKED NEXT TO THE ONLY OTHER CAR IN THE LOT OF THE LARGE warehouse. The building was painted a dull gray, but the sign on the door told her she was in the right place—Pacific Production Lighting.

Pulling open the glass door, she was pleasantly surprised by the interior. Inside, pale wood floors greeted her, along with a waiting area of dark-blue furniture in mid-century style.

Dead ahead, the company's logo was projected on a tall white wall in brilliant color. She glanced up, expecting to see some kind of projector, but she saw a light fixture instead. It was long, maybe two and a half feet, and eight inches in diameter. The light coming from the back was white, so some kind of lens was creating the projection.

Moments later, a voice called out from across the room. "Greta Donovan?"

She looked over and inhaled sharply. The man was young, like she'd guessed from the phone call, mid-twenties maybe. He watched her silently, hands tucked in his jeans pockets. His slim black T-shirt emphasized his well-muscled arms and broad shoulders. He was at least an inch or two taller than she was, six-three maybe.

Her scalp tingled; her body warmed. She wanted to run her hands up his chest and wrap them around his neck, pulling him to her until they touched. She had never felt this way about a guy. The college boys were too annoying, and the few physics geeks she was friends with weren't so blatantly attractive.

Too attractive for her.

She looked away before her face gave away too much. "That's me."

Chapter Four

TIMMY

When Timmy Eisenhart, owner of Pacific Production Lighting, first spied the woman he was supposed to interview, he immediately had second thoughts. Not because she was a woman—no, she was tall and obviously strong, her top revealing well-toned arms and shoulders. She looked like she could sling gear as well as anyone.

The problem was that she was gorgeous.

He'd watched her from the doorway between the waiting room and the warehouse. Okay—he'd spied on her. She'd stood below a wall-mounted Source Four ellipsoidal fixture that projected his company logo, her head tilted back, eyes scanning it as though she were learning all its secrets.

Timmy was desperate for help because Julius, his right-hand guy, had quit unexpectedly the week before. Julius had auditioned for a part in a television pilot and got the job. Timmy hadn't even known Julius was interested in acting. But this was L.A., and he should have expected it.

Every damn person secretly wished they were an actor.

Only last month, Timmy had renovated the front of the warehouse. He and Julius (the jackass) laid wood floor and painted the walls and trim, adding a seating area too. Now, clients had a place to wait that was free of lights, light boards, cables, and truss.

As a finishing touch, Timmy had considered having a sign made with his company name to hang on the wall across from the front door, something impressive for clients to see when they first walked in.

Instead, he'd hung the Source Four, a stage light with a focusable lens, and used it to project the name and logo on the wall. Light shone through a gobo—a piece of specialized glass that held the image, kind of like a photographic slide. Timmy had spent a lot of time designing the image and paid three hundred dollars to have the gobo made. It was worth every penny. When you walked into the warehouse now, his logo glowed on the tall white wall, the letters alive with light.

When Greta tilted her head at the light fixture, examining it more closely, Timmy knew he had to hire her. When most people entered the shop, they stared at the projection, its arrays of blues and golds, fascinated by the magic the light created. Greta was fascinated by what was making the magic happen. That's what this work was about —the behind-the-scenes stuff that other people found boring.

It wasn't boring to Timmy. He smiled to himself. Working behind the scenes is what got him into this business in the first place. He enjoyed mystifying others. Working his magic.

He enjoyed making people happy.

"Greta Donovan?"

Quickly, the woman trained her eyes on him, bright green flecked with gold, and he was startled by their beauty.

At that point, Timmy got really worried. If he were smart, he would glance at Greta's resume, tell her she didn't have enough work experience, and send her away. Timmy was self-aware enough to know that he was instantly, wildly attracted to her. To her green eyes, her slender body, her direct stare, and her long, long legs.

"That's me," she said.

"Timmy Eisenhart. Come to my office, and we'll talk."

They sat across from each other at the large wooden table that served as his desk. Greta ran her hand down the rounded edge of the mahogany surface. "Wow," she said. "This is a nice piece."

Timmy drummed his fingers. "I got it from a developer who was tearing down a burned-out building near downtown. It was an old bank's conference table. It has some damage here." He pulled aside a file, revealing a water stain and a cloudy black spot where the finish had burned.

The developer was his Uncle Brian, now an L.A. city councilman. He'd always been close to his uncle, his father's brother. Uncle Brian had stepped in during the tough times of Timmy's childhood. Timmy's father, Brian's brother, was a semi-functional alcoholic. Sure, Timmy's father held down a job with a consulting firm, but at home, things could get bad. He'd had affairs—Timmy never asked how many, and he'd spent way too much money on things they didn't need.

But the worst part was when he would lose his temper with Timmy's mom. Frequently, his father would storm out after a fight, his mom begging him not to leave. He'd hear her crying in her room late at night. When Timmy was a little kid, he'd climb into bed with her to snuggle because she said his snuggles made her feel better. As he got older, he'd comfort her in other ways—cleaning the kitchen really well, doing the laundry, mowing the yard, and anything else he could think of that would make things better. Uncle Brian knew the score, and Timmy suspected the only reason their mortgage got paid during the toughest years was Brian's help. He also paid for his dad's rehab, which fortunately stuck, during Timmy's senior year of high school.

So now, whenever Uncle Brian came across something he thought Timmy might want, he gave him a call. The tall racks in his warehouse came from a superstore that got torn down. Lots of extra lumber that Timmy needed to build scenery. And the table that Greta was now caressing.

"The burn improves it, I think." Greta traced the outline of the burn. "Gives it history. Before the fire, it was just a table. Now it's something more."

Transfixed by her strong, slender fingers as they ran across the burned surface, Timmy wondered what they would feel like touching him. This woman was doing something to him. It was more than just simple attraction, although there was plenty of that. No. There was something more. The gobo, the table—she saw the things he loved the same way he did.

Greta spoke, pulling his thoughts from the gutter. "Would you like to see a resume?"

Grateful that Greta had spoken, since he'd apparently forgotten how, Timmy nodded. Digging into her bag, she pulled out a brown leather portfolio and handed him a single sheet of paper. He read that she was just out of college—a very nice college—and had worked as a research assistant in a lab while a student. She'd just moved to L.A. and had an address off Melrose, a spot not far from where he lived. She'd majored in physics, but she had no experience in production. Most of his crew, even those with no paid experience, had worked for their high school or college theaters before coming to him.

"Why do you want to work with lights?" Timmy asked.

"I don't know a lot about your equipment, but I know a lot about electronics and power usage—I can wire things. I also know about light projection and color." She laughed. "However, most of *that* knowledge is theoretical."

Timmy paused a moment to soak in the sound of her laughter. It lit him up. When he found his voice again, it sounded gruff to his own ears. "You know this is physical work. The gear is heavy."

"I can lift it." Greta didn't bristle at the implication that she might not be strong enough. Instead, she made an unemotional statement that the implication was wrong.

With that, she passed his final test. She had to be confident and emotionally tough. She'd be the only woman on his crew in a field that was predominantly men, and he didn't want her getting upset if one of the idiots on a job said something stupid about girls and production work.

Of course, if that happened, he'd fire the asshole on the spot.

And now his heart was racing at the thought of this theoretical mistreatment of Greta by a faceless crew guy at some random point in the future.

He drew a deep breath to calm down. He was a laid-back guy, but Greta's presence was screwing with his head.

Again, he wondered if he should send her on her way. Seriously. If she were this distracting during a job interview, he couldn't imagine what it would be like to have her around all the time.

It would either be fantastic or a total disaster.

Uncle Brian would tell him to take a chance. Be brave.

So he told her the starting rate for his full-time crew—desperately low for such an expensive city—but she didn't balk.

"Can you start tomorrow?" Timmy asked. "We have a show this weekend to prep for."

"Sure," she said.

He gave her some tax paperwork. "Just bring it with you when you come in tomorrow."

She slid the papers into her portfolio. As she moved, Timmy couldn't keep his eyes off of her. Her hair fell forward when she tilted her head, and she tucked a loose curl behind her ear. He had to sit on his hands to prevent himself from touching her.

He wanted to tuck that curl back himself. He wanted to skim his fingers up Greta's arm to her bare shoulder. He needed to know if her creamy skin felt as good as it looked.

He glanced away, annoyed with himself. He needed to get a grip. He was having completely inappropriate thoughts about a woman he'd just met. Thoughts about wanting to remove the woman's clothes and lay her down on his soot-stained mahogany desk.

He stood abruptly. This wasn't like him. She deserved better from her boss, and he would act professionally. He could give her that.

She stood as well, holding out her hand. They shook. Slowly, and with regret, he let go. Her hand felt just like he imagined it would— both strong and delicate at the same time.

Greta seemed confused when he released her. She looked down at the hand he'd shaken, as though expecting it to have changed color.

"Thanks for the job," she said. She eyed the doorway, as though getting ready to dash through it.

Timmy took a calming breath. "I'll show you out." He walked with her to the entrance. "The guys usually roll in around ten and stay till seven."

"Oh, that's perfect," she said, face brightening. "My roommate's work hours are the same. She and I can carpool. We live off Melrose— but you probably know that since you just saw my resume." She trailed off.

When their eyes met, her face flushed, and she quickly glanced down. She's nervous, he realized. He felt a spark of protectiveness ignite inside him. He wanted to make her comfortable. Happy, even.

He walked over to the light fixture that projected his logo and stopped. She examined it once more.

"You like the gobo?" Timmy asked her.

"What's a gobo?"

"It's a funny acronym—*goes before optics*. A piece of metal or glass that's placed between the lamp and the lens of a fixture. This one is made of glass."

"It must be a borosilicate glass, right?"

"I have no idea," he said with a laugh. "I flunked chemistry."

"It's a type of glass that has high thermal resistance. Ordinary silicate wouldn't work because of the extreme heat of that halogen bulb."

"Sure, that makes sense." He gave her a smile. "I'm starting to see how you will be very useful." He kept his smile reassuring and stepped back to give her more space. "You know, I have a little more time. Do you want a tour of the shop before you go?"

"Um, sure. I'd like that." She returned his smile, and it warmed something inside him. Glancing around, she said, "Where is everyone else?"

"We were out late at a show last night, so the guys won't get here till noon."

Greta glanced at her watch. He could see that it said eleven a.m. He didn't want her to feel nervous in the shop alone with him. "If you'd rather wait till tomorrow when the rest of the guys are here, that's fine too."

She shook her head. "No, I like how quiet it is. Let me call my friend to tell her I'll be a while longer."

He expected her to take the call outside, away from him, to tell her friend that she was alone with some strange dude, but she didn't.

She dug a cell phone from her bag and dialed. "Hey, Daph. Yeah. It went great, actually."

Timmy smiled at that.

"I'm going to stay a little while for a tour. Oh. It's called Pacific Production Lighting. Yeah. Near the airport, like you said. I'll call when I'm leaving. Yeah. Bye." Dropping the phone back into her bag, she turned to Timmy. "All set. She doesn't need her car back anytime soon."

"Cool. This way."

He led her back through the door, past his office, and into the warehouse. Glancing over, he watched her scan the racks that towered high with gear, the rolling ladders everywhere to let them access it.

"How big is the shop?" she asked, sounding surprised by the expanse in front of her.

"About ten thousand square feet."

"You have a massive amount of gear. It will take me a while to learn how all of this works. I hope that's okay."

Of course it was okay, Timmy thought. But a physics major from a top-five university probably held herself to some high standards. When she met some of the guys who worked for him, she'd feel a lot better about things.

"What are those?" she asked, pointing to two large shelves filled with two different types of lights—long, narrow ones like the one in the lobby projecting the gobo, and short, squat ones on stands that looked like small cauldrons with glass across the top.

"These are our conventionals," he said.

"What's conventional about them?" Greta asked.

"They're not automated. They just fart light."

"Fart?" She laughed, and he wanted to make her do it again.

"They're powerful, but they don't move like our automated lights."

As Greta followed Timmy on the tour, listening to his explanations and asking intelligent questions when he used unfamiliar words, he found himself drawn to her even more. It was the most enjoyable tour of his shop he'd ever given. A brilliant, gorgeous woman who wanted to know all about him and his work?

That was every man's dream.

"How did you get started doing this?" she asked. "You seem young to have such a large company."

Timmy laughed. "That's a direct question." When Greta said nothing, just chewed her lip, Timmy saw more of the awkward nervousness he'd noticed earlier. He found it utterly charming.

He explained. "When I graduated from college, I got a job with this guy named McGee. He'd been running Pac Lighting for over a decade. I was responsible and learned the complicated stuff quickly, so he promoted me to his second-in-command. Five years ago, McGee told me he was, quote, too old for this shit, and sold me the company."

This time, they laughed together.

It wasn't long before they were back at the front of the shop, and Timmy wished he could come up with another reason for her to stick around.

"Tomorrow at ten?" Greta asked.

"That's when I get here. And I have the key." Patting his pocket, he smiled.

As he took in her serious face, Timmy prayed he'd made the right choice hiring her. Julius's leaving had pissed him off, and the last thing he wanted was to waste his time training another employee who'd walk out. Greta was young and thus flighty by definition. But she seemed steadier than most people her age. Besides, he was only the ripe old age of twenty-seven. At her age, he was already preparing to take over for McGee.

Glancing at her green eyes again, he knew that the only problem with Greta's employment would be him and his ability to keep his hands to himself.

They said goodbye, and he watched her strong shoulders as she pushed open the glass door and stepped into the harsh sunlight. Through the open door came the roaring engines of an airplane taking off from nearby LAX. Then the door closed behind her, blocking the light and noise.

He knew Greta was inexperienced. For a while, he'd miss having Julius and his knowledge. But she didn't seem like someone who would walk away from a commitment unless she had a really good reason. His Uncle Brian had taught him that most people are decent, and the ones who aren't, well, you can just feel it.

But he needed to be honest with himself: he thought Greta was sexy as hell, and he would have to deal with those feelings sooner rather than later.

Chapter Five

GRETA

Greta struggled to focus on the directions back to Daphne's work. After making a second wrong turn, she pulled into the parking lot of a fast-food restaurant to look at the map. At least, that's what she told herself.

Be honest, she scolded herself. You're distracted by Timmy Eisenhart.

She really needed this job. But these thoughts—about Timmy's broad shoulders and gorgeous smile—were distracting her far too much.

Besides, a crush on Timmy was pointless. Not only was he her boss, which was wildly inappropriate, but he was out of her league. She had crushes over the years, but she never revealed her feelings because she knew they would never feel the same way about her. Guys might want to be her lab partner, even her friend—especially the other physics dorks—but none of them ever looked at her the way guys looked at Daphne, with heat in their eyes and hope on their faces.

But she really liked Timmy. Not just because he was handsome. During the tour, Timmy called the place his *shop*, as in workshop. She liked that word. It sounded practical, like *lab*. And she didn't expect to enjoy learning about the gear so much. After that tour, there was no way he'd ever feel attracted to her. Not only was she plain looking (and he was so, so not), but she would have freaked him out when she went on and on with questions and ideas.

She always screwed up conversations when she was nervous. She spent years saying too much, not realizing that her babbling made others uncomfortable. So, she learned to say very little, sometimes nothing at all. People thought she was standoffish, but that was better than being a supermassive loser, as her father once called her when no one asked her to prom.

Prom. Seriously.

At Timmy's, after she'd rambled on about how she'd love to chip in to help repair broken lights because she really enjoyed taking things apart and, oh god, she didn't want to even think about all the things she said, Timmy had watched her silently, his hands stuffed in his jeans pockets. Gradually, her words had petered out.

She wanted to touch him, but it was an impossibility.

Angry at herself for thinking such ridiculous things, she decided to put all thoughts of Timmy and touching and how hot he was out of her mind. He was her boss, and she was herself. Because even if he did feel that way about her, what then? A boss and a boyfriend, all in one? She couldn't bear the thought of one person having that much control in a relationship. Nothing would ever be in balance.

Closing the map, she pulled back out on the road to Daphne's work. She arrived at Marco Bertucci's office around noon.

From the outside, the building looked like a run-down brick warehouse, but when she pulled open the door, she gasped.

The inside was marvelous. The cement floors had been rubbed with a dark brown stain with a shiny finish, creating a rich surface marked with a half-century's worth of scrapes and divots. The walls were raw brick. The tall ceiling was painted black, and the beams and ductwork were exposed. Pendant lights hung every few feet from long cables that disappeared in the shadows above. The place was a superhero's lair: dark, sleek, and designed to intimidate.

"There you are!" Daphne said, standing behind her desk, a Scandinavian-style table easily three meters long. "Marco isn't here yet. He had a lunch meeting."

Greta shook her head in awe. "I can't believe how amazing this place is inside. The outside is a dump."

"Marco deliberately keeps the outside looking grim. He likes to think it throws people off, keeping them from knowing famous people might be inside."

"Ah, the anti-pretension," Greta said.

"The worst sort of pretension," Daphne finished for her. "But he has his good points too. You'll see."

Greta felt doubtful.

It must have shown on her face because Daphne piped up. "He gave me a chance in a tough business. He has his flaws, but he's harmless."

Across from Daphne's desk stood a set of tall double doors, closed. Unable to help herself, Greta rubbed her hand across the surface. "These are clad in copper," she said. "Incredible."

"Isn't it?" Coming around her desk, Daphne placed her hand next to Greta's. "And the color gets such depth from the verdigris."

"Oxidization, and the attendant coating of copper carbonate."

"Wasn't that what I said?" Daphne laughed, elbowing Greta.

Greta knew she had a strange way of viewing the world, but she also knew it wasn't entirely her fault. Her father was a precise man, and he trained his daughter to be precise as well. She was raised using metric measurements—inches were not permitted in the Donovan household. Their thermometers read only Celsius. *Fahrenheit*, her father used to say, *is for dummies.*

To survive in the regular world, Greta learned to perform metric conversions in her head, like a bilingual person translating. But the language the rest of the world used never stopped feeling awkward. The only person who never seemed to mind her awkwardness was Daphne.

"Help me with these," Daphne said. They opened the doors, propping them with stone doorstoppers shaped like Egyptian obelisks. Daphne turned on the lights in Marco Bertucci's private office.

Inside stood another large desk and the building's only window, enormous. It must have once been a loading dock.

Backing out of the room, she stood by Daphne's desk, which only had one chair. There was no waiting area. "Where should I sit?"

"Next to me," Daphne said, motioning to one end of her long

desk. She grabbed one of the two armchairs on casters facing Marco's desk and rolled it out for Greta.

Beyond Daphne's desk, in the back half of the narrow warehouse, a pale young woman with white-blonde hair sat at a desk, talking in a low voice on the phone.

"Who's that?" Greta asked.

"Olivia," Daphne said, smiling and waving at the young woman.

Greta waved too. From what Greta could hear, Olivia was scheduling a delivery.

"Tell me about the job interview." Daphne bounced in her chair with excitement.

"He hired me. I start tomorrow."

"What? That's amazing! I knew it would all work out."

Greta laughed at Daphne's incessant optimism.

Right then, the front door flew open. "Good afternoon!" The man's voice boomed off the hard surfaces of the warehouse. He was about Greta's height, with thick dark hair combed back from his forehead and restrained with some sort of pomade. He had pale blue eyes, and the crow's feet around them suggested he was in his late forties or early fifties. He was handsome, but he made her want to flee.

Greta sensed it in a heartbeat.

Narcissism. Just like her father.

"This must be your East Coast friend." He smiled, but not with his eyes.

Daphne jumped from her chair with enthusiasm. "Marco Bertucci," she said, gesturing dramatically at Greta. "This is Greta Donovan."

Greta stood slowly, cautious.

"Fuck, you're tall," Marco said. When he shook Greta's hand across the desk, they were eye to eye.

"It appears so," Greta said stiffly, startled by Marco's profanity.

He held her hand a moment too long and a bit too tightly. The handshake was a challenge—or a warning. Greta held very still.

Suddenly, Marco released her hand and let out a big laugh, his whitened teeth the brightest objects in the room. Then, abruptly, he stopped laughing. "Daphne. In my office."

Daphne picked up a notepad and pen and followed him into the office, kicking aside the obelisks to shut the double doors. She smiled at Greta before the doors closed.

Greta sat back down, exhaling heavily.

"I think he likes you," Olivia said, her small voice barely projecting from the back of the room.

Greta turned to her in disbelief. "Why do you say that?"

"Because he laughed."

To Greta, Marco's laughter seemed more mocking than joyful. "He doesn't laugh a lot?"

"No. Mostly, he grunts or nods or barks orders. Daphne makes him laugh sometimes, though."

"But you don't?"

"No." Olivia turned her pale blonde head toward the phone as it rang again. She took a reservation. "Yes—yes, sir. It is nice to hear from you again. Two for dinner? Eight o'clock? It's always a pleasure, sir."

Greta knew from Daphne that many of Rivet's clientele were big-time in the industry. Marco ruled the place with an iron fist—you had to be approved by Marco before you could get in.

So, Marco Bertucci liked to assert control over other people. It wasn't surprising, but it made her even more wary.

Twenty minutes later, when Daphne emerged from his office, Greta said, "I'm going to head out. Find a coffee shop or someplace where I can read. Take a walk."

"Marco said I could leave early today, so you won't have to wait too long." She handed Greta her mobile phone. "Take this. Just in case."

"See you soon." Greta stepped from the dark warehouse and into the summer sun.

———

WHILE SHE WALKED DOWN THE BOARDWALK OF VENICE BEACH, GRETA wondered once again if she'd made the right decision moving to California. Yes, she had a job and a place to live. Yes, she was with Daphne. But she'd left behind her dying mother.

And she'd left behind her path to avenge her mother by taking down her father.

The desire to expose Jim Donovan clawed at her.

When the mobile phone rang, it startled her. The caller ID indicated Princeton University.

When they'd set up their home answering machine, Daphne had put her cell number on the outgoing message in case someone needed to reach them in an emergency.

Hi! Daphne had recorded. *Aren't you lucky! You've reached the home of Greta and Daphne. But wait! We're not here. Leave a message, or try us at...*

Greta was unsure if she was doing the right thing, but she answered the phone.

"Greta Donovan," a man said on the phone. "Great to hear your voice. It's Phil Blue from the Princeton physics department." Professor Blue had taught Greta at Cameron, but left to chair the department at Princeton when she was a sophomore. She never called him anything but Professor Blue; the man was a legend. She certainly never called him Phil.

"Um. Hi."

"I'm wondering what your plans are for this fall."

"My plans? Um." Greta's head spun, trying to keep up with this conversation that felt like it was speeding away from her. "What do you mean?"

"This is an unusual situation, but we had someone drop out of the physics program at the last minute. The first person I thought of to fill the spot was you."

Greta couldn't suppress a gasp.

She could start her doctoral work in physics now? At Princeton? No waiting for an application cycle, no wondering if she'd get good funding? Everyone at Princeton got good funding.

All she had to do was say yes, and she would be doing right by her mother instead of running away.

Her gut churned as anger at herself rose to the surface. Running away was exactly what she'd done. She betrayed the promise she made to herself to get her mother the credit she deserved.

But another voice inside her pointed out that she'd just signed a lease. She'd accepted a job.

And how could she abandon Daphne? Leaving Daphne wouldn't mean just ditching her friend, but also leaving behind the only person who ever loved her without conditions.

The thought of losing that love made her panic. In her panic, an image of Timmy Eisenhart rose in her mind, the moment when he gave her a half-smile before she left.

She needed more time. She needed to think. "Can I have a day or two to consider it?"

"Take a week. The semester doesn't start for another month. Plenty of time."

After ending the call, Greta stared at the phone in her hand, wondering how her life could change so dramatically in a moment.

Instead of returning to Daphne's work or even finding a quiet place to read, Greta sat on a grassy hill facing the ocean, phone still gripped in her hand.

Betray Daphne or betray her mother? The decision was impossible.

Chapter Six

TIMMY

After Greta's first whole week on the job, Timmy knew two things for sure.

First, she was one of the best shop workers he'd ever hired.

Second, he really, really wanted her.

He wasn't sure how he was going to handle the situation. She should be off-limits. She was his employee. No. She was his best employee, and he'd be an idiot to screw that up.

At the moment, he stood in the doorway between his office and the shop, watching her. She already fit right in.

She was working with two of his regular guys, Romero and Dell, prepping a rental package for a small production company that would be picking it up later that day. Greta maintained the pack list on a clipboard, the guys readily ceding that responsibility to her, which was a wonder in itself.

As Greta started to lift a particularly heavy light to load in a road case, Romero stopped her. "G, let me help you with that."

The light weighed nearly a hundred pounds. Even Timmy struggled to load it. Usually, two people loaded them together.

But Greta stiffened at the offer of help. "I got it."

Romero wasn't insulted at all. "We always load it four-handed. After this idiot," Romero jerked his finger at Dell, "dropped one on his foot."

Greta's shoulders relaxed. "Oh. Okay."

Together, she and Romero slid the light into the black road case, along with three more.

Timmy had watched similar scenes play out all week; the guys offering to help, then Greta rejecting it. Most of the time, she truly didn't need the help. She worked with quiet, self-sufficient precision. But something about her self-sufficiency troubled him. As though everyone in the shop could just disappear, and she wouldn't even notice—everyone, including him.

Later that day, just after seven p.m., Timmy was finishing up a quote while Greta wrapped up another pack for a client. The rest of the guys had left for the day, but not Greta. She never left till her task was completed.

As she checked an item off on her clipboard, he tapped her on the shoulder.

"Oh, wow," she said. "I didn't even hear you."

"I'm not complaining," he replied. "I didn't think we'd get this pack finished till tomorrow."

Greta just blinked at him, her green eyes flashing.

"Right." He rubbed the back of his neck. "I'm leaving now, so."

"Oh!" She flushed. "I'll grab my stuff and get out of here."

He smiled at her. "No rush."

Following her out of the shop, Timmy locked up. Instead of heading off, she waited for him, talking about an idea for a new system for organizing the shop's power cable. It was brilliant.

"So yeah. We're totally doing that," he said. "What supplies do you need?"

She flushed at his compliment. "Just a label maker that can make waterproof labels. I think." She met his eyes. "What do you think?"

When she asked his opinion, he paused, resisting the urge to lean closer to her. "I think we can start with the label maker, and whatever else comes up, we can buy later."

They strolled toward their cars, her old pickup truck parked next to his car. The truck had to be at least twenty-five years old, and the years weren't easy on it. As he took in the truck's faded paint, he thought about how many miles she was putting on this clunker every day, how much she must be spending on gas. He got an idea—a terrible, wonderful idea.

The logical part of his brain told him to say nothing and kick the idea to the curb. But he seemed unable to avoid what he was about to do, even though it was an epic gamble.

If things went badly, he'd lose his best shop hand. But if things went well, he'd have so much more.

Uncle Brian used to talk to him about the importance of taking risks. Buying a company in his early twenties had been a risk, one he never regretted. But back then, it had been scary. As scary as what he was about to do now.

Stopping, he touched her arm to get her attention. The moment his fingers brushed her skin, fire erupted inside him.

Epic, epic gamble.

When Greta turned and met his eyes, he nearly lost his nerve. But then he glanced at her old truck again, and he couldn't bear the thought of her driving that unsafe thing on the freeway every day.

"What's up?" she asked.

"You know I live just north of Melrose, too?"

She shook her head. "No, I don't think you ever told me."

"Yeah, just a few blocks northeast of you."

Greta tilted her head, her question unspoken. The setting sun glinted off her red curls, turning them gold.

Oh god, what was he doing? "We're basically neighbors." He hoped he didn't sound like a creep.

"Okay," she said, but her brows still drew together in confusion.

"Right." He paused. "Um, so I was thinking we might carpool." He tried so hard to sound casual.

But he didn't feel casual. He felt like he was going to jump out of his skin.

When she was working in the shop, and he was in his office, he'd invent reasons to check on her. When she was joking with the other guys, jealousy ate at him.

He was a goner.

"Oh." She met his eyes but gave nothing away.

Damn it, but this not-talking thing Greta did made him crazy. "I drive right past your place on my way home anyway."

That's right, he thought. Make it seem like it's no big deal. She doesn't like accepting favors.

Meanwhile, he was dreaming of spending a private hour with her every day in very close quarters.

While she pondered his offer, a breeze picked up, carrying her scent to him, spicy and citrus. Maybe her skin lotion. Maybe her hair. He didn't care—he just wanted to bury his nose in her neck and breathe her in.

He cleared his throat, trying to get himself under control.

She cocked her head. "It does seem like a good idea. Let me talk to Daphne."

Right. The mysterious Daphne. He was dying to meet this person. Part of him wondered if Greta and Daphne were a thing, except Greta didn't talk about Daphne like she was a girlfriend. No, their relationship seemed more like sisters.

"Great. Let me know what you decide."

"Can I call you later tonight?"

"Sure thing." This was the best he could hope for. A chance.

———

LATER THAT NIGHT, WHILE HE WAS EATING MICROWAVE CORN DOGS AND drinking a beer, his cell phone rang. It was a number he didn't recognize. "Yeah?"

"Timmy?"

"Greta." He cleared his throat, and his heart started racing. "Hey. Um, hi."

"I talked to Daphne about carpooling. What if I ride in with her in the morning and then home with you at night? Since we might work late or something? Does that sound good?"

It sounded fucking fantastic. "Yeah, sure," he said, trying to play it cool. "I'll see you at work tomorrow."

"Okay, great. Um, bye."

Timmy resisted the urge to pump his fist, but it was a near thing.

While waiting for her to call, he'd accepted that he was going after Greta. There was no point in lying to himself about his feelings for her. He was all in.

But she was like a gazelle, liable to bolt at any moment. So, his approach had to be slow and careful. He could do it, and she was worth it.

Chapter Seven

GRETA

Sitting on the thrift-store yoga mat they'd put on their living room floor as a pretend couch, Greta hung up the phone. Daphne sat next to her, painting her toenails a midnight blue.

"Now we can split the cost of gasoline," Greta said. "This is going to save us a ton of money. Plus, my truck won't rack up mileage and croak."

"I wonder why your boss wants to drive you around. Is he creepy?"

"No!" Greta shouted. "Oh, wow. That was loud. No, he's not creepy. He's totally normal."

"Where's he from?"

"He grew up in Woodland Hills. His parents still live there."

"Right. He probably had a bright blue pool in the backyard and a chocolate Labrador Retriever. His parents gave him whatever he wanted, but he didn't ask for much. He graduated from Southern Cal and then stayed to make a life in the big, bright city."

"He went to UCLA," Greta said, annoyed at Daphne's judgmental tone.

"How old is he?"

"Still in his twenties, I think."

"Oh, I see." Daphne stretched out the vowels into a song. "He's young."

"Timmy doesn't feel *that* way about me at all."

"Would you know if he did?"

Greta picked at a cuticle, then grabbed the cuticle clippers from the yoga mat. Had Timmy given her any signs that he liked her in that way? Daphne was right—she had no real experience with guys. She was a virgin. She'd never even kissed anyone. A chasm of ignorance was opening in front of her.

She needed Daphne's help.

Daphne screwed the lid back onto her nail polish. "The real question is, do you feel *that* way about *him*?"

Greta squirmed. "I don't know. How do I know?" She leaned back, wincing as her head hit the wall. "I'm like a middle schooler."

Boys in college never seemed to be interested in her. But, if she were honest, she put out vibes telling them she wasn't interested in them, either. Her fear of rejection ran deep.

She exhaled deeply, trying to let go of her father's judgment. But it wasn't easy, even from thousands of miles away.

Daphne peered down at her. "You'll know because he makes you feel tingly."

"Seriously? Tingly?" Greta snorted. "We really are in middle school."

"Well? Does he?"

Greta thought about how it was hard to breathe when Timmy stood near her. How her belly grew warm, and the hairs on her arms rose. When his hand brushed against hers while they were working, it felt like a minor electrical shock.

Tingly.

Shit.

And now she was going to be riding alone in a car with him for their commute every day. "I've made a terrible mistake. I can't carpool with Timmy. I might have a cardiac event in the car." She covered her face with her hands.

Daphne squealed. "Greta, you have a crush on your boss!"

Greta absorbed Daphne's words, not wanting them to be true because her feelings would never be reciprocated.

"I know what you're thinking," Daphne said. "And you're wrong."

Greta didn't question that Daphne knew her thoughts. Their

conversations were like icebergs, most of the words hidden beneath the surface. "You can't know that. He could just be a nice person who wants to do an environmentally friendly thing."

Daphne hooted with laughter. "He wants to be friendly, all right, but not with the environment." Daphne took Greta's hand in hers. "Guys do everything they can to be around a girl they like, including making up bullshit excuses. And they always make up bullshit excuses if it isn't clear that the girl feels the same way. Helps protect them from rejection."

"What do I do?"

"You say yes." Daphne paused, smiling. "To everything." She turned back to her nails.

But Greta still struggled. "Relying on Timmy for a job and a ride seems like too much. He doesn't drive Romero, Dell, or any of the other guys. And I know he won't let me split gas with him." She and Daphne were already splitting the gas for the Civic because Daphne drove them most of the time.

Daphne met her eyes. "You've spent your whole life with your dad taking things away from you, holding money over your head. It's not surprising that it's hard for you to let a guy do something nice." She picked up Greta's hand and squeezed. "And that's okay. But you should let him do this for you."

Daphne was rarely wrong. If she told Greta to agree to the carpool, then Daphne believed it would all work out.

And Greta believed Daphne.

Greta glanced at her friend, who still had no idea about the far bigger decision Greta was agonizing over. She'd kept her grad school offer a secret, and guilt was eating her up.

Could Greta abandon the one person who'd always been there for her?

Greta was well aware that one week had passed since she spoke to Professor Blue about graduate school, giving her a pathway to begin her quest to avenge her mother. Was she so shallow that a crush on Timmy would cause her to forsake everything she'd been planning since she was old enough to suspect her father's wrongdoing?

Greta stood, her back aching from sitting on the floor so long. "I'm going to take a walk."

Not looking up, Daphne nodded, so she didn't notice when Greta snagged Daphne's cell phone on her way out the door.

A block away from the house, she dialed. Professor Blue answered on the second ring, and Greta was relieved. She didn't know when she'd find time for another private conversation with him.

"Do you have good news for me?" he said.

"I need more time," she blurted out. "I just signed a lease, and I'm in California…"

"Don't worry," he said kindly. "I sprang this choice on you. Take a month. I'll be able to fill the spot, even at the last minute. And if you have to miss the first week or two of classes, I have no doubt that you'll get up to speed with no trouble."

Greta paused. "I have one question."

"Just one?" he chuckled.

"Did you ask me because of my father?"

"No." His voice was firm. "Any program in the country would be lucky to have you. I'm just trying to get the jump on them."

Greta exhaled, relieved. "Okay. I appreciate the extra time."

After the call ended, Greta realized the sky was unusually clear. When she looked north, the Hollywood sign shone like a golden beacon in the setting sun. She stood on a precipice. One way lay what she always believed she wanted—revenge. The other way lay uncertainty (oh, how she hated that), but also possibility. She had no idea how she was going to choose.

Chapter Eight

TIMMY

After only two weeks of carpooling with Greta, Timmy felt like they had a regular rhythm. Greta seemed relaxed in his car next to him.

He, on the other hand, was completely wound up. With immense effort, he'd held back from doing the things he wanted to do, like ask her out, or kiss her, or literally anything that involved letting her know how he felt about her.

He exited the freeway, heading north on La Brea toward her apartment. "You know, I hired you because this guy Julius quit on me with no notice when he got an acting job."

"Really? How long did Julius work for you?"

"Three years."

"That's immensely rude." She sounded upset on his behalf. It was adorable.

"That idiot hung his hopes on a pilot, and I was forced to hire someone quickly. You called first. What's funny is I was scared to hire a woman. You know, because the equipment is heavy, and I didn't know if you could do the job."

She glared at him, and he barked with laughter.

"You know I'm kidding," he said. "You could probably deadlift Dell."

"That's not saying much. He's five-five."

Timmy hooted again. Everyone gave Dell a hard time about his height, but only because Dell never had any trouble getting girls. The guy might not be tall, but he had charisma for days.

"So," Timmy continued. "Julius called me today. Turns out the pilot was canned."

"That's terrible, right?"

"That's terrible for Julius. He asked for his old job back. I turned him down."

He glanced at Greta. He would have turned down Julius a hundred more times just to see the small smile that crossed her face.

When he pulled to a stop in front of her duplex, she made no move to open the door. All of the other days they'd carpooled, it seemed like she was ready to dive out while the car was still rolling to a stop. He tried not to take it personally.

A gazelle, he reminded himself.

Today, though, she turned to him. "Daphne and I really need a couch."

"You don't have a couch?"

"We don't have any furniture." Greta paused. "Well, except one chair."

"Wait, you really don't have any furniture?"

"Are you listening to me?" Greta sounded exasperated.

"Yes, sorry." Timmy kicked himself for letting his surprise get the better of him. But seriously. No furniture?

"Never mind." Greta reached for the door handle.

"No, really. Tell me what you need."

He hoped she could hear the echo behind his words. He wanted to help her get a couch. More than that, he wanted to help her with everything she might need.

When she looked back at him, her eyes were tight at the corners. It wasn't easy, it seemed, for Greta to ask for help.

He wanted to know why.

Patience.

"Let me help you," he said, reaching out to touch the back of her hand. Risky, but he couldn't help himself. Her freckled skin was smooth, and he wanted to see everywhere those freckles went.

Next to him, Greta froze in place, looking at his fingers on her hand, her face flooded with color.

But she didn't pull her hand away. And when he took the next step, wrapping his hand around hers and squeezing, she exhaled slowly. "Okay," she said. "I really could use the help."

At her words, Timmy let out a breath he didn't realize he'd also been holding.

She turned her bright eyes toward him. "Where can we get a couch? Used, but not too shitty? We saw this leather one on the side of the road last week, but someone's dog—well, I hope it was a dog—had obviously urinated on it." She scrunched up her nose.

Her nose was adorable. He wanted to kiss it.

He was still holding her hand. That single touch was blazing a path all the way through him, sending blood straight between his legs.

He cleared his throat, trying to remove his thoughts from the gutter. "Cheap, good furniture? I'm a single dude in L.A. I'm an expert."

"Can I use your phone? I need to call Daphne."

To get his phone from his pocket, he had to let go of her, and his body screamed at him in response. As he reached into his pocket, he tried to adjust himself so that she wouldn't be able to tell that he was getting hard just sitting next to her.

He handed her the phone, and she dialed quickly. "Daph—listen. Timmy's gonna help us get a couch. He says he knows some places. I'll pick something good." She paused. "Yes, of course I'll make sure it's ugly." Another pause. "Okay, but I'm not sacrificing structural integrity for appearance." She said goodbye and handed him his phone back.

"As ugly as possible?" he said.

"We don't do pretty furniture. It's a long story."

"I'm not in a hurry."

Greta paused, as though weighing what to share. "Something happened once with my dad and some furniture that was supposed to be mine. The furniture was beautiful."

"Supposed to be yours?"

Greta nodded.

"But then something happened to make it not yours."

"Yes." Both pain and anger reverberated in that single word.

He was grateful to learn a little bit about why Greta would be all right leaving behind her family thousands of miles away.

At the same time, her words made his chest hurt. He wanted to make that pain go away, to take her in his arms and hold her. To provide her with anything she might need. He knew what it was like for a father to turn his back on those who needed him. He wanted to show Greta that she could rely on him.

But not yet. She wasn't ready for that yet.

"Ugly makes our job a lot easier," he told her, trying to act cool. "Gives us a wider selection."

"My truck's around back." Greta got out of his car and headed down the walkway that ran alongside the duplex.

As she walked away, he stared at her ass in the Levi's she always wore. Transfixed.

He was a disaster. He was never going to make it through an evening with this girl.

After parking his car, he followed her around back to her pickup. Keeping his hands to himself and his thoughts on the task at hand, he gave her directions while she drove.

At a thrift shop in Glendale, she zeroed in on a long, atrocious orange vinyl couch. Timmy had never seen a piece of furniture so ugly.

Greta looked it over, dropping to her knees to check out the legs and frame. "It's structurally sound. But," she paused, tapping her lip, "it might be too well-designed to suit the ugliness requirement." She babbled some words about mid-century modernism and Knoll and Eames and shook her head. "I just don't know. It has classic lines."

"Greta," Timmy said, wondering if she were losing her mind. "It's eye-bleed orange."

"I know. It is such a wonderful color." A smile lit her face, one he wanted her to shine on him all the time. "We should probably take it."

Greta paid one hundred dollars for the couch. They carried it out to the truck and headed back south to Melrose.

At Greta's apartment, Timmy helped her carry the couch inside, setting it along the wall in the living room after Greta moved a yoga mat out of the way.

"The yoga mat was our metaphorical couch," Greta explained, as though that made perfect sense.

Once the couch was in place, he stood next to her, staring at the orange monstrosity. "It looks like a lifeboat."

"Agreed," Greta said as though his words were a compliment. "It's perfect. Thank you."

Timmy waited awkwardly in the silence, hoping Greta would ask him to stay, wondering if he should invite himself.

After a moment that seemed to last twenty years, Greta asked, "Do you want to look around?"

Of course he did. And then he wanted to take her clothes off and take her right there on the lifeboat.

He needed to get a grip, but it was impossible. "Sure. I'd love to."

Greta showed him the bedrooms. He couldn't believe how empty the place was. One bedroom had no furniture or decorations, only some clothes in the closet. By the looks of the clothes, they were Greta's—jeans folded on the top shelf, black tank tops and t-shirts hanging on the rod.

"This is my room," she said. "But I don't spend much time in here."

The second bedroom had bedding on the hardwood floor. His stomach lurched—Greta slept on the floor? Every night? Not even an air mattress?

This bedroom also had a desk and endless clothing—both hanging up and piled on the floor. These sparkly clothes clearly belonged to Daphne. He hadn't known Greta long, but he knew that she'd never be caught dead in sequins.

The living room had one chair, as Greta had mentioned before, and now the lifeboat.

"Let's test it out," he said, nodding at the new couch.

And no, he told himself, "testing it out" did not mean stripping her naked and properly christening the couch.

As he sat, he was surprised by how comfortable it was. "I think you made an excellent choice."

Greta brightened. "You think so? I love it." Then she flopped down next to him, letting her feet fly into the air like a little kid.

Carefully, he rested his hand on hers once more. She didn't stiffen this time, and she didn't pull away. No. She trained her green eyes on his, knocking all thoughts from his brain.

He coughed, pretending to clear his throat. "So, uh. You guys have been living here for weeks," he said. "How can you have so little?"

She immediately stiffened, even her fingers under his palm. "We have what we need," she replied, looking at the floor.

Shit. He'd upset her. He squeezed her hand.

"I'm sorry. I wasn't judging you. I just want to be sure you're okay."

At his words, she relaxed, turning her palm over and squeezing him back. "Thank you. For saying that. And for helping me."

Warmth suffused him. He had it bad for Greta, and he wasn't afraid to own it.

He liked making her happy. He wanted to do it all the time. He imagined helping her find furniture for her entire apartment, taking her to all the best thrift shops. Even garage sales on the weekends. The ones in the Hills were incredible.

Grinning and tucking his hands in his pockets, he made himself a deal.

It was time to be honest with her about how he felt. If it was meant to be, he'd have his girl.

Chapter Nine

GRETA

Two weeks later, Greta sat on the steps outside of Pac Lighting, waiting for Daphne to pick her up. It was mid-August, a little after seven p.m., and everyone else was gone but Timmy and her. That was the usual schedule these days, but she didn't mind. Ending the workday with some peaceful alone time in the shop gave her time to tinker on projects that required concentration, like rewiring lights. Sometimes, Timmy would join her, but he would work silently, too, as if he were enjoying their quiet time together as much as she was.

God, I wish that were true, she thought.

When she heard the door open behind her, she turned to see Timmy in the doorway.

"Don't you want to wait inside?" he asked. "I'm pretty sure the waiting room chairs are comfortable."

"I like sitting outside at night because it's cool. Dry." She gestured around her. "No bugs. Summer nights in North Carolina are so miserable."

Stepping outside, he let the door close behind him. "Do you want some company?"

"Okay." Greta was grateful Timmy had asked because she was still too afraid to invite him herself. And she really wanted to. After her conversation with Daphne, she'd accepted that she had a crush on her boss.

After he'd helped her with furniture shopping, she was afraid she felt something more than a crush.

For a while, they sat without speaking, the only sound the airplanes taking off and landing at LAX. She glanced at him. He sat with his arms resting on his knees, looking at the horizon, his handsome profile illuminated by the building's exterior lights. Greta couldn't fathom that he would feel anything more for her than what an employer feels for a good employee—and she was a very good employee.

Well, maybe he saw her as a friend, but surely that was all. Those times when she caught his gaze on her were merely happenstance. When he touched her, taking her hand in his, it was only to comfort her. When he helped her buy the lifeboat, he was just being supportive.

She wished his actions meant more, but she needed to be realistic, no matter how comfortable she felt sitting next to him in the twilight, embracing silence.

"It was a good show last night," he said after a while.

Yesterday evening, they'd had a corporate event at a hotel in Santa Monica, where they'd turned the hotel ballroom into a 1950s Cuban mambo club. They'd brought in uplights to splash the walls with tropical colors. Ellipsoidals with metal gobos covered the ceiling with the texture of palm trees. Stage lights washed the band in gold, magenta, and purple, glinting off brass trombones and trumpets. A single follow-spot lit the young singer channeling Tito Puente.

"Was the client happy?" she asked.

"Very. They want to hire us for their next event."

The party ran late, so they struck the gear today. Back at the shop, they quickly unloaded the truck and repaired any damaged gear— burned-out lamps, cracked lenses, frayed cable. Then they put together another package for a local theater. The theater people had just left with a truck full of stage lights. Quick turnarounds like these were exhausting, so everyone but Timmy had already headed home as soon as they were done. Timmy, Greta knew, needed to stay late to run payroll.

"What are your plans tonight?" he asked. "You and Daphne are going to dinner, right?"

She nodded. "We're going to Rivet with her boss. He owns the place. It's my first time."

"Dinner at Rivet." He whistled. "Must be cool."

She shrugged. "I don't really fit in with Daphne's Hollywood friends. I feel like a goose among swans."

He chuckled. "They can't handle your honesty. Your brains, either."

"That's not what I meant."

He exhaled. "I know what you meant." He drummed his fingers on his knee.

"What is it?"

He met her eyes, and her breath caught.

Timmy shook his head. "Goose among swans. Just…" He paused. "That's just such crap. I think you're…" He stared at the sunset for a moment that stretched on and on.

Greta held her breath, waiting for him to finish his sentence.

Timmy met her eyes with an intensity she'd never seen before. "Greta. Listen to me. You're worth more than a hundred of them."

"I…" She bit her lip. "Thank you."

"It's the truth," he said.

Before she could say anything more, Daphne pulled up. She rolled down the window. "Get up! Can you not see me?"

"Do you want to meet Daphne?" she asked him in a low voice, giving him a chance to politely decline.

"Of course." Timmy stood, approaching the driver's side of the car. Greta stood by his side, nervously digging her toe into the ground.

Daphne hopped out and shook Timmy's hand. "So nice to finally meet you!" Daphne gave him her biggest smile.

"Likewise," Timmy said.

For a moment, Greta felt something she'd never felt before— jealousy toward Daphne. Daphne, who dazzled. How would Timmy feel about her, plain Greta, after meeting her friend?

He walked with her back to the passenger side and opened the door for her.

He leaned close. "Have a wonderful night."

She could feel his breath on her neck as he spoke, and the hairs on her body rose in response.

Breathless, she managed, "Thanks. Um. You too."

Shoving his hands in his pockets, he strode back inside, leaving Greta wondering what just happened.

Daphne bounced in the driver's seat. "He is *way* cuter than I thought he'd be."

Greta buckled her seatbelt. "Be quiet. I'm having thoughts."

"But I want to talk!"

Greta sighed. "About what?"

"Apparently, we're in for a special treat."

"Marco said that?"

"I have no idea what he's referring to. I guess we'll be surprised!"

"I hate surprises."

"Still?"

"People don't change, Daphne."

Daphne pouted. "Tell me about these thoughts you were having about your hot boss."

Greta blushed at Daphne's words. She was, of course, thinking about Timmy. What he said to her before Daphne pulled up. How he spoke to her before going inside. "Timmy just gave me a big compliment, I think."

"You're not sure?"

"I think he was going to say something else, then changed his mind. It's hard to explain."

Daphne laughed. "It would be easier if you told me what he said."

Greta wondered whether she should tell Daphne—Timmy's words were basically an insult to Daphne's entire industry.

But this was Daphne, who often insulted the industry herself. So Greta recounted the conversation.

Daphne was silent for a while. "He's right—about what he was going to say, and what he actually said."

"How do you know—"

"Please. He knew that you were saying you weren't pretty enough. He was going to say that he thinks you're gorgeous, scintillating, striking, and amazing."

Greta couldn't speak.

"But, he chose not to say that because he knew you would gape like a fish." Daphne gestured at Greta. "Like you're doing right now. So instead he said the other thing, which is also true." Without taking her eyes from the road, Daphne took Greta's hand in hers. "We are worth a hundred of them, Greta. Don't let the bright lights fool you."

Greta scoffed.

"I'm serious. Sometimes, even I get fooled."

Greta was quiet. For Daphne to admit such a thing was a big deal.

"We're worth more than a hundred of these bottom-feeders. The vain ones who seek notoriety at any cost. Who will sell anything to walk through the golden gates at Sony. God, these people make Faust look like a winner."

"They can't all be so awful."

"Here and there, you'll find good ones. And you'll know who they are because you're you—you see things for what they are, especially when they're trying to be something else. It's your superpower, Greta."

"Like how Marco invited us to the club tonight under the pretense of welcoming me to L.A., but really, he wants an opportunity to see you outside of the office?"

"Oh, please, even I know that. But the food at Rivet is delicious and way out of our price range. I could use a break from oatmeal and ramen."

Greta nodded. "I want an enormous steak."

"Try to act surprised, but steak is the only thing on the menu."

"You can't be serious."

Daphne just quirked an eyebrow.

While Daphne drove, Greta kicked off her sneakers and socks. She pulled her duffel bag from Daphne's back seat. Inside were her snakeskin stilettos, carefully wrapped in soft fabric. Her favorite shoes. She'd found them on sale, the last pair in the store, marked from six hundred dollars down to ninety-five, and large enough to fit her feet. She didn't think twice before buying them, and she always thought twice. But these shoes did what years of Daphne's coaching could not—they made her feel beautiful.

She pulled the black t-shirt with the Pac Lighting logo over her head and stuffed it into the bag, revealing a navy blue camisole underneath, one with lace sewn around the neckline. She slid the ponytail elastic from her hair and used her fingers to arrange her curls. Then she applied some of Daphne's lip gloss, kept in the car's center console.

Lip gloss was a compromise Greta had made with Daphne back in college. She tried some of the clothes Daphne suggested and even liked some of them. But Greta refused to wear makeup. Daphne insisted on the lip gloss, saying, "Nothing else really matters as long as your smile shines." When Greta agreed to wear it, Daphne said, "Of course, this also means you have to smile, Greta."

Greta smiled at her reflection in the visor mirror. "Good enough."

"Way better than that." Daphne pinched Greta's cheek without taking her eyes off the road.

Daphne, consistently going fifteen miles above the speed limit, drove north past Santa Monica on the 1. Greta was accustomed to Daphne's driving, but she still marveled that Daphne had avoided speeding tickets for so long. It's not that Daphne never got pulled over. It happened all the time, but no cop would give her a ticket. The police officer—man or woman—would see Daphne's wide-set brown eyes and pleasant smile, hear her genuine apology for causing them trouble, and let her go with a warning. This was part of Daphne's magic, and Greta accepted it.

"Marco said he's excited to see you again," Daphne said.

"He's lying."

"Marco likes quirky. That's why he likes me."

"He certainly does like you," Greta said. "And your quirkiness might be one of the reasons. But it isn't the main one."

Actually, Daphne told her that Marco Bertucci was obviously and unashamedly infatuated with Daphne. About once a week, before Daphne left for the evening, he would ask her some version of the same question: "When are you going to realize we're perfect for each other?" She would laugh at him and say something like, "I'm not perfect for anyone."

Greta was surprised that Marco's overtures didn't make Daphne uncomfortable, even though she was employed at his whim. But Daphne never worried about losing her job. As she told Greta, "I'm the best assistant he will ever find, and he knows it."

Plus, everyone in the business knew Marco could be a creep and wouldn't blame her for quitting if he crossed a line. So Daphne would be able to find another job even without his reference.

But Greta also knew Daphne kept a careful distance from Marco. Daphne explained that Marco wanted power first and foremost, and he wanted sex—specifically, sex with her. He also wanted to be seen with a beautiful woman. But if she gave him sex, she would lose whatever tenuous power she held as a new-in-town production assistant to a has-been producer. So she withheld sex but let him squire her about, meeting one of his needs while denying the other, treading a tightrope of power.

Greta worried, though. Did Daphne realize that it was only a matter of time before the tightrope snapped?

"Where are we?" Greta asked.

Daphne had pulled off the Pacific Coast Highway and turned inland, passing some frankly gorgeous homes and then, strangely, turned into an undeveloped area with some warehouses and an empty parking lot.

"We're here." Daphne pulled into a circular drive in front of one of the smaller warehouses.

Greta climbed out of Daphne's car as a valet approached, a Latino man with a warm brown complexion. His red jacket was cut perfectly, custom-tailored to his small frame. Daphne handed him the keys and spoke to him in Spanish. They laughed together.

Daphne spoke fluent Spanish. Greta knew that when Daphne was growing up, she cleaned her parents' motel alongside two Guatemalan maids employed by her father. Daphne had spent a lot of time with them when she was a child, more time than she'd spent with her parents.

Greta hated Daphne's father as much as she hated her own.

Greta envied Daphne's linguistic skills—not just her fluency in three languages, but her ability to communicate deeply with every person she spoke to. At this moment, Greta knew, the valet believed he and Daphne shared a connection. The crazy thing was, he was right.

She turned her gaze to the square building before her. Rivet was very unassuming on the outside, a plain box with no windows. "Another ugly warehouse," she observed.

Daphne nodded. "It used to be a storage facility for surplus city road equipment."

"No sign, either."

"Nope, just the street number, there." Daphne pointed to the spot-lit digits of the street address, chrome numerals above the entryway.

The dumpy facade gave Rivet the aura of a speakeasy. "I'm guessing the inside will be as gorgeous as the outside is ugly," Greta said.

"I'll tell Marco you're onto him."

Greta snorted. "Please don't."

She followed Daphne to the wooden double doors. Two tall, broad-shouldered men flanked the entry. They were handsome and young, dressed in impeccable black suits and silk ties, but they were bouncers nonetheless.

Greta wondered what Marco was trying to prove, and to whom, by dressing his bouncers and valets in suits they obviously could not have afforded to purchase for themselves. As she studied the bouncers while they spoke to Daphne, she frowned.

Marco Bertucci liked owning people.

It seemed that Marco also liked to surround himself with beauty. Daphne, the bouncers, Olivia—they were all such good-looking people. And Daphne was the most beautiful of all.

Suppressing a smile, Greta wondered what Marco must think of her. She threw off the logic of his universe. For him, she would be unexplainable, like dark matter. By any and all logic, she shouldn't be standing next to Daphne, about to enter the most exclusive restaurant in Los Angeles. Yet here she was. And she felt powerful for the first time in her life.

Chapter Ten

GRETA

The interior of Rivet echoed Marco Bertucci's office so closely that Greta figured the same decorator had done both buildings. "Marco is no dummy," she whispered to Daphne.

"Well, no," Daphne said. "But are you thinking of something in particular?"

"He got Universal to pay for this upfit, claiming the work was for his office. Those are the same pendant lights." She nodded to the bar.

Daphne grinned. "I will not confirm or deny."

To the left, a gleaming mahogany bar stretched the entire length of the wall. To her right were square dining tables, and tall-backed booths of dark brown leather lined the walls. She tapped her foot on the wide-planked hardwood floors buffed to a deep luster. Straight ahead was another doorway, and she could just make out the twinkling festoon lights of an outdoor patio.

From a booth in the far corner of the room, Marco stood and waved to Daphne. Daphne smiled at him and waved back.

"Come on." Taking Greta's hand, Daphne led her to the table.

Marco sat across from another man, also in his late forties, Greta guessed, his graying hair pulled into a short ponytail. Daphne slid in next to Marco. For a moment, Greta stood by the table, uncertain whether she was supposed to sit next to this strange man.

"So good to see you again, Greta," Marco said. He sounded genuine. He gestured at the man across from him. "This is an old friend of mine, Sandy." Sandy, whose eyes were the most piercing blue Greta had ever seen, stood to shake her hand. The gentlemanly gesture disarmed her, and she relaxed, sliding into the booth next to him after he'd sat back down.

"You girls are right on time," Marco said. "The food should be out any minute. I went ahead and ordered for you."

Greta bristled.

On the rare occasions her family dined out, her father always ordered for her mother and her. When the server would begin handing out menus, Jim Donovan would interrupt, saying, "We just need one." Taking it from the server's hand, he would make the server wait while he scanned the menu and ordered three entrees.

Neither Greta nor her mother ever complained, but sometimes Greta would glare at him, angry at his high-handedness. He would ignore her, confident she would give in. Beatrice Donovan would smile lightly and stare at the salt and pepper. After years of this treatment, Greta grew angrier and angrier. She wanted to scream at both of her parents, but she never did. What was the point? Her father held all the power. Fortunately, the Donovans didn't eat out as a family very often.

And my father doesn't hold the power anymore, she thought.

"What did you order?" Greta asked.

"Steaks, of course. It's what Rivet does. Good ol' red meat." He pounded the table with his fist for emphasis. "Are you a vegetarian? That would be a disaster."

Greta wondered whether Marco would prefer it if she answered yes. "No," she said. "I'm not."

"I'll never understand the vegetarian thing. It seems selfish, if you ask me. Forcing everyone else around you to cater to a dietary fad."

"That's ridiculous," Daphne said, slapping Marco on the arm. "It's selfish that our country consumes such a large amount of beef that we force other countries to chop down rainforests to raise it for us."

Daphne delivered this set-down with a smile, as always, and Greta could see that Marco didn't mind being corrected by Daphne.

"Of course," Daphne continued, "I'm still a serious carnivore."

"You sure are, babe." Then Marco turned his gaze on Sandy and Greta. "Wine, people? Let's have some wine." Marco gestured at a server, a young man with a fashion model's face who stood by the wall a couple of feet from their booth. His only apparent responsibility was Marco's table. Marco requested a specific bottle and four glasses, and the server scurried off.

"Did you find a job, Greta?" Marco asked.

"Yes."

There was a long pause, and then Marco guffawed. Daphne's eyes met Greta's, saying, *Please forgive him.*

"Are you going to tell us what this job is?" he asked. "Or should we play twenty questions?"

Greta's face turned red. She hadn't offered to describe her job because she had no reason to think Marco would be interested. In fact, the contrary seemed far more likely. "I work for Pacific Production Lighting," she said.

"I know that shop. We use them all the time," Marco said. "What's the guy's name who runs it? Tom?"

"Timmy," Greta said.

"Right. Tim."

Greta resisted the urge to correct him. Timmy was not *Tim*, not to her, not to anyone. Certainly not to Marco Bertucci. But she tried to let it go, squeezing her hands into fists under the table.

During that dinner, Greta began to notice a change in herself. She was having a harder time letting it go when someone like Marco Bertucci made snide or obtuse comments, the kind her father used to make and that she spent her whole life ignoring.

She didn't feel like ignoring them anymore. She could hear Timmy's voice, *You're worth more than a hundred of them.* It didn't matter whether the words were true, she realized. It only mattered that Timmy believed them.

Timmy believed in *her.*

She watched while Daphne handled Marco like a pro. She didn't put up with obtuseness, but she still managed to get along with everyone. Greta wondered what her secret was. She would ask her about it later.

The wine came, and the steaks shortly thereafter. Each plate was identical—a thick cut of filet mignon cooked medium-rare, wilted spinach topped with crushed sea salt, and sweet potato fries.

"Rivet's menu is American through and through," said Marco. "Three simple items on a plate. None of those fusion sauces or any trendy crap. We do classic."

"It looks delicious," Daphne said. Clutching her knife and fork, she proceeded to wolf down her dinner.

After a stretch of silence while everyone ate, Marco turned to Daphne and began talking to her about work, and then moved on to other things, like her apartment. He shouted in disbelief when she said that she and Greta were sleeping on the floor.

Daphne replied, "It's doing wonders for my posture," and the two of them laughed. Daphne seemed to sincerely like Marco.

Every day after work, Daphne told Greta stories about the pompous or self-centered things Marco had done that day. But despite his boorishness, Daphne insisted he was charming and harmless.

He was certainly charming, but Greta suspected that he was not as harmless as Daphne supposed.

"Hey there," Sandy said, jerking Greta's attention from Daphne and Marco. Leaning his head toward hers, he said, "You aren't from here, correct?"

"Correct." Greta lifted a bite to her mouth, then stopped. She'd almost repeated her earlier conversational mistake. She lowered her fork. "I'm from North Carolina, like Daphne."

Sandy smiled, and it struck Greta that he was extraordinarily handsome. The faint lines on his skin accentuated what must have been a film idol's face twenty years before.

With a shock, she realized who he was—a genuine *movie star*. She knew what the name Sandy was short for and what surname followed it. *Alexander Martin.* She couldn't draw breath.

Eyes jerking toward the exit, she had to restrain herself from running.

She didn't belong here.

Blood rushed to her cheeks, and she took a sip of wine to cover her embarrassment. Unlike Marco Bertucci, this man was truly famous, despite his absence from headlines and film billings over the past few years. If Harrison Ford had stopped making movies in his early forties, he would be Sandy. How could she not have recognized him?

A special treat, Marco had said.

Now, she looked around Rivet and saw the other patrons stealing glances at their booth. Some of them—even the ones she recognized from their own sitcoms and primetime dramas—openly stared at Sandy. He had at least two Oscars that she knew of, and she didn't pay attention to the movies.

She wanted to sink beneath the table and hide from all of those eyes. Her hands shook, so she concentrated on stilling them. Was this what it felt like to be starstruck? But no. She didn't want to be closer to the spotlight; she wanted to run. She would run if she were certain Daphne wouldn't mind.

She didn't belong here. At all. Nausea hit, her appetite gone.

Then Daphne and Marco stood. They were holding hands.

"We're going outside to dance," Daphne said. "Wanna come? There's a great band about to start."

"On a Tuesday?" Greta asked, confused. She couldn't move her eyes from their clasped hands.

"Every night," Marco said. "It doesn't cost me a dime—they're dying to play here."

Sandy said, "Maybe in a little while. I think we'll sit here and finish our wine." He turned to Greta. "If that's okay with you?"

"Yes," she managed. "Of course."

Marco and Daphne headed out to the patio. Greta clutched her glass with both hands, the wine trembling as her hands shook.

How could she make conversation with Alexander Martin? She was a little odd at her best. Now? She felt like a freshman in college, when every word she spoke was so weird that Cameron students laughed in her face.

"You all right?" Sandy whispered.

"What?" she said, startled.

"You looked a little pale there. Figured you wouldn't want to dance."

She nodded. Dance? She wasn't sure her legs would work.

"So how'd you and Daphne meet?" Sandy asked.

Is this what they were doing? Small talk? As though everything were normal?

Well, at least the question was normal. People often asked how she and Daphne became friends. She knew what they were really asking—how come a gorgeous girl like Daphne was friends with an awkward geek like her.

"We were roommates in college. Now we live together here."

Sandy nodded, sipping his wine.

Reaching for any small talk she could manage, she said, "How do you know Marco?"

"We're old friends," he said. "Tonight he wanted to discuss a project with me."

Project meant some sort of movie, Greta figured, but she couldn't imagine what sort of project Marco might have that would interest an actor like Sandy.

"If you're having a meeting," Greta asked, "then why are Daphne and I here?" She gestured toward the patio. "Is your meeting over?"

Sandy smiled, as though something were funny. "Apparently."

"I guess Daphne is technically his production assistant," she said. "So it would make sense for her to be here. But not me."

Sandy drew his eyes together in confusion. "Are you serious? Can't you tell this is classic Marco?"

"I don't know classic Marco," she said. "I just moved here."

"Marco implied you and Daphne were two of his girls."

Greta began to slide toward the edge of the booth. She didn't care about embarrassing Daphne. She'd run.

Sandy laughed. "It's not what you think. He's not running a brothel."

From the edge of the seat, she asked, "What is he running, then?"

"He's a producer."

"That means nothing to me." Blessed anger was quickly replacing her embarrassment.

"I can see that." He smiled. "I think it's awesome."

Greta relaxed. Unlike Marco, Sandy seemed truly harmless. A part of her mind wondered how Daphne felt about being one of *Marco's girls*. She filed the thought away for later.

"So Daphne and I were part of some plan for the evening."

Sandy nodded. "Entertainment. And bait. Motivation for me to agree."

Relaxing back into the booth, Greta shook her head.

"What?" Sandy asked.

"Daphne being bait? Sure. She's gorgeous and funny. But not me. I'm terrible bait."

Sandy leaned back, his eyes turning cool, his mouth pulling down into a frown.

Greta grew uncomfortable under his piercing stare.

Finally, he spoke. "You're not starlet material, true."

Although Greta knew his words were fact, they stung nonetheless.

"But you are a lean and elegant woman with extraordinary eyes and beautiful hair, and legs that go on forever." Sandy raised his eyebrows. "You know, *bait*."

The word hit Greta like a body blow. Tears stung her eyes. "I don't know you," she said, hating the rising pitch of her voice. "Why are you talking to me like this?"

"Like what?" Sandy said, coolly sipping his wine.

"Like you're trying to hurt me." A tiny sob escaped. She turned away from him, embarrassed beyond bearing.

"Ah, so you weren't fishing for compliments, then."

"What?" She whipped her face back toward him, anger quickly replacing her humiliation. "What are you talking about?"

"I hoped not. But since literally every other person in this building would have been, it seemed improbable that you weren't." His face softened.

Anger still coursed through Greta's veins. "Daphne doesn't fish for compliments either." Greta spat out the words. "She'd rather eat dirt." She wiped the tears from her cheeks, and this time she didn't try to hide them. Let the jerk see that he hurt her.

"I'm sorry, Greta," Sandy said. "Forgive me." He sounded sincere.

"You were testing me, Mr. Martin."

"Yes."

"Why?"

"I'm old. It's a terrible habit."

"That's not a good enough reason." Her anger was abating, but she liked how it made her feel. Powerful. Able to stand up to a man like this. She cocked her head, meeting his eyes directly for the first time since they started speaking. "People want things from you a lot."

He nodded. "And please call me Sandy."

Greta snorted. "We're friends now?"

Sandy gave her a small smile. "I think we could be. If you wanted."

Greta relaxed back against the booth. "Sure thing, Sandy." A laugh escaped as she said his name, and she slapped her hand over her mouth. The whole situation was too surreal.

"Good." He sounded like he meant it, his gaze sincere.

She took a sip of wine. "Even if those things you said about me were true, I'd still be terrible bait."

"Why's that?"

"Because I'd rather eat dirt than talk bullshit to curry favor."

Sandy picked up his glass of wine and held it aloft. "Fucking cheers to that."

Grinning, Greta lifted her glass as well and touched it to Sandy's.

She finished her wine, one she guessed came from the priciest position on the wine list.

Ordering a five-hundred-dollar bottle was Marco's prerogative. But he seemed to believe he could order her and Daphne as well. What amazed her most was how relaxed Daphne was about the situation.

"What else is classic Marco?" Greta asked.

"There's a long list for you." Sandy chuckled. "Let me see. Arguing the superiority of New York City to Los Angeles in the tone of a native son, even though he's from New Jersey. Giving you his opinion first and checking facts later." Then, Sandy's tone turned serious. "And always calling his oldest friends first when he has a new project, to give them first refusal, even when he could pull more funding with a hipper star."

Greta heard the loyalty in Sandy's voice, and genuine gratitude—from this man, the kind of person the bouncers were literally outside to protect. She better understood why Daphne felt more than just tolerance for Marco.

Then Sandy asked Greta about college, and she told him about her studies. He seemed impressed.

"Does a physics major help with your work in lighting?"

"All the time." She was getting excited, and for a moment she feared she would frighten Sandy with her geekiness. But then she decided he probably wouldn't mind, and if he did, she wouldn't care.

The not-caring was a new feeling for her, and she liked it.

"I studied electricity, of course, and part of our job in lighting involves running power. Optics helps with lenses. And then there's the inverse square law."

Sandy raised his eyebrows, questioning.

"The law says that as a light source gets farther away, its brightness falls off in a squared relationship to the distance. So, if you double the distance a light has to shine, it doesn't become half as bright, but rather one-fourth. Physicists use the law to talk about stars, but you can apply it to any lights."

Sandy paused. "And to metaphorical stars, I guess." He sounded wistful.

He was talking about himself.

Sandy's humility, combined with his loyalty, suddenly made him very appealing to Greta. Sure, he was an ass earlier, but he sincerely apologized. She didn't know what it was like to be him. But she did know that he was wrong about his own brightness.

She leaned closer to him. "That's true. But only to a certain point."

"What do you mean?"

"Trendy celebrities do fade quickly as their fame grows distant. But the law bends, I think, for those who have, we'll say, permeated the cosmos with their stellar radiation."

After a long moment, Sandy leaned over and kissed her on the cheek. Her face turned red once more, but this time she didn't try to hide it.

———

Twenty minutes later, Daphne and Marco returned. Despite Sandy's excellent company, Greta was tired, the day's hard work weighing her shoulders down. Daphne raised an eyebrow at her, and she nodded.

"That's all, folks," Daphne said. "We're off to bed—and by bed I mean floor!"

When Greta stood, Sandy did so as well. He pulled her close for a hug. "Let's do this again."

"Dinner with Marco?" Greta asked, stepping back. "I'm not one who can make those plans."

"I am," he said, squeezing her hand that remained in his.

She tried to hide how much his words dazed her. This man, so accomplished and famous and frankly stunning, wanted to hang out with her. She spoke the only word that came to mind. "Why?"

Sandy chuckled. "The fact that you asked that question is your answer."

She took in his words. "Because I didn't presume that someone like you would want to hang out with someone like me?"

He shook his head. "Because you're not hoping that I'll help you get your foot in the door."

Greta frowned. "I don't even know what door to put my foot in."

He laughed again. "You are the most refreshing person I've met in a decade." His expression grew serious. "Do not let all of this nonsense change you." He gestured around the room. "Please."

Greta shrugged. "People don't change, so you have nothing to worry about. Besides, I don't think I could if I wanted to." She smiled now. "And I don't want to."

At her words, Daphne butted in. "She's always saying that people can't change. It's one of the few things we disagree on."

"That," Greta interrupted, "and whether I should grow my hair long, which is never going to happen." What on earth would she do with even more unruly hair?

Sandy waved goodbye as he took his seat again. Meanwhile, Marco escorted her and Daphne to the door. There, Daphne stopped by the bar to say good night to the bartender, and Marco pulled Greta aside, his hand gripping her elbow a little too tightly.

He spoke close to her ear so Daphne couldn't hear. "You two are sleeping on the floor?"

"That's right. We're saving up to buy beds."

"But that's crazy."

Greta didn't respond. Their plan wasn't crazy; it was smart. She couldn't imagine an alternative that didn't involve credit cards with unconscionable interest rates.

Marco went on. "I'm going to buy a bed for Daphne. It's a surprise."

She hid her shock behind the same blank face she used with her father.

Marco went on. "I'm telling you so that when the deliverymen arrive, you'll let them in, okay? Tomorrow night." He rubbed his hands together, excited by his plan. "Don't tell her," Marco said. "It's a surprise."

"I won't tell her."

"Good girl." Marco squeezed her arm once more. Turning, he grabbed Daphne, kissing her on the lips and saying goodbye.

Greta smiled stiffly, aggravated by his patronizing tone and his ridiculous gift. Buying a bed for a woman was too intimate. Worse, a bed was large and expensive—a person would feel obligated to the person who bought it for her.

That's exactly why he's doing it, she thought.

But Marco miscalculated. She refused to feel obligation, ever since she left her parents' home. No bargains. No exchanges. Not after her father bargained her teenage body to a guest to pay off his debts.

When Daphne shared the horrible secret with her one night during their first summer together, she'd sobbed in Greta's arms. Greta was the first person she ever told outside her family. She'd kept the secret for nearly a decade, from every boyfriend, every friend she never fully trusted. But she trusted Greta.

Marco could spend all the money in the world on Daphne, but Daphne would never be bought. The thought brought a smile to her face.

But then she frowned. Marco's gift meant that while Daphne slept on a bed, Greta would be sleeping on the floor. Sleeping on the floor without Daphne seemed far less palatable. In her mind, Greta quickly designed a platform bed she could build with some plywood and two-by-fours at Timmy's shop. Maybe she'd paint it orange.

———

THE NEXT DAY, TIMMY DROPPED GRETA OFF AT THE DUPLEX BEFORE Daphne got home from work. She'd only been home a few minutes when the delivery truck arrived. Two men assembled the metal bed frame and then placed upon it a mattress so thick and plush that Greta was certain Daphne would have to special order the fitted sheets.

Daphne got home shortly after the delivery team left. Greta sat on one of the loungers in their courtyard, waiting for her as she often did, a cup of coffee in her hand.

"There's a fresh pot if you want some," Greta said as Daphne walked up.

"Great. I'll be right back, so don't move."

When Greta heard Daphne pull a mug from the kitchen cabinet, she called to her, "Could you bring me that book I was reading? I think I left it in your room."

She waited for Daphne's reaction. Moments later, Daphne screamed, calling for Greta.

Daphne was jumping on the bed like a child. "What the hell is going on?" Daphne asked, grinning. "Did you buy this?"

"It's yours," Greta said, tucking her hair behind her ears. "From Marco."

"He's such a freak!" Daphne said, falling to her back, a huge grin on her face.

A few hours later, when it was time to go to sleep, Greta headed to her own room. She dug her bedding from her closet and spread it on the floor.

Daphne called from where she sat on her new bed, typing on her laptop. "What in the world are you doing?"

"Making my bed," Greta said.

"Don't be ridiculous. Come in here."

Greta entered Daphne's room. Marco's extravagance made her uncomfortable. Daphne took it in stride, as though she believed she deserved all of these wonderful, beautiful things men bought her. And Greta agreed—Daphne did indeed deserve them.

But she didn't think she deserved them, too.

"I can't believe you think I'd let you sleep on the floor," Daphne said. "I'm insulted."

"It's your bed."

Daphne rolled her eyes. "You're sleeping here," she said, patting the surface next to her.

"I don't think Marco intended to buy a bed for me, too."

"Who cares?" Daphne said. "Besides, he'll think it's hot."

"That's obscene." Greta walked over and fell back on the mattress, pulling the comforter up to her chin. She sighed in comfort.

"I'm concerned, though," Daphne said. "We're going to have to find a truly ugly headboard to make up for how nice this mattress is. Maybe something with carvings? French Provincial? With gold leaf?"

"Gold leaf is the worst. We definitely need gold leaf."

After a while, Daphne closed her laptop, then stood to turn off the overhead light. As she climbed back into bed, she leaned over and kissed Greta on the cheek.

"What's that for?"

"If Marco asks if we made out in the new bed, I can say yes."

While Greta made puking noises, Daphne laughed until she cried.

But later that night, after Daphne fell asleep, Greta thought about Professor Blue's offer. Dinner at Rivet had taught her one thing for sure. Despite Sandy's kindness, she did not belong in Hollywood, and never would. This wasn't her world.

Chapter Eleven

The last week of August, Greta entered Timmy's office at 9:45 a.m., before anyone else arrived for work. "Good morning," she said to him, giving him a small smile. "I'm going to work on cable."

When he looked up and smiled back, her heart rabbited in her chest.

Timmy had a great smile, and a closely clipped beard accentuated his jawline. He was handsome, but he didn't behave like most handsome men in Los Angeles. He didn't talk about himself, mistreat those who were less good-looking or less important than he, or fixate on his appearance.

She figured that Timmy didn't realize how appealing he was.

But over the past few weeks, ever since he'd helped her buy the lifeboat, after he'd complimented her before her night at Rivet, he'd grown very, very appealing to her.

And she hated it.

He didn't feel the same way about her. At first, she thought he did. She believed Daphne when her friend tried to convince her that Timmy must feel something special for Greta. But a week had passed since he sat outside with her waiting for Daphne, and he had done nothing to convey those feelings again. If he did find her attractive, he would have said something by now. They saw each other five days a week, sometimes more. He'd had ample opportunity to make his feelings known, but he never treated her any differently than the other guys in the shop.

She was as invisible to him as she was to everyone else.

Usually, she didn't mind being invisible, or at least away from the center of attention. But Timmy had flipped her world upside down, and she didn't know if she could take it anymore.

The ache in her chest. The wanting.

It was awful.

"Good morning to you," Timmy said, his smile only growing brighter. "Can I help? I'm sick of desk work. I've been here since eight o'clock."

She shrugged in assent and headed into the shop to the cable bins. If she'd spoken, she was afraid she would have told him no, that she didn't want his help. That she didn't want him near her at all.

And then she'd get fired. Or he would ask why.

She couldn't decide which would be worse.

Today was supposed to be a satisfying shop day. All the shows and rentals were already prepped, so Greta had time to work on her backlog of special projects: road case repairs, gel organization, and cable labeling.

She often worked alone on these projects, able to zone in and focus despite her coworkers' goofing off.

But a few days ago, she'd overheard Timmy tell another guy on the crew to leave her alone while she was color-coding truss couplers. Rather than letting him help, Timmy said, *Don't mess with Greta right now, man. She's a machine.*

Timmy was right—she was indeed about to focus better than most other people, and she worked fast. But his words bothered her. Sure, he meant them as a compliment, but hearing him talk about her that way made her feel like a weirdo again. She didn't want him to think about her as a strange lab partner who didn't talk but got the answers right.

After the Rivet night, she let herself believe that he felt something more for her. But nothing had changed. She was wrong. It hurt.

She'd imagined the whole thing. His intense stare. His words of praise. What seemed to go unspoken, too.

Worse, her feelings for him had grown stronger in the days since, which made being around him nearly intolerable.

He was polite and kind, and she wanted to scream at him to just leave her alone.

To stop thinking about Timmy, she focused on the cable. Pac Lighting had thousands of power cables of various lengths, gauges, and types, ranging from eight to a hundred feet. Cable could make or break a show, and being able to quickly identify it was essential. So they were labeling it all.

They stored their cable in circular loops tied with Velcro straps. She grabbed a cable from the storage bin and showed it to Timmy. He glanced at the cable and said, "Twenty-five feet." After working with cable for as many years as he had, he no longer needed to measure.

Timmy punched some buttons on their label maker, and the machine churned out two pieces of label tape printed with the words "Pac Lighting 25." He handed her the labels, and she wrapped one around each end of the cable. She tossed the loop of cable into a bin, and they began the process again.

They worked like this all morning, barely speaking to one another. Greta was grateful for the silence because she had no idea what to say to him. But that didn't stop her from stealing glances at how well his black t-shirt fit across his broad shoulders. At his strong forearms, muscular not from time wasted in a gym but from the hard work he did every day. At how well his jeans fit his long frame, accentuating his athletic build—he'd played soccer in high school and sometimes joined friends for a game on the weekends.

The ache in her chest returned. She was never going to be more to him than an employee, a good worker, *a machine*. She heard echoes of her father's voice, criticizing her appearance and her choices.

After she labeled the cable in her hand, she hurled it into the bin.

"Whoa. Are you okay?" Timmy asked.

Horrified, Greta found herself on the verge of tears. "I need to go." She dashed off to the bathroom before she could finish her sentence.

Once behind the locked door, she pulled herself together. Her father was gone. And if all she could be to Timmy was a friend, that meant a lot, because she didn't have many friends, and Timmy was a good one. She considered calling Daphne to ask her to drive her home tonight. The thought of being alone in a car with Timmy today tore her up. She'd be okay tomorrow.

He was a friend, she reminded herself. A good one.

So she didn't call Daphne. She could be his friend. She could.

After a few minutes, she returned to Timmy and picked up another cable. She held it out to him with a weak smile.

"Fifty feet," he said, returning her smile.

She couldn't go on this way. She had a doctoral program waiting for her. She didn't have to force herself into the ill-fitting world of Los Angeles any longer.

Tonight, she'd call Professor Blue, and she would figure out how to help Daphne find another place to afford on her own.

She held up another cable to Timmy, and he told her the length. She watched him type in the numbers, overcome with regret about what might have been.

Chapter Twelve

TIMMY

Timmy worked with Greta on her cable project all morning. Sure, he had other stuff to do, and one of the other guys could have helped her. But he didn't want another guy helping her. The very thought made him want to fire his entire crew.

Shortly after noon, he announced to Greta, "I'm hungry. Do you want to go to lunch?" He prayed she would say yes. He had an important question to ask her, and he was going to ask her today, even though she seemed off. He was done procrastinating.

The first time he asked her to lunch, she'd been working for him for a month. A few weeks after that, they started having lunch together regularly. Now he asked her out to lunch at least twice a week. But building up to a regular lunch schedule with her had been difficult.

The first challenge had been her sandwiches. She packed a sandwich every day, usually peanut butter like a little girl. Her sandwiches were adorable.

The first time he asked her to lunch, she told him about her sandwich. But she said, "Don't worry. The sandwich won't go to waste. I'll just eat it for dinner."

So Timmy asked, half-joking, "Am I paying you enough to live on?"

When she replied, "You pay me more than the mean salary for a worker in my position with my level of experience," he couldn't tell if that was a yes.

The second challenge was that she was frugal and didn't like to waste money dining out.

"I still don't have a bed," she told him, explaining why eating in restaurants wasn't within her budget. The day after her Rivet dinner, she told him the story about Daphne's boss buying Daphne a bed, and now Greta was putting pressure on herself to find one of her own. She didn't want to keep relying on Daphne, despite how close they were.

As Greta told him about the bed situation, he spent the rest of the conversation thinking about Greta in a bed. Naked. After getting his mind (and other body parts) back under control, he offered to help her find a bed at an estate sale. He explained how you could get a nearly-new bed from the mansions in the hills, even one that was still in plastic, if you got there early enough.

He figured she would go to lunch with him if he paid for the meal, at which point he encountered the third challenge: She didn't want him to pay for her. Of course not. She was proud and independent.

God, he loved that about her. But it was also frustrating. Why couldn't she let him do small things for her? At the very least, she deserved a pay raise. But she'd balk at that too, he knew, saying some nonsense about how she'd only been there two months and had less experience and on and on until he would pull his hair out.

To get her to let him treat her to lunch, he told her he deducted their lunches as a work expense.

This was a lie.

Figuring out how to spend time with Greta took some hard work, and perhaps a white lie now and then. But she was worth the effort.

She didn't seem to hear today's lunch invitation at first, because she was studying a frayed piece of cable.

"Well?" he asked.

"Well, what?" she said, looking up.

"Lunch?"

"Oh."

And then it seemed to him that, for some reason, she was

blushing. He knew he must be wrong. He asked her to lunch all the time, and she never blushed before.

"Sure," she said. "Let me go wash the cable funk from my hands."

She emerged from the bathroom, running her clean fingers through her hair and then tucking it behind her ears. The color had lightened since she'd been living here, the L.A. sun turning the reddish brown curls into bright copper. He loved the color and her curls. He wanted to be the one running his fingers through them.

Timmy drove Greta to a retro-style drive-in near the shop, a place she really liked. He rolled down his window to order.

Greta spoke. "I'd like a burger with all the veggies, bacon, and cheddar cheese."

Timmy hid his smile as he placed their order. Greta always ordered the same thing, but she always told him what she wanted. Surely she knew he was aware of her preferences at this point. But Greta liked precision. It would be hard for her to take anything, including lunch, on faith.

He was hoping she would put her faith in him, though.

After he finished ordering, he asked, "Do you want to sit on the hood? It's finally getting cool outside."

"That sounds nice. Not long, though. I'll get a sunburn."

"Don't worry," he said. "I'll keep you safe."

At his words, her back seemed to stiffen. What had he said wrong?

A gazelle. He reminded himself. A gazelle.

After climbing out of the car, they leaned back on the warm metal hood, feet on the bumper, the autumn sunshine bright but not overbearing.

An airplane roared overhead, lifting into the sky, then banking sharply south. Timmy took the jet as a good omen, its majestic metal body defying the laws of physics. It was like a miracle, even.

"What are you doing tomorrow night?" he asked.

"Going home first, as you know, since you're driving me. Making dinner. Hanging out with Daphne in our back courtyard, like we do every day, drinking our evening coffee."

"What's evening coffee?"

"It's a Daphne thing. She likes to drink a cup of coffee when she gets home to signify that the real start of her day occurs after she's finished work. Then she goes into her room and works on her own screenplays for an hour or two. She's amazingly productive."

"What do you do while she writes?"

"A lot of times I'll read. Sometimes I'll go running if the air seems less gross than usual. Or I'll wash our cars. After she's done writing, we head over to this bar near our apartment, Iguana."

"I know that place," he said. And good god, it was a total dump. What were Greta and Daphne doing hanging out there? It was below even his single-dude standards.

"We go there two or three nights a week," she said. "It's our second home."

"It sounds like you have your evening planned."

Greta shrugged. "I'm merely predicting based on past events. Daphne might have to work late."

"Or you might have other plans," Timmy said.

"But I don't," she said, looking at him with unblinking eyes.

"How about dinner with me?"

"Did a last-minute show come up? I can work late tomorrow."

"There's no last-minute show. Just dinner. A date, actually. With me."

"A date?" Greta repeated, brows scrunched together.

He'd been planning to ask her out ever since last week, when he'd almost shown his entire hand, pushing her too far, too fast. But he hadn't been able to help himself. When Greta had started bagging on herself because she didn't fit in with Hollywood types, he'd lost his mind. "You're worth more than a hundred of them," he'd said, but he'd wanted to say so much more.

Then he dashed inside like a coward.

He spent the next week playing it as cool as he could, hoping he hadn't scared her off for good. He needed to rebuild her trust. No creepy comments. No staring. No heartfelt confessions.

But now, he was tired of waiting.

Early that morning, sitting at his desk, he decided today was the day. If she said no, he'd have to figure out how to be her boss without wanting to kiss her, because there was no way he was letting her quit. She was the best shop hand he'd ever had.

But it was one thing to speculate about her saying no, and another thing to sit on the cliff's edge like he was doing right now. He just asked his best shop hand out to dinner, and she wasn't answering.

He was trying not to freak out. "What do you think?" he asked.

"You like me in that way?"

Greta said *that* with such incredulity that Timmy decided to be as clear as he could.

"Yes, I do like you. In fact, *like* is too lightweight a word."

He was putting himself all the way out there. If she turned him down, it wouldn't be because there was a misunderstanding.

"I like you too," she blurted, then quickly looked down at her lap, tucking her hair behind her ears. "But after the past week, I thought you didn't feel the same way about me."

"What do you mean?"

"That night, when you told me I was good enough for Rivet—"

"I'm so sorry I said all of that. I was way over the line."

"What do you mean? It was the nicest thing you've ever said to me. But then you just…stopped."

Timmy dropped his face into his hand. "I think we've had a terrible misunderstanding."

"Please explain." She pulled at a curl, a nervous habit he recognized.

"Are you saying that I didn't freak you out that night?"

"You surprised me, but no freaking out."

"So you're saying I wasted an entire week trying to earn back trust that I never broke in the first place?"

A smile pulled at her lips. "Is that what you were doing?"

He looked at her hands, where they lay on her thighs. Calluses had formed on her palms and fingers since she'd started working for him. They looked a lot like the calluses on his own hands. Taking her hand in his, he squeezed. She gave him a sideways glance, a smile crinkling the corner of her eye.

He leaned over and kissed her temple. She turned to face him, and they kissed for real, a small kiss, but one that lit a fire in Timmy like he'd never felt in his life.

He cradled her face, feeling the soft hair on the nape of her neck. Pulling her face to his, he kissed her again, deeply this time. He tried to show her how much he'd been wanting to do this ever since she'd first walked into his shop.

The cough of the waitress holding their tray startled them apart. He wiped his face with his hand, then he pulled some cash from his wallet and paid the waitress. After handing him the tray, she skated off, her red and white striped skirt flapping around her thighs.

He set the tray on the hood between them, then handed Greta her burger.

"Yes," she said.

"What?" He was still dazed by their kiss.

"To dinner. Yes."

Timmy leaned back on his elbow, holding his burger with one hand, smiling. "Great. Just." Should he hold back? No, he should not. "Amazing, actually."

She graced him with another of her secret smiles, and he felt like a hero.

Chapter Thirteen

GRETA

The next day, Greta arrived at the shop feeling more nervous than she had on her first day of work. Last night, she didn't share with Daphne that Timmy kissed her or asked her out to dinner. She didn't like keeping secrets from Daphne, and now she had two. It felt awful, breaking Daphne's trust with secrets. It wasn't their way.

But Greta was overwhelmed. She needed time to think about the immense change that had happened to her, and she didn't have a lot of alone time these days.

She never appreciated how much she liked her alone time until it was gone. In college, she'd had plenty. But now, working in a busy shop, living with Daphne, going out with Daphne after work—unless Daphne had a date with one of her many boyfriends, she was never alone.

Last night, she realized she needed to tell Timmy something important. She found him in the shop programming a light board. "Um, can I talk to you in your office about something?"

"Is everything okay?" He looked concerned.

She nodded. "Just need to talk."

Once they were in his office with the door closed, she dug her toe into the concrete floor. She was so nervous.

Timmy leaned against his desk. "What's the matter?"

"I don't want the other guys to know." She gestured toward the workshop. "We have to keep you and me a secret."

Timmy nodded slowly. "I can respect that. But, can you tell me why?"

"I earned my place here. I work really hard."

"Too hard probably," Timmy interrupted, "but go on."

"I didn't flirt my way into this job."

"Of course not." He sounded far too calm. Couldn't he see how upset she was?

"There's no of-course anything when you're fooling around with the boss," she hissed. "If you flirt with me, hold my hand, even touch me around them, they'll sense it."

Timmy paused a long time before answering. "We can keep things under wraps. That's fine."

But Greta had a feeling it wasn't fine for him. She let it go, though, because she didn't want a fight. "Thank you."

He nodded, and she left with the sense she'd just hurt him deeply, though she couldn't figure out how.

———

Later that evening, Greta didn't even realize that the shop had cleared out until she leaned back to stretch her shoulders. She had taken over programming the light board for an upcoming show and had been too focused to notice that all the guys had left.

She checked her watch. It was only six-thirty.

"Timmy?" she called out.

He appeared around a rack of gear, grinning.

"Where is everyone?"

"I said I needed to close up early today." He approached her as he spoke.

"Oh," she said, standing. "I didn't realize."

He took her hand in his, lacing their fingers together. "You're the reason I need to close early."

She blushed at her mistake. "Right. Dinner. I forgot."

Timmy laughed. "I didn't."

"That's not what I meant," she said, trying to fix her stupid words.

Before she could go on, he said, "I know." He tugged her hand. "Come on. I want to show you something before we leave."

He led her out onto the loading dock to a set of wooden stairs built along the side of the building. Up they climbed until they reached the roof and a deck built atop it. He rested his arms on the western-facing railing, and she joined him there, looking outward. "Oh, wow," she said. "We can see the ocean from here. Did you build this?"

"Yeah. Shortly after I bought the company, I needed a private place to think. Back then, I was mostly thinking about how stupid I was for believing I could run a business like this. Later, I started coming up here just to get away from the noise. I thought you might like it. No one else is allowed up here but me."

At first, Greta was amazed that Timmy shared his special spot with her and offered to let her use it. But then she frowned with worry. "But what will the others think? If they're not allowed up here and I am?"

"You'll have a reason. You know how much I hate running payroll?"

She nodded.

"Congratulations. You're the new payroll person of Pacific Production Lighting. I thought about giving you a new title, but figured you'd hate that."

Greta felt a small pinch of shame. "Am I so easy to read?"

"No, not at all. But I'm beginning to figure you out." He took her hand in both of his. "And don't worry. Literally every person who works for me has heard me bitch about payroll. They also know you're a math whiz who could probably do it in her head. So you can work on it up here. Or, at least use it as an excuse to do so."

She ran the scenario in her head. A plausible excuse for time in this isolated spot. More job responsibilities. These were good things. So why was she feeling trepidation?

"And one more thing," Timmy said. He pulled a cell phone from his pocket. "Here."

She held the phone, a plastic block with large buttons like a children's toy, designed by some Finnish technology company she'd never heard of.

"Why?"

"It's a work phone. In case you need to reach me or anyone else. But really, use it as much as you want."

"I...I can't accept this. It's too much."

He raised his brows. "It's a phone, Greta."

She couldn't speak, torn between the kindness of Timmy's gifts and her instinctive need to refuse them. She felt like a rabbit in a trap, just as her father used to make her feel.

"Does Daphne have a phone from her boss?" he asked.

Greta nodded. "But it's not the same. Marco's a slimeball. I call it her Hottie Tracking Device."

Timmy cradled her face in his hands. "I'm not trying to track you or trap you. I just want you to have a cell phone. Honestly, it's mostly selfish because it'll make my life easier. I don't think you realize how much I count on you here."

She swallowed hard. He was saying all the right things.

"And if having a phone makes your life easier, too? I want to do that for you. I like you, Greta. Can you see that?"

She nodded, at a loss for words.

"I'm going to kiss you now. Okay?"

"Okay."

As they kissed, she let all of her fears fall away, leaning against his strong body. She wrapped her arms around his neck, holding on for balance as she went light-headed. When they broke apart, she was breathless.

"Yesterday was my first real kiss," she blurted out.

He hugged her to him, and she rested her head on his shoulder. "How is that possible? Were you in a convent? Were the guys at that fancy college all assholes?"

She couldn't stifle a laugh. "There was a high asshole ratio at Cameron, for sure, but that's not why. It just never...happened for me."

"My father was an alcoholic," Timmy said. "He is sober now, but for most of my childhood, things were pretty chaotic."

"Oh, that's awful. I'm sorry." Greta wondered if she should tell him about her own parents. But he seemed to be making some kind of point.

"It was pretty awful for a while. I have an uncle, Brian, my dad's brother. He helped out a lot back then, like a second dad. I turned out all right, I think."

She stood on her toes and kissed his cheek. "I agree."

He squeezed her tighter. "Anyways, things were always disappearing from the house to pay for his addiction, which also included a string of mistresses. The television. Some of my mom's jewelry." He pulled back so he could meet Greta's eyes, resting his hands on her shoulders. "Let me do nice things for you, okay?"

Greta quickly made the connection. Every time she pushed him away, rejected a gift, even a small one, she hurt him.

She never wanted to hurt Timmy. "Okay," she said, turning back to the railing and the view. "I really like it up here. Thank you." She paused, wondering what to tell him about herself. She could see her father's fingers meddling in her life, still. "Remember, back when you helped me buy the lifeboat, I told you about why we only buy ugly furniture?"

Timmy, who held her from behind, resting his chin on her shoulder, said, "Something about how your father took away some nice furniture that was yours."

As he spoke, his warm breath kissed her ear, and she shivered. Being with Timmy felt so natural. So *right*. "Heirlooms, actually. Hand-made for my grandmother, handed down to my mom, then to me." She told him about that awful day at her parents' house, how she held onto that precious drawer, then smashed it.

Timmy let out a low whistle. "I can't even picture you doing something like that."

Greta surprised herself by laughing. "Me, neither, honestly. A first and last time for everything, I suppose." She turned in the cage of his arms, her back against the railing. "Thank you for the phone. And the hiding spot."

Gathering her courage, she pulled his face to hers and kissed him, darting her tongue into his mouth, feeling the desire flood her veins.

Timmy groaned. "You're a fast learner in everything." He pulled her tight. "We should get going if we're going to make our reservations."

She nodded. "I just need to stop by home first. Is that okay?"

"You could ask me for anything right now, and I would agree." He took her hand, kissing the back of it. "Let's go."

Chapter Fourteen

GRETA

When they arrived at Greta's apartment, Timmy asked her, "Do you want me to come in with you?"

Greta shook her head. "I'll just be a minute. Wait here." Greta wanted to talk to Daphne without Timmy there. She needed to tell Daphne about Timmy and the kissing and the date tonight. She'd kept it all a secret and hoped Daphne would understand. Because she really needed some advice about whether she was making the right decision.

"Sure," Timmy said. He got out of the car when she did and leaned against the driver's door to wait.

She looked down at her dirty t-shirt and jeans. "I'll try to do something about my outfit, but don't expect a miracle."

"I'd take you out just like that and have no problem with it."

Greta blushed at the compliment. She wondered if she would ever stop blushing around Timmy.

Not any time soon, she thought.

She walked briskly down the pathway to her apartment. Thankfully, Daphne's car was already parked in the carport. Inside, Daphne sat on the lifeboat, her feet perched on the coffee table that Greta had built with leftover wood from some scenery she'd made for a show, reading a book.

"Hello, dear," Daphne said, closing the book and setting it on the table.

"Timmy's waiting with the car," Greta blurted. "We've kissed twice, and now he wants to take me to dinner."

To Daphne, who could read Greta's moods better than anyone, she must have sounded like she was announcing an impending Richter eight earthquake.

"He invited you on a date." Daphne didn't seem surprised. "And you've kissed."

"We kissed at lunch at a drive-in yesterday. Then again today. Daphne, what do I do? I'm so sorry I didn't tell you last night."

Daphne waved her hand. "You didn't tell me because you were still trying to wrap your head around it. It's not the first time. It's just who you are. Sometimes you need some time." Standing, Daphne squeezed Greta's shoulders. "In order to make a decision, we have to think about worst-case scenarios," she said. "We need to write a list."

Daphne pulled a pad of paper out of her shoulder bag and unsnapped a fountain pen. "What would happen if your relationship goes south? Will it affect your job?"

"Worst case scenario, I'll have to find a new job." Greta's stomach tightened at the thought of leaving her job. She loved the work. The shop was her new laboratory. And she really, really liked it there.

The shop was her new laboratory. Wow.

Daphne wrote "Leave job" on the list. "What if you didn't leave your job?" Daphne asked.

"It would be horribly awkward at work, and Timmy wouldn't talk to me." The idea of working for Timmy without the camaraderie she'd grown to love made her feel physically ill.

Daphne pushed back. "He'd have to talk to you if you still worked there."

"But he wouldn't want to."

Daphne wrote "Awkward at work" on the list, and then below that, "Timmy won't like me." Then she asked, "Can you think of anything else?"

"No." Greta took the list from Daphne's hand. "I guess this isn't so bad. These don't seem likely. Except for the awkward part, and things are already awkward now because I like him and act stupid around him half the time."

Daphne nodded, thoughtful. "He's waiting outside?" She looked at Greta's dirty T-shirt and said, "For you to change clothes?"

Greta nodded.

Daphne tapped her chin. "Go have dinner," she said. "You can tell a lot over dinner. If you pay attention, you'll learn if you really like him, and if he's right for you." Daphne paused. "Remember: Just because you like him doesn't mean he's right for you." She placed both hands on Greta's face, right where Timmy's hands had been earlier that day. "There are a lot of likable people out there, but there's only one Greta."

Greta threw her arms around Daphne's narrow shoulders. "I do really like him," she said. "But what if it all goes to shit?"

"You won't have to leave your job if you only have dinner."

"But what about the kissing?"

Daphne shrugged. "What's a kiss between friends?"

Greta sat back on the lifeboat, tugging nervously at one of her curls. "There's something else. Something big."

"Bigger than your first kiss? Your first date?"

Greta nodded, then she told Daphne about Professor Blue's offer. "I'm so sorry I kept this a secret, too. I didn't mean to."

Daphne inhaled deeply. "This offer is your dream come true, right?"

Greta shrugged. "That's the problem. I don't know anymore. I don't want to hang you out to dry with this lease. And I'm not ready to leave my job—well, Timmy."

Daphne raised her brows. "You're going to turn down the offer?"

Greta nodded, shocking herself. "Yeah. I am." Wow. She couldn't believe it. This decision felt huge. Even bigger than moving out to L.A. in the first place. She had her revenge in the palm of her hands, and she was letting it fall. "I can always apply for next year. Maybe even to a university out here. Caltech's program is pretty good, I hear." She snorted. Caltech was fantastic, and it wasn't so hard to get to Pasadena. She could still live with Daphne. "I think a break from school, from my family, is a good thing."

Daphne squeezed her hand. "I'm glad you decided to stay. And I agree—maybe someday we can let our families back into our lives, but not right now."

Daphne nudged her book with her toe, seeming crestfallen. Sure, they usually went to Iguana together, and Daphne was probably counting on going tonight. Iguana was a dive bar just up the street, nicely within stumbling distance. It was the anti-Hollywood: a dark, strip-mall lounge with Christmas lights staple-gunned to the ceiling, full of men who laid asphalt for a living and women who changed motel sheets, just like Daphne used to.

Greta and Daphne were frequent guests, spending two or three nights a week there, eating stale peanuts and drinking High Life with migrant workers—because Daphne spoke their language—and electricians—because Greta spoke theirs. Greta liked it because the guys didn't seem to mind that she wasn't beautiful. She never felt pressure to be someone she wasn't.

But Greta knew that Daphne wouldn't go to Iguana alone, because the walk was just a little too dangerous, and because she'd be lonely, just like Greta would.

For a moment, Greta considered telling Timmy she needed to postpone. She shouldn't have dropped this bomb on Daphne at the last minute.

"I can see what you're thinking," Daphne said. "I'll be fine. Go put on something cute. Let me know if you need help."

After Greta changed, Daphne handed her a tube of lip gloss. "Remember to call at midnight."

The midnight call was a policy they'd instituted in college. If one of the girls were going to stay out late or all night, she'd call to let the other know she was safe. They didn't have many people caring whether they lived or died, so they created a way of caring for each other. After all these years, the call was sacred.

Greta wrote down Timmy's number and address in the notebook they kept by their phone. "Don't worry," she told Daphne, squeezing her hand as she walked out the door. "You know where he lives, and you know where he works." She paused. "And I love you, Daph. I don't know what I'd do without you."

At her words, Daphne's face softened. "Back at you."

Chapter Fifteen

TIMMY

Timmy had spent all afternoon figuring out where to take Greta to dinner. The decision required careful consideration. The restaurant would have to be anti-Hollywood, because Greta hated Hollywood types—they made her self-conscious. It couldn't be too expensive, because she would go nuts and not let him pay for her if it were pricey. It would have to be delicious because he wanted them to enjoy the food and have the warm feelings a good meal together creates. And if he were lucky, those warm feelings might carry them into the night.

And finally, the restaurant would also have to be casual, because he was going to wear the jeans he'd worn to work with the dress shirt he'd hung in his car a few days ago, hoping that she would agree to dinner, once he got up the nerve to ask her. He put on the shirt while Greta was changing in her apartment.

He was leaning against the car when Greta emerged from the back of the duplex, striding down the walkway toward him. She'd put on a black spaghetti-strap top and long black pants that hugged her thighs and hips and flared out at the knee, hanging low over high heels. He'd always thought she was sexy, but he'd never seen her like this— striding toward him as though the world belonged at her feet.

If he weren't leaning against his car, he would have fallen to his knees.

She stopped in front of him, as though waiting for him to say something. Instead, he stepped close to her. Slowly, deliberately, he tucked his fingers into her hair and kissed her, letting loose all of the emotions he'd kept contained since the first moment she'd walked into his shop. When she opened for him with a gasp, he wrapped his arms around her and crushed her against him.

Eventually, he broke the kiss and pulled her close, dropping his head on her shoulder, glad to see that she was as breathless as he.

"Damn," he said.

"Yeah," she whispered.

He opened her door for her, and she sat, pulling her dazzling legs into the car. When he started the engine, he had a crazy urge to drive straight to his apartment and skip the restaurant. Once there, he would rip her clothes off, and after he made love to her, they would order pizza.

With regret, he set the idea aside. Instead, he settled for another kiss in the car, fisting his hand in her hair. She opened for him again, delicately tracing his tongue with her own.

He was going to die right here on the side of the road.

He dragged his lips down her neck and nibbled, pleased to see goosebumps rise all over her.

"Sorry," he said, nuzzling where his teeth had been. "Couldn't be helped."

She giggled. Then her face turned serious. "That sounds like a problem you should have checked out by a professional. Biting people might give them the wrong idea."

He raised a brow. "Or they'll get the right idea."

Flushing red, she cleared her throat. "Right. Yes."

He shouldn't enjoy making her flustered, but it was just so adorable. "Let's eat," he said, taking her hand in his.

He drove to the restaurant on Melrose. He'd selected Amelia's, a dimly lit joint with black tables and red-upholstered chairs. It was small and quiet, specializing in Latin American cuisine. Growing up in the Valley, he'd learned to love the food of the cultures that sprang up all around him—Mexican, of course, but also Guatemalan, Costa Rican, and Honduran. So he knew what empanadas were, tostones and pupusas, and pretty much everything else on Amelia's menu. Plus, his buddy Kristof was a bartender there. Having bartender buddies around town was an incidental benefit of being a dude in your twenties and lighting a lot of private parties.

The valet took the keys, and Timmy offered Greta his arm. She placed her long fingers through the crook of his elbow and smiled at him. He stood up straighter. She made him feel strong, like he could keep her safe. He liked it.

Leaning close, he kissed her bare shoulder, and she shivered. Even that small reaction was gratifying.

Amelia's was long and narrow, formerly a storefront among the array of shops down the avenue. The owners had knocked out the entire front wall and installed tall glass doors. The doors were now folded back, accordion-style, opening the restaurant to the pleasant evening air and the foot traffic of the shopping district. Greta stopped to admire the doors.

"Wow," she said. "Cool." She pushed on the doors with one finger, watching them slide.

He could guess what she was thinking. She would note the well-designed track mechanism that allowed the heavy doors to slide so easily that even the rail-thin hostess could operate them with one hand. She would admire the double-paned reinforced glass panels, strong enough to resist a well-thrown rock, and insulated enough to keep out the desert heat in summer. And she would notice the copper-clad steel they used to build the frame that held the glass, the copper turning green with oxidation.

He loved that Greta noticed the doors. He also loved that she wouldn't notice the Kahlo painting hanging on the back wall, a piece from the restaurant owner's private collection. Kristof told him that the guy locked the painting in a special safe every night before he left. Kahlo had been a family friend, and the painting was a treasure.

It wasn't that Greta didn't notice beautiful things. On the contrary, Timmy could still picture the transfixed expression on her face when she first saw the Pac Lighting gobo at the shop. But she didn't care about status symbols or ostentatious shows of wealth. In this, she was different from every other woman he'd met.

He loved that about her.

Loved. Oh, wow.

Soon after Timmy and Greta were seated, Kristof sent a bottle of wine over. Timmy nodded to him in thanks. Kristof gave him a wink.

The server poured the dark drink into Cabernet glasses nearly six inches in diameter. Greta held the large glass with two hands as though it were a cup of warm tea.

"Cheers," Timmy said, holding his glass out to her.

She tapped hers against his so softly he could barely hear the clink. She took a sip and smiled at him over the glossy rim. Right then, Timmy knew things with Greta were going to be serious.

Timmy had four phases of relationships with women.

First, there was plain sexual attraction. You saw someone and realized you wanted to touch that person all over. Then, either you did the touching, or you didn't. Touching was phase one.

If there were no obstacles in phase one, you moved on to phase two, which most people call dating. Examples of obstacles that might prevent you from entering phase two: The person turns out to be an idiot. The person turns out to be a jerk. One of you, for whatever reason, is not interested in a relationship.

Up until Greta, the not-interested person was usually him.

Phase three started when you realized you could build a life with this person whom you found sexy in phase one and fun and charming in phase two. You wanted to share an apartment and put her name on the company letterhead. Phase three was truly breathtaking.

Technically, there was a phase four. When it was over. When someone left. When someone died. Phase four was purely theoretical at this point in Timmy's life, but he felt like he should acknowledge its existence.

During dinner at Amelia's, Timmy felt himself fly right past phase two and land squarely in phase three. He knew Greta was sexy. He knew she was fun and smart, and a hard worker who loved the same work he loved. What he was wondering over dinner was how, once they were married, they would apportion the business responsibilities at Pac Lighting. For example, he wondered whether she would take on the invoicing as well as the payroll, since he really hated it and she was much better at math than he was.

Of course, he was also thinking about how much he wanted to see her naked.

Patience, he told himself. We have all night.

———

AFTER THEY ORDERED AND RETURNED THEIR MENUS TO THE SERVER, Timmy wondered how to get Greta to open up to him more. She'd told him a lot about her dad the night before, but he wanted to know everything. Normally, on a first date, he'd ask a woman about her family. But he knew her family was as tricky as his. One of the many reasons he liked L.A. was that people rarely asked where you came from. Few people were actually from here, but they came to reinvent themselves.

Plus, he already knew so much about her. They'd spent hours together every day for nearly two months now. Taking a breath, he dove right in. "So you're from North Carolina," he said. "I'm from the Valley. I went to UCLA, and you went to Cameron. Neither of our fathers is winning an award anytime soon." He reached across the table and took her hand. "When I was growing up, I had to spend a lot of time comforting my mother. It sucked. In retrospect, my family was barely holding it together, and I could sense that even as a kid. I still resent him for it. We barely speak."

"That's awful," Greta said, squeezing his hand. "No kid should have that burden."

"I'm thinking you know a little about that kind of burden, though. I just don't know why. Do you want to tell me about your mom?"

Greta frowned. "I'm not sure." She paused. "It's a long story."

Timmy squeezed her hand this time. "We've got time."

Greta told him a heartbreaking story of a childhood with a father who redefined "manipulative" and a mother who was chronically ill. She told him about how they attended graduate school together, but that her mom dropped out while her father became famous by stealing her research. "Famous for a physicist, I mean." Then she paused for a long time, taking another sip of wine.

"I'm so sorry about your mother," he said. "Why didn't you ever say anything? Do you need time off to go visit her?"

"No." Her quick response stopped him cold. "I…I left her behind on purpose. We agreed, I guess, that I wasn't going back."

He leaned back in his seat, still gripping her hand. "Greta, that's awful."

She shrugged, but he could tell her shoulders were stiffer than usual. "She knows how hard things are with my father. I think she was setting me free. She said something a little funny that day, though." Greta paused, as though she wanted to get the words just right. "When she was trying to convince me to move out here with Daphne, she said, *This seems like a path that will change you in unpredictable ways. I took a path like that once, and I've never regretted it.*"

"Do you know what path she was talking about?"

Greta shook her head. I mean, I can't imagine she's talking about marrying my dad and his parade of grad student mistresses." She made a face like she smelled something gross, her nose scrunching up. He could hear the anger in her voice. Then her face fell, and she took a huge gulp of her wine. "I have to tell you something, and I'm afraid you'll get mad at me."

Timmy's heart stopped for a moment, but he didn't let his fear show on his face. Or, at least he hoped it didn't. "Of course."

Whatever she wanted to share with him, he could be there for her. Help her. It was what he did best.

"The same day I interviewed for the job at Pac Lighting, I got an offer to start my physics Ph.D. at Princeton." She paused. "This fall."

Releasing her hand, Timmy let out a whoosh of air as he leaned back in his seat. She was leaving him. Of course she was. Greta didn't belong in his shop slinging gear.

"Tonight, after I got dressed, I turned them down." She scraped the tablecloth with a finger. "I don't want to go back east. I could go to school here, maybe next year or the year after. But I can't let go of what my father did. I can't just let him win." She squeezed her hand into a fist.

Timmy struggled to find the right words. He wanted to support her more than anything—he would do anything for her, it seemed. But if supporting her meant letting her go? Never seeing her again? He acknowledged that he was too selfish for that.

"I want to go to school here," she said. "I don't want to leave Daphne—she's the only family I have left."

Again, Timmy's heart lurched. Would he ever be able to compete with Daphne in Greta's life?

"And," she said, her face flushing while her green eyes met his. "I don't want to leave you, either."

Timmy leaned forward again, this time taking both of her hands in his. "Jesus, Greta, you scared me." He paused. "I don't know what I would do if you left."

"Your pack lists would be a disaster," she said, deadpan.

"That's not what I meant."

She gave him a half-smile. "I know."

His heart raced, and this time he knew why. He was in love with this woman.

But he couldn't tell her, not yet. He didn't want to overwhelm her. But he knew what he felt, and he would do anything to keep her.

He was her first kiss. She was his first love. He wondered if he looked as dazed as he felt. For a long while, they sat like that, hands clasped on the tablecloth. He wondered if he looked into her eyes long enough, whether he could convey everything he was feeling.

A throat clearing caught their attention. The server had arrived with their meals.

"Wow," Greta said, looking down at her plate. "This looks amazing."

"I love this place," he said. He wanted to say *I love you* but that was as close as he could get.

They ate for a few minutes in silence, until Greta asked, "Tell me how you got interested in production."

He said, "Life in the Valley could have been suburban life anywhere. Safe. Boring. But good-boring, you know? With all the chaos my dad was bringing home, having an easy town to grow up in helped a lot. But once I got my driver's license, I headed into the city every weekend to explore and to get away. When my dad was home on the weekends, there was a lot of fighting. It wore me out."

"I don't like fighting either," Greta said. "Usually, I just hide from problems instead of facing them. Probably not healthy."

Timmy said, "I'm not judging. Kids aren't supposed to manage adults' feelings. At least that's what my Uncle Brian always said, and he's usually right about stuff like that."

"What did you do in the city?"

"I went to underground parties, mostly raves. The parties are why I got interested in lighting." Timmy laughed. "Most people think it's because of the movies."

"I've never been to an underground party."

"You would hate it." He said. "They're loud and chaotic. But it's fun to look at the lighting rigs. If you want to go, I'll take you to one." He hoped she could hear that he was promising more than a night out at a party. He was offering to be her friend. To watch out for her. To be there every morning when she showed up for work and to drive her home every day if she needed him to. To take care of her. To love her.

"I'd like that," she said.

Around nine-thirty, they finished up. Timmy insisted on paying and was surprised when Greta didn't put up a fuss.

While they waited for his car at the valet stand, he put his arm around her waist, and she leaned into him, sharing warmth. She made him feel bold.

"Should we go to your apartment? I'd like to see it." She spoke quietly, but not timidly.

Hiding his delight, Timmy nuzzled his face against her hair. "Absolutely."

Chapter Sixteen

GRETA

As she climbed the exterior wooden steps leading up to Timmy's second-floor apartment, Greta held tightly to the handrail. Her heels weren't ideal footwear for the aging lumber. Ahead of her, Timmy unlocked the door.

His studio apartment was sparsely furnished. The space was large, probably ten meters long, the entire half of the square stucco building's second floor. At the near end was a kitchen, at the other end, a bed. Next to the bed stood a chest of drawers that looked to be made out of the same birch plywood that they used at the shop, the same plywood that she'd used to make the coffee table for her own apartment.

Glancing at the wall above the bed, she gasped. Hanging on the wall was a circular stained-glass window, at least five feet in diameter, a light fixture illuminating it from behind. The central image depicted a small white lamb sitting in a green field, the sun rising behind it, greenish-blue hills rolling all around. A circular border of a multitude of colors radiated from the central image, as though projecting from a prism. Each piece of glass, even the tiniest, contained rich pigment.

She crossed the room to examine the window more closely. Its metal edges looked raw, as though scraped free of mortar.

"Where did you get this?" she asked.

"Do you like it?"

"It's amazing." She slid her finger along the rough outer rim.

"A church near my parents' home was set for demolition for a freeway extension. It was an old Episcopal church, so I'm amazed the state got away with it. A contractor took the old stones to repurpose, and I got the window."

"It must have cost you a fortune."

He shrugged. "My uncle had connections with the freeway contractor."

"What are you using to light it? Fluorescent tubes? It looks like daylight."

"Nope. It's an LED array I built."

Greta placed her hand on the glass. The surface was cool to the touch.

But she felt warm, very warm, toward Timmy. She had come to count on this man almost as much as she counted on Daphne. He was no longer just her boss. In fact, he'd become more than just her boss weeks ago. Once he'd started driving her home, once he'd helped her buy the lifeboat, once he'd started giving her greater responsibilities at the shop, once he'd started taking her to lunch—she knew she was his friend.

And after this week, he'd become something so much more.

She pulled him to her, running her fingers through his hair.

"Greta," he whispered, his voice a plea. He wrapped his hands around her and kissed her deeply, his tongue lighting her up inside. He ran his hands under her top camisole, pulling it over her head, groaning when he gazed at her nearly bare torso. Kissing her neck, he let her tug his shirt upward, then helped her yank it over his head until they were skin to skin.

"Is this okay?" he asked. "We don't have to do anything you don't want to."

She shook her head. "But I do want to. I'm just nervous."

"Then let me take care of you, okay?"

Biting her lower lip, she nodded.

He turned off all of the lights in the apartment except the stained glass. Then, he led her to the bed, and she sat. Kneeling, he slid off her shoes. Then he leaned forward, kissing along her collarbone, down, until he reached the top of her bra, lighting a fire inside of her that she'd never felt before.

She liked it. A lot.

She reached behind her back to unfasten her bra, but he stopped her with his hand. "Let me do it," he said. "Please. Let me do everything."

"Okay," she said, unsure what he meant by *everything* but willing to find out.

He unfastened her bra and let the straps fall down her shoulders, dragging his lips down the center of her chest. "Lie back, baby," he said.

She did, feet still on the floor. Above her, Timmy rested his arms on either side of her body. Instead of feeling trapped, she felt safe.

He kissed her breasts, one, then the other, then dragged his lips down her belly and to the top of her pants. Then he unbuttoned her pants and slid those off as well, leaving her panties in place.

"You are so gorgeous," he said. "I could stare at you for hours."

Her instinct to refute his compliment leaped to her lips, but she shut it down. Because she believed him. To Timmy, she was gorgeous, and that's all that mattered.

He ran his hands up from her knees to her thighs, parting them so he could kneel between them. He put his hands on her panties and began to tug. "Is this okay?"

She nodded. "Yes." She was nervous, but not afraid. Heat pooled in her belly and lower.

He pulled her panties down her legs and tossed them aside. Shirtless, the light from the stained glass painted his muscular torso in a rainbow of color.

Then he kissed her between her legs, and her back arched from the bed in surprise and intense pleasure. "Holy shit," she said.

She could feel, rather than hear, Timmy's chuckle.

Unbidden, her hands tangled in his hair. As she stared at the ceiling, she began to see stars.

"Please don't stop," she said.

"Never," he growled.

The stars exploded.

While she caught her breath, he stripped down to his boxers and climbed onto the bed next to her.

"Come here," he said, tugging her to him, placing her on a pillow like she were a fragile, precious thing.

He kissed her again, and she locked her arms around his neck. "I want the rest, too."

He pulled back. "Are you sure? We're not in a rush."

"I'm sure." And she was. "I know it might hurt at first, but I trust you."

At her words, a grin tugged at his lips, one that she loved. She pulled his boxers from his waist, and he finished the job, kicking them to the floor.

"I'm going to put on a condom," he said. "I'm guessing you're not on birth control."

He fished a foil packet from his bedside table, and she watched him put it on. So many new things, but he didn't make her feel silly for being inexperienced.

He rested on his elbows by her head, holding himself above her. "I don't want to hurt you."

"I know."

"I'll go slow, okay?"

She nodded.

As he entered her body, her muscles tensed involuntarily. She drew a deep breath, relaxing around him.

He groaned. "You feel amazing."

He didn't feel amazing, not yet. But the deeper he went, the fuller she felt, and she really liked it.

He held steady, meeting her eyes. "How are you?"

"It didn't hurt. Just a little uncomfortable."

"I hear it gets better," he said with a grin.

She snorted with laughter, and he groaned again, shutting his eyes. "I'm sorry—did I do something wrong?"

"Literally nothing you do right now would be wrong, babe." He opened his eyes again. "Why don't you move? See what feels good? Torture me a little bit?"

Greta might be a virgin, but she knew plenty about sex. Daphne told her anything she wanted to know. She knew Timmy was staying still for her sake. She knew the torture he was referring to meant he was holding back his own pleasure for hers.

She lifted her hips, and that felt good. So she wrapped her legs around him and pulled his hips even closer to her.

"Oh my god, Greta. Please say I can move now."

"Please move now. I want you to."

When he did, the sparks she'd felt earlier returned. His weight and warmth surrounded her, enclosing her as she enclosed him. She ran her fingers up his smooth back, feeling his muscles move around his shoulders as he propped himself over her, gazing into her eyes. She buried her face in his neck and smelled the delicious salty sweetness of his skin.

She was desperately happy.

Within her, something stirred, then lit like a fire. The pleasure was so intense she started to shake. When she cried out, she couldn't have stopped it even if she wanted to.

Timmy groaned and shook, falling next to her, out of breath.

She pulled him to her, their skin glowing green and blue.

Burying his face in her neck, Timmy said, "You are incredible." More deep breaths. "My Greta."

Greta's heart stuttered, old wounds rejecting the possessive words. But she refused to let the past taint the present.

Chapter Seventeen

TIMMY

Timmy woke to Greta in his arms. She was still sound asleep. Placing a kiss on the back of her neck, he climbed from bed and moved to the bathroom as quietly as he could. He pulled a spare toothbrush from the drawer and placed it on the counter, then brushed his own teeth.

"Hi," she called from the bed, wrapped in his sheets and comforter. He wanted to keep her there all day.

But no, they needed to get to work. And she didn't need him pawing at her after losing her virginity.

"I have a toothbrush here for you, and a towel for the shower." He pointed them out. "And I put one of my t-shirts on the bed if you want to slip that on."

She glanced at the folded shirt he'd placed by her pillow, then pulled it over her head. When she stood, it fell to the top of her thighs.

God. Those thighs.

"Thank you," she said, glancing at her watch. "I need to stop by my apartment and get clean clothes before work."

"I figured. Come on in, the bathroom's yours. I'll be ready to leave in a moment."

She looked grateful for some privacy, and he didn't blame her. He expected some of her bashfulness this morning and did everything he could to make sure she felt safe. Cared for.

Twenty minutes later, he was driving toward Greta's apartment, holding her hand in his. Her damp curls hung longer than when they were dry, and he wondered what she would look like with long hair, curls hanging down her back.

The few blocks passed in silence. In front of her apartment, he parked on the street. "Stay put," he said, then trotted around to open her door for her. He wanted her to feel like a princess. He wanted to be her prince.

He had it bad, and he didn't even care.

On the front porch of the duplex, an older man with dark hair was drinking coffee. As they passed him, Greta waved.

Timmy stopped. "Good morning." It was a fucking fantastic morning.

Greta stopped next to him, standing close. He could feel the warmth of her body in the cool morning air. "This is Marcellus, my landlord."

Before she could finish the introductions, Marcellus asked gruffly, "Who are you?"

Surprised by the man's abruptness, but not really bothered by it, he said, "I'm Timmy, Greta's boyfriend."

She immediately stiffened at his words—boyfriend. They'd never spoken about it, but how could he be anything else to her?

"No long-term guests," Marcellus barked, and Greta smiled, giving the gruff man a nod.

She led the way down the sidewalk to her door.

"Wait out here." She pointed at the loungers. "Have a seat if you want. I'll be right back."

He sat back in one of the chairs and crossed his arms over his chest. Last night had been amazing, but if she felt shaky about the thought of being his girlfriend, where did that leave him? In love with someone who didn't feel the same?

She entered her apartment, leaving the wooden interior door open.

"Daphne?" he heard her call.

An interior door slammed, and Timmy jumped to his feet, dashing to the steps. "You didn't call at midnight!" Daphne yelled.

At midnight, Greta was sound asleep in his arms. What was Daphne talking about?

Greta sounded surprised by Daphne's anger. He could see them facing off in the living room. "That's what you're saying to me this morning? Really?" Greta took a step back. "You had his number and mine—you could have called me."

"That's not how the midnight call works!" Daphne fumed. "You should have called. I never, ever forget, and you've never forgotten either."

Daphne was furious.

"Daphne, I…" Greta trailed off, and Timmy could hear the anxiousness in her voice. "I stayed over at Timmy's." She plucked at the t-shirt she was wearing. But she refused to apologize, and Timmy wanted to applaud. "If you were actually worried, you would have called Timmy or me instead of breaking our phone."

That's when Timmy noticed the shattered plastic remains of a cordless phone on the living room floor.

Greta went into her bedroom.

Daphne stood in the doorway, continuing her tirade. "You don't care that I waited for you to call, do you? You don't care about me at all." Daphne crossed her arms over her chest. "All you care about is your little crush."

Greta stepped out, dressed for work. "Stop thinking about yourself for once." Her voice was as cold as the dry ice they used for scenic effects.

Daphne ran to her room and shut her door with a resounding slam, one that Marcellus would probably hear from his porch.

Greta stopped outside of Daphne's room, looking annoyed. She said, loudly enough to be heard through the closed door, "I'm sorry I didn't call. I'll catch a ride with Timmy."

"Whatever!" Daphne yelled back.

Greta paused once more, reaching for Daphne's doorknob. But then she shrugged and turned to leave.

As Greta stepped outside, she noticed Timmy standing close. "I suppose you heard all of that."

He nodded. "It was hard to miss."

Greta shook her head. "I'm sorry. You have to understand,

Daphne and I, we're the only family we have anymore. I should have set an alarm to call her at midnight—it really was my mistake."

Timmy wasn't so sure about that. As Greta had said, if Daphne were truly worried, she could have called two different cell phones.

But after what he just witnessed, Timmy had a feeling that inserting himself between Daphne and Greta wasn't something he should be doing. At least, not any time soon.

Chapter Eighteen

GRETA

For a week, Greta avoided Daphne, staying most nights at Timmy's. For the first time since she and Daphne became friends, she was vividly angry at her. Greta wondered just how often she'd overlooked Daphne's self-centeredness. Greta had apologized for not calling, but Daphne hadn't apologized at all. Not for losing her temper, not for breaking the phone. Most painfully, she didn't apologize for failing to support Greta after one of the most important nights of her life.

When she did see Daphne, they spoke in short sentences and only about logistics. Greta rode to work with Timmy in the mornings and home with him at night.

With a lurch in her heart, Greta realized she missed her friend. Her sister. She was at work reviewing a pack list, trying to focus on the details, but it was hard.

Her phone rang, and she fished it from her back pocket. "Daphne?"

"Hey, G."

G. Her nickname, the one only Daphne used. "Hey, Daph."

"Do you think we could have lunch today? Talk stuff out?"

"Yeah," Greta said. "I'd like that."

After hanging up, she knocked on Timmy's office door to let him know she was going out with Daphne so that she wouldn't be eating with him.

"That's okay. Of course it's okay."

"So, I don't have a car, though."

Without pausing, Timmy tossed her his car keys.

For a moment, Greta wondered what the others in the shop might think of her taking the boss's car on a personal errand. She stared at the keys in her hand.

"I know what you're thinking," Timmy said. "And it's fine. Dell drives a Ford Fiesta. He uses mine all the time."

"Thank you."

He gave her a quick smile. "No problem."

She met Daphne at a small cafe in Santa Monica that also served sandwiches. Daphne already had a table and two coffees. "Order whatever you want," she said. "My treat."

"Is this an apology lunch?" Greta asked.

Daphne nodded.

"Okay," Greta agreed. "Your treat."

After she ordered at the counter, she joined Daphne at the table. But she didn't speak. This was Daphne's apology. Daphne had hurt her badly, and she wasn't going to make it any easier on her.

In their years together, she and Daphne only had a few fights, and never one that lasted this long or hurt her so badly. But she was willing to forgive Daphne because she understood her so well.

This fight wasn't about the midnight call. It was about unconditional love, and how little of it either of them had ever had.

Daphne met her eyes. "I should have called you at midnight when you didn't call me."

"I agree."

"After you left that night, I didn't realize how disappointed I was that you were going out."

"You go out with guys all the time, Daph. I don't flip out or get jealous."

"You're right. I was jealous." Daphne rested her face in her hands. "God, I was horrible to you that morning. And the thing is, I knew. I knew, Greta, that you had…been with him. How could I have ignored something so important? You needed me." When Daphne met Greta's eyes again, her eyes were filled with tears. "Instead of checking on you, I tore into you for forgetting the midnight call."

"You made it all about you."

Daphne nodded. "I did. I hate myself."

"Here's the thing. That night with Timmy changed my life. I woke up that morning in Timmy's bed—my boss's bed. My relationship with him and my own body changed forever. I needed you, Daph. After all of these years, you should have been reaching out to me, helping me understand everything that was messing with my head. But you didn't."

No, Greta thought. Daphne hadn't been thinking about Greta at all. She was only thinking about herself—at the time when Greta needed her most. Greta was still really angry about it, too.

"That night, after you left with him. I went out to the courtyard and tried to read. But I couldn't. I stayed out there a long time, until it grew dark. I looked for the stars, but they're so hard to see because of the glow from the city."

Greta wondered where Daphne was going with this story.

"But I've been out to the high desert, where the Milky Way paints the sky, so I knew they were there. The stars." She took a sip of her coffee. "I don't blame you at all for staying away this past week. After what I did? I wouldn't be surprised if you stayed away forever."

Greta snorted at the absurdity. "No, Daphne. No. You are my family. Sometimes, we annoy each other. Sometimes we fight. I realize we're both completely dysfunctional, but our friendship isn't."

"You're saying you forgive me?"

"Don't you miss seasons?" Greta waved outside at the September sky, the same as it was in August and July. "Back home, the leaves are changing color. Temperatures are dropping."

"I mean," Daphne laughed, "mostly. Plenty of hot days left in September."

"True. But here, sometimes it's easy to feel oppressed by the constant sameness. When the weather changes, and the trees turn color, you can feel hope. Possibility, I guess. The point is, cycles are important. They remind us that even when things seem to be falling apart, the world will inevitably revive."

"So you are saying you forgive me."

"Of course I do."

"Will you tell me about Timmy?"

Greta nodded. "How about tonight? Iguana?"

Daphne's face relaxed for the first time since they sat together, and she nodded.

———

BACK AT WORK, GRETA SPENT THE REST OF THE AFTERNOON IN THE SHOP, with Timmy working alongside her and the other shop hands. As the other guys said goodbye around seven, she and Timmy stuck around to wrap things up. This had become their habit over the past few weeks, with Greta taking on more and more responsibility.

As Greta came out of the bathroom after washing the shop funk off of her hands, Timmy was waiting for her. "Everyone's gone," he said, and pounced.

At first, she panicked. What if someone saw them? Come back?

But no, Timmy wouldn't put her reputation at risk like that. She trusted him.

Relaxing into his arms, she kissed him, running her lips down his strong neck. She breathed deeply, inhaling his sweet scent, and he pulled her even tighter to him.

"I have a present for you," he said. "In my office."

She pulled back. "I'm not having sex with you in your office. I don't care what you say."

Timmy guffawed. "As much as I have actually imagined that scenario—"

"You *have*?"

"I'm a guy who has to work with his gorgeous girlfriend and pretend nothing is going on. I should get a medal for making it through the day without taking care of personal business in the bathroom."

"That's so gross."

"Is it? Honestly, I can't tell anymore."

She shoved him playfully, and he caught her in his arms again.

"Come on. Let me show you."

In his office, they sat across from each other, the scorched wooden table between them. Timmy pushed a white box across the table toward her.

Curious, she opened it—and then her heart stuttered in panic. He'd had business cards made with her name on them, and a new title—"Production Manager."

Greta knew she should feel elated. She just received a promotion. Probably a raise. The cards were lovely, and the only person who had them before now was Timmy. Her panic was unreasonable.

She forced a smile onto her face. "Manager?"

"A mere formality at this point. I actually discussed it with some of the guys, and they thought it was a great idea." He grabbed a card and looked at it. "It's official—you're mine now."

Timmy's tone was joking, but Greta could see how serious he was by his gaze. She needed to handle this gift correctly.

And Greta did feel warm toward him. But she also felt like there was a catch, that she would owe him something now, more than she was capable of giving.

"Thank you," she said. "I don't know what to say." At least she was being honest. Sort of.

"Greta, babe." Timmy ran his hand through his hair, causing it to stand on end. "I love you." He held up his hand. "I just want to tell you. I don't expect anything in return. I've loved you for a while."

Greta nodded, chewing her lip.

"You don't have to say it back. That's not what love is about, right?"

"Right," she said, as though she knew anything about love, and tried to ignore the rabbiting of her heart. For Timmy's sake.

"Should we head home?" he asked.

Home. He meant his apartment, where she'd stayed all week. "I made plans with Daphne for tonight."

"Ah," he said, tilting back in his chair.

"Yeah," she said. "I'm glad she and I aren't fighting anymore."

"Yeah," he said. "I'm glad, too." But Timmy was lying to her. He sounded disappointed, not glad at all.

Greta's life was about to get complicated.

Chapter Nineteen

GRETA

On a Friday in mid-September, Greta was riding home with Timmy after work.

She and Daphne were going to cook dinner while Timmy and Federico, Daphne's current boyfriend, watched a baseball game on TV. She was thoroughly uninterested in professional sports, but lately she was looking for ways for all of them to spend time together.

Greta felt torn between Daphne and Timmy. Whichever one she chose, whether for a ride to work or for dinner out, the other ended up annoyed with her. She'd never had two people vying for her time before, so she had no idea how to handle it.

But she was sure that she was handling it badly.

As they headed north up La Brea, Timmy placed his hand on top of hers, lacing their fingers together. He squeezed her hand in silent communication, sending warmth throughout her body. The feeling was still so new and strange that sometimes she didn't trust it at all. She knew Timmy was a good person. She admired his honesty, his reliability, and his skill at programming a light board. She really wanted to learn how to program like that. He barely even looked at the buttons.

But she was afraid. She was pretty sure she was falling in love, and it terrified her. She wanted to talk to Daphne about it, hopefully tonight. She needed her best friend's help.

"Have you thought about your birthday?" Timmy asked, one hand on the wheel and one holding Greta's. Her birthday was in less than a week. "Is there anything special you want to do?"

"Daphne already mentioned it to Marco, and he said we could have a small party at Rivet." She was delighted to have the party at Rivet. It was a sound financial decision because Marco would cover the cost of the food and drink. Plus, it would be fun to see Sandy again.

Timmy abruptly took his hand from hers and placed it on the steering wheel. "I thought you and I could do something special together."

"You're invited, of course."

"I don't want to be *invited*," he said. "Jesus. I want to do the inviting."

"Why does it matter? Especially if Marco's willing to host?"

"Don't you think Daphne should have asked me first?" Timmy ran his hand down his face. "I'm your freaking boyfriend, Greta. I get to plan your birthday party. At the very least, I get to help. Can't you see that she's trying to cut me out of things?"

She hated it when Timmy talked to her about Daphne. Or when Daphne talked to her about Timmy. They rarely had anything kind to say about one another. When they acted like this, she just wanted to get away from them both.

She sighed. "If Daphne had asked you first—if she'd told you that Marco Bertucci wanted to host my birthday party at his exclusive restaurant and foot the bill—what would you have said?"

Timmy didn't answer her, and that was answer enough.

But Timmy had planted doubts about Daphne's motives. A small inner voice suggested that perhaps Timmy was right, and Daphne was indeed trying to undermine him.

Timmy took the cutover to Highland Avenue, an alternate route north. Taking Highland was slower, sure, but it had its perks. Highland was one of those grand, old Los Angeles avenues, with a grassy median dotted with palm trees. The homes were old and stately, Spanish colonials with red tile roofs surrounded by tall iron fences with intricate curves.

She rolled down her window. The evening air was cooling as the sun neared the horizon. Timmy reached over, picked up her hand again, and squeezed.

———

WHEN THEY ENTERED THE APARTMENT, DAPHNE WAS PULLING A SOUP kettle out of the cabinet. On the counter, Greta saw the maki that they liked from the local Asian market, the rolls sliced into bite-sized pieces. Federico sat on the lifeboat, munching on edamame, watching the pregame show. Udon noodles sat on the counter, uncooked, and vegetables lay next to them, unwashed.

When Daphne looked up, annoyance showed on her face. "You're twenty-five minutes late."

Greta suppressed a sigh. "There's beer in the fridge," she said to Timmy.

"Hi, Daphne," Timmy said.

Daphne didn't reply.

Grabbing a beer, Timmy headed over to the lifeboat and took a seat, clinking his beer bottle with Federico in greeting.

Daphne's boyfriend, Federico, was extraordinarily handsome, with olive skin and brown eyes that were nearly black. His features were Pre-Raphaelite in their beauty: straight nose, full lips, and strong cheekbones.

"Hola, brother," Federico said in his deep Colombian voice.

"What's up?" Timmy replied.

Leaning back against the orange vinyl, they were two normal guys hanging out with their girls, Timmy's light brown hair next to Federico's black, two guys from very different places who weren't very different at all.

Greta sighed again, this time loudly. "You couldn't even bother being polite?" she said to Daphne.

Daphne tilted her head back and drew a deep breath. "You're right. I'm sorry. I'm being a shitty friend and need to do better."

"You need to figure out how to get along with Timmy."

"I do. I like him. It's just I feel like I never see you anymore, and I miss you. But if he makes you happy, I'll work on it, I promise. That's all that matters, G."

"Okay." Greta washed her hands and grabbed a knife to slice the green onion.

"I just thought you'd be home sooner." Daphne ripped open the package of noodles and dropped them into the pot. "Traffic must have been terrible."

"We took Highland," Greta said.

"Greta, Jesus. Highland was not the way to go when you are running late and have people counting on you."

Greta's annoyance flared higher. "I thought this was a casual dinner, not a five-star meal."

Daphne set down the uncooked noodles and turned off the stove. "Can I talk to you for a moment? Outside?"

Once in the courtyard, Daphne paced, hands on her hips, obviously at a loss for words.

"Just spit it out," Greta said.

"I'm upset because Timmy made you late," said Daphne. "I needed you to help me get this meal prepared. I expected you at seven, not seven-thirty."

"We arrived at seven-twenty-two." Yes, she was being overly precise. But it was either that or raise her voice.

Daphne tugged at her hair. "You know what I mean."

"You shouldn't blame Timmy. I'm just as responsible."

"Did you tell him to take Highland?"

"No." Greta paused for a moment, then said, "But he didn't make us late intentionally."

"That's irrelevant," Daphne said.

"I disagree." But secretly she wondered. Had he made them late on purpose? The seeds Daphne planted began to sprout.

"You always say your loyalty is to the facts, right?"

Greta nodded. At least, she thought that was always the case.

"Here's a fact: Timmy might be gone tomorrow," Daphne said. "But I won't be."

Greta shook her head with impatience. "Timmy owns his own company, plus his family lives here. He's not leaving L.A."

"I didn't mean he would relocate."

"I see," Greta said, temper flaring. "You're saying that he might break up with me."

"Or you with him."

Here, Greta paused again, making the connection that Daphne wouldn't say directly. "You want precedence because I've known you longer, and because you are less likely to break up with me?"

Daphne fidgeted under Greta's directness, then looked at her feet.

Greta softened. "I'm not going to break up with you, Daph."

"I know that." She was trying to play it cool, but Daphne had a tell —she chewed her thumb, shredding the nail.

Greta changed the topic to the other seed of doubt growing inside her. "Did you arrange a birthday party for me so that Timmy wouldn't be able to?"

Daphne's eyes flared in anger. "That's ridiculous. Did he accuse me of that?"

"Yes." Greta pinned her with a level, green-eyed stare. She wanted the truth. "Do you?"

"I don't know." Tears welled up, spilling down her face.

At that moment, their house phone rang. Through the open doorway, Greta heard Federico answer. "Hola, home of Daphne and Greta."

After a moment, he stuck his head outside. "Greta, it's for you," he said, adding a slight *szh* to the front of *you.*

Chapter Twenty

TIMMY

Timmy watched his woman's face as she listened to the caller. He had never seen this expression on Greta's face before.

Her bright eyes were opened wide, her lips parted. The knuckles of the hand clutching the phone were white and bloodless. Grief, shock, and anger showed on her expressive face.

One of the things he loved most about Greta was her levelheadedness. She rarely lost her cool or got angry. But whatever she was hearing on the phone right now was killing her.

After a terse goodbye to the caller, Greta turned to Daphne.

"That," she said to Daphne, "was my father." Tears spilled down her face.

"Oh!" Daphne said, throwing herself at Greta and wrapping her in a hug.

Timmy wanted to know what was happening, but he knew that if he interrupted, neither woman would even hear him.

Federico was clearly uncomfortable, unsure what to make of the sobbing and whispering.

Timmy suddenly realized what must have happened. "Was that about your mother?"

Greta looked at him over Daphne's shoulder and nodded. "She died."

He'd known Greta's mother was sick, of course. But being sick and being dead were totally different things. He wanted to drag her into his arms and hold her like he was supposed to. It was his right, as her man, as her lover, to comfort her now. But Daphne was between them, like she always was.

He understood there were girl things Daphne and Greta liked to do together, things sisters would do. He didn't mind that. But it was his job to plan his girlfriend's birthday party. And it was his job to comfort Greta when her mother died. Wasn't it?

He hated feeling jealous.

Daphne spoke to Greta in a low voice, "She was a beautiful, wonderful, brilliant woman, and she loved you so much. She loved you."

"I should have been there," Greta said, sobbing now. "I should never have left."

"Remember what she said the last time you saw her? She understood that you needed to leave. She told you to go."

He hadn't known Greta's mom. He certainly didn't know what her last words to Greta were. Daphne had been there, and he had not. He slumped his shoulders in acceptance.

Glancing at the spread of uncooked food across the kitchen counters, he called out to Federico. "Here," he said, handing the guy forty bucks. "Go down the street to the Thai take-out place. Get a bunch of food and bring it back here. Just get anything."

Federico gave him a grateful look and left.

Greta and Daphne sat on the lifeboat now, holding hands. Timmy pulled a chair from the card table that served as their dining table and joined them.

"When's the funeral?" he asked.

"Sunday." Greta sniffled.

"But that's only two days from now," Daphne said. "Can't he give you more time to get home?"

He, Timmy figured, referred to Greta's father. He knew a lot about him from Greta, but Daphne actually knew the man.

"If I were going home, it would be plenty of time. I could be there tomorrow."

"You're not going?" Timmy asked, surprised. No, shocked.

"No." Greta sounded certain on this point.

"I'm happy to give you the time off," he said. "As much as you need."

"I'm not going." She paused. "But I'll take some time off. Thank you."

He mostly listened as Greta recounted the phone call with her father, Jim. He felt out of his depth as Daphne showed just how much she knew about Greta's life, and just how much he himself did not.

When Federico finally returned with dinner, Timmy was grateful to have something to do.

"Can I fix you a plate?" he asked Greta.

"I'm really not hungry."

"You should eat anyway," Daphne urged her.

Greta nodded. "Okay."

Federico stood by the door with his hands in his pockets. "I should go," he said, clearly uncomfortable with the situation.

Daphne nodded at him, and he disappeared out the door.

Timmy didn't leave. After they ate, he washed the dishes. He stuck around until ten that night.

He wanted to stay with Greta in her room. Sleep on the lumpy futon that she bought from one of her neighbors. Hold her close while she grieved.

But she didn't invite him to stay. After he rejoined them in the den, she said to him, "You should go."

"Are you sure? I can sleep on the couch if you need space." Desperation chewed him up. "Let me be here for you, babe." He yearned to do more for her, but she was shutting him out.

It hurt.

Greta shook her head. "My mother died alone, and it's my fault."

Daphne interrupted. "That's not true. Stop saying it."

Sitting next to Greta, he pulled her stiff body toward him and kissed her forehead, whispering in her ear. "Take as long as you need. I'll be waiting."

But he didn't feel as patient as he tried to sound. Inside, he was raging. The worst thing that could happen to his girl just happened, and she was shutting him out. He wanted to help, and she rejected him.

When she slipped out of his embrace, he hurt like nothing he'd felt before. He tried to remind himself that this moment wasn't about him. It was about Greta.

Silently, he ducked out of the apartment. He hated to leave her in pain; it went against every one of his instincts.

But she didn't want him. Not tonight.

Frustrated, he shoved his hands in his pockets as he walked to his car. The tighter he tried to hold onto Greta, the more she slipped away.

Chapter Twenty-One

GRETA

After Timmy left, Daphne locked the door and tugged Greta to the lifeboat. "Let's talk about Beatrice. Tell me a story I don't know."

"Okay." Greta felt surprisingly relieved by this idea. She wouldn't be alone with her ghosts after all. "When I was a freshman in high school, my mom was in treatment for ovarian cancer. She was really sick from the chemo. My dad made me visit with her for two hours a day, one hour in the afternoon when I got home from school, and one hour in the evening after dinner. He took my backpack so I couldn't read or study while I sat in her room, even though she was barely conscious."

Greta continued recounting the memory for Daphne. How she could hear her father downstairs, talking jovially with his research assistant, a blonde woman from South Carolina with small brown eyes and an upturned nose. She reminded Greta of an opossum, clinging to Jim with painted pointy claws.

Her mother's fingers would twitch, clutching the sheet spasmodically. Spasms caused by pain, nausea, or any other suffering. The morphine drip, programmed by the nurse who visited twice a day, kept her mom semi-conscious much of the day. Greta wished there was something she could do for her.

Many times over those months, Greta wondered how her mother and father had come together, her mother so small and frangible, her father so large and ursine. They were both highly intelligent and good-looking, but surely that wasn't enough for a marriage.

When the hour was over, she always hoped that her father and the opossum would retreat to his office to do things a married man shouldn't be doing. If they were out of the way, at least she wouldn't have to speak to them. She'd grab her backpack from the kitchen, lock herself in her room, and proceed to read about stars.

"She recovered from the ovarian cancer, but only a few years later was diagnosed with leukemia, likely caused by the cancer treatment. And now she's dead."

They sat side-by-side, letting the grief settle around them. Greta was more grateful for Daphne than she'd been in a while. To have someone to talk to who knew Beatrice and their complicated relationship. Who knew her father and his philandering and didn't ask questions she didn't want to answer.

After a while, Daphne picked up the television remote. "Let's find something that won't make us cry." They sat on the lifeboat watching reruns of *Good Times*.

Meanwhile, Daphne called Rivet to cancel Greta's birthday party, which relieved Greta immensely. The thought of celebrating anything in the next few days made her nauseated.

Around three a.m., Greta was still awake, staring at the bare ceiling of her room. Daphne had gone to bed hours ago, but Greta wasn't sure how she would ever sleep again.

It would be easier with Timmy's arms around me, she thought, and realized how true it was. He made her feel safe, and she loved that about him.

But as she replayed the evening's power struggles between Daphne and Timmy, she realized how frustrated she was with both of them.

She didn't understand why she couldn't just exist peacefully between them, a covalent electron creating stability rather than turmoil. No one needing more or less than what she was able to give.

Daphne was demanding more and more from her now that Timmy was in her life. And now that they were dating, Timmy wanted her to back away from Daphne and give more time to him.

There was no balance. Couldn't they see that she couldn't carry on like this? She didn't have enough energy for their demands.

The only person who seemed to expect nothing from her was her father. How strange.

He had sounded surprised when he'd heard her voice on the phone, almost as surprised as she'd been to hear his. "I called the number for Daphne Saito. I wasn't expecting to speak to you."

"Well, here I am." She'd surprised herself, and likely him, with her snappy tone.

He hadn't asked her any questions, not about where she was living or how she was getting on. He'd simply told her the facts. "Your mother died last night in her sleep. The funeral is on Sunday." Then he'd paused. "I don't suppose you're coming."

He already knew that she wasn't going to the funeral. She'd told him so the last time she'd seen him.

She assumed he would marry Anna Lopez now, who'd practically been living with him by the time Greta graduated. A wedding at this point would only be a formality.

Right then, she hated Anna and her father. But she also hated Daphne and Timmy. The only person she didn't hate was her mother. She wished she had called Beatrice after moving here. She'd avoided calling because she'd been afraid of getting her father on the phone.

She was a coward.

She would give anything to hear her mother's voice one more time.

Her breath caught. *The notebooks.*

On her closet floor, she dropped to her hands and knees, tossing shoes behind her until she could reach the old cardboard box. It had gone undisturbed since the day they'd moved in.

She berated herself for forgetting about her mother's work. About her mother, full stop.

She dragged the box out into the light.

Inside were sixteen laboratory notebooks, covered with brown cardstock and filled with green, square-ruled, acid-free paper. The covers were numbered with a black permanent marker: 2 of 16, 6 of 16, and so on, as though her mother expected someone to read these later and wanted to be sure they were read in order.

Greta found the one labeled 1 of 16 and opened it to the first page.

She'd been expecting physics. Course notes, ideas for experiments, even lab reports. Instead, she found words. Just words.

No numbers, no equations. No science at all.

The first entry was dated March 1, the year Greta was born: "Today, I discovered I'm pregnant. I've been trying to decide whether to finish my doctorate, and I'm taking this pregnancy as a sign that I should not."

Greta wasn't sure which shocked her more—that her mother voluntarily left graduate school rather than being forced to quit by her father, or that her mother believed in signs.

Greta read on: "I've decided to keep a diary as a letter to you, my small unborn thing. Since I've never been much of a writer, I'll probably fail to fill this volume. But I think it is worth a try."

Her mother always underestimated herself, and this sixteen-volume diary was no exception.

Greta leaned against her headboard and read on, her entire existence taking on a new valence. Her plan to avenge her mother fell to dust. A mere fantasy.

She'd majored in physics so she could one day prove that her father stole her mother's research. She'd wanted to look through the archives of her mother's work and find a way to show her father's colleagues that her father was a fraud, that he'd built his whole career on Beatrice Donovan's ideas.

It was hard to let go of long-held beliefs. She had to let them die, and then she had to mourn them. She realized she was grieving more than her mother. She was also grieving the story she had always told herself about her parents. She needed her father to be the bad guy and her mother to be the victim. It was the only way her life made sense.

But now nothing made sense. She'd been so wrong about her mother and her father. No wonder her mother wanted her to move away. She must have sensed Greta's desire for revenge—she didn't exactly try to hide it from her—and wanted something better for her daughter than a fruitless quest.

And if she was this wrong about her mother, could she be similarly wrong about Timmy? Timmy, whose face carried so much pain when she forced him to leave earlier that night. Who only wanted to do nice things for her.

Greta flipped ahead to the first entry after her birth. September 14, 1977: "Too much to narrate. Will list. You were born at 6:30 p.m. Beautiful and perfect, with strong Apgar scores. 7 lbs., 12 oz. Skinny fingers like mine, skinny legs like your father, and just like him in the face, a perfect angelic copy. I know I'm spewing hyperbole, but I don't care. Moments like this are what hyperbole is for."

Greta opened another book. The first entry was from when Greta was eleven years old: "Now that I've been diagnosed with cancer, I'm doubly grateful that I've been keeping this diary for you. I'm working hard to shield you from this illness. It's difficult, but I think I'm succeeding. I hired two students to play with you during the day, Thad and Darla. Darla comes on Tuesdays, Thursdays, and Fridays, Thad on the other four days. They are taking you to the pool, quizzing you in math and science, and discussing books you've read. They are kind to you, too. I make sure of that. I also make sure you don't notice me spending more time in bed, or eating less because the treatments make me ill."

She grabbed another, from when Greta was in college: "I've just now given up on my leukemia treatments, deciding to go into hospice care instead. You were really angry with me when you found out. You said I was giving up."

Greta swallowed back tears of guilt. She had been angry, so angry.

"You seem to think that I don't have the heart to beat this new cancer. You see me ending treatment as capitulation—to cancer, to your father, to everything. Dearest Greta: You'll figure out some day that I have kept a few secrets of my own. It might be in a few years or many years from now. And you'll learn that sometimes giving in can be the best decision."

Greta dropped the volume on the floor and dug for volume sixteen, the final book. She turned to the last entry, dated shortly before Beatrice gave her the notebooks. The handwriting was pale and angular, as though Beatrice kept losing control of the pen mid-letter: "This is the last entry I will write to you. I'm pretty sick now, and it's getting harder and harder to write or to keep my thoughts in order. I want the last entry to be something you're proud to read, not the ramblings of an invalid."

Greta felt deep shame, now. She'd often thought of her mother as an invalid.

'The next time I see you, I will give you these notebooks. I know you've seen me write in them over the years, and I let you believe they were part of my research. I think you wanted me to be a brilliant scientist far more than I ever wanted to be one myself. But what you really wanted was a role model who wasn't your father."

Greta thought how Beatrice Donovan was indeed a brilliant woman, and an astute observer and collector of data.

"If you learn anything from these notes of mine, I hope you will learn to understand and forgive Jim. He never wanted to be a father, but he was proud of you when you were born. He was proud of everything you did. He just didn't know how to tell you. Alone in this room so much, tied down with these tubes, I start to feel like a sequestered oracle. It's so easy for me to see what keeps you two from speaking sense to one another."

Her mother was right, of course, but Greta was still amazed. She and her father—two supremely rational individuals—had always lacked the facility to engage rationally with one another.

Her mother wrote: "I know you think you hate him, and that he hates you. You are wrong on both counts. You'll probably figure out on your own that you don't hate him. So let me explain how your father feels about you.

"When we brought you home from the hospital, your father was scared for the first time in his life. He wasn't just scared—he was terror-stricken. He dragged your crib into the living room next to his desk so he could monitor your breathing and heart rate. He measured the length of your feet and the circumference of your wrists and kept charts in a lab notebook much like this one. You were the only thing in his life he wasn't completely certain about.

"As you got older, and it became clear to me that you were simply a newer version of Jim, I knew there would be trouble. As hard as he ever was on himself, he directed that hardness at you. He couldn't help it. And I think, deep inside, he knew one day you would stop letting him bully you. He hoped for it as much as he feared it. I'm certain you will stand up to him one day, if you haven't already."

Greta thought of a desk drawer shattered on the floor. Of a promise to never return.

Suddenly, she felt exhausted. Reading her mother's words had sucked the tension from her. It was nearly five o'clock in the morning. Even though she didn't have to go to work that morning, she needed to sleep.

She took off her clothes and climbed into bed in Timmy's t-shirt that she'd never returned, falling asleep to his comforting scent.

Chapter Twenty-Two

GRETA

Greta woke the next morning to Daphne's singing in the kitchen. The diary she'd fallen asleep reading lay next to her.

"Daph?" she called.

Daphne appeared in her doorway. "How are you feeling, besides completely shitty?"

Greta shrugged. "That sums it up. But what are you doing at home?"

"I told Marco what happened and that I'd be missing work today. I'm cooking breakfast for you. Frittata with spinach and chorizo."

Greta loved frittata with spinach and chorizo.

"Look what I found last night," Greta said, picking up the diary.

"Isn't that your mom's research?"

"That's what I thought." Greta choked on her words. "But I was wrong. It's a diary. Written to me when I was a kid."

"Holy shit," Daphne said, caressing the front of the notebook as though it were a precious treasure. "That's amazing."

"And completely unexpected." She met Daphne's eyes, and for the first time in weeks, they were in perfect accord.

Daphne said, "I thought we'd just relax around the house today if you wanted."

"I'd rather go out." Greta definitely wanted to get out of the house. Hollywood could be fun, but it was horribly claustrophobic.

Out of her open window, through the black iron bars, she could hear a couple chatting in their apartment, their window only two meters from hers, their conversation punctuated with deep male laughter.

This is how it was to live here: everyone isolated in separate buildings, separate vehicles, yet pressed together, bees encased in individual combs.

"Anywhere in particular?" Daphne asked.

"Yes."

———

GRETA PULLED HER SWIM GOGGLES OVER HER EYES AND LEFT DAPHNE IN the shallows. She dove under wave after wave until she passed the waves entirely, past the surfers bobbing in the swells, then turned north.

She still could not believe how cold the water was, especially compared to the ocean back home. In North Carolina, the water was at least 25 degrees in late summer. Here, it could be no more than seventeen or eighteen.

The coldness reminded her of early-morning summer-league swim practice. Ever since she was seven years old, practice started in May at the outdoor pool near her home, the water nearly as cold as this.

In her ten years of competitive swimming, her mother had never missed a meet. When she could no longer walk, she'd come in a wheelchair.

Greta swam north along the shore. When she breathed to her right, she counted the lifeguard stands to keep track of her location. She kicked hard to ignite every muscle in her legs, so hard that her toes tightened with cramps. She was out of shape.

She didn't tell Daphne why she wanted to swim because she knew it would hurt Daphne's feelings. Daphne had stayed home from work that day to keep her company, but Greta wanted to be away from Daphne. She didn't want to worry about anyone's feelings but her own.

Out here, Daphne couldn't follow her. Daphne would splash

around in the shallow water and then sit under her umbrella, deftly deflecting the surfers who asked her out until Greta returned.

Greta pulled through the water with cupped hands, using all of the force of her back and shoulders with each stroke. Her speed built, and she was aware of nothing but the pain growing in every major muscle group. She knew falling levels of adenosine triphosphate caused the pain, and her body couldn't produce it fast enough because she didn't exercise like she used to. This pain made her angry, mostly at herself, for failing to keep up her training. So many things had changed since she'd moved here. She vowed to swim three times a week, minimum, for sixty-minute sessions.

She swam faster. When she couldn't take the pain anymore, she took a deep breath, gave one powerful kick, and propelled herself to the ocean floor three meters down. With both hands, she grabbed fists of sand and squeezed until the sand slid through her fingers. She squeezed again and again. Finally, she relaxed and let the air in her lungs lift her back to the surface.

For a while, she floated on her back, resting, eyes closed and mind empty, letting the ocean rock her like a mother rocks a baby.

Turning south, she swam slowly back to Daphne. The waves to her left churned up sand as they broke. To her right, the depths of the big ocean were as dark as a cloudy night.

Grief washed over her. She sobbed, choking on water. She stopped swimming and coughed, treading water and crying for her mother and also for herself. She felt immense guilt for not being there when her mother died. On the shore stood Daphne's yellow umbrella, the same umbrella Daphne used in college when they first met. Daphne sat in one of their blue loungers, her face hidden behind large sunglasses.

She knew that Daphne, like her mother, only wanted the best for her.

And so did Timmy. God, Timmy. She owed him so much better than what she'd done yesterday when she pushed him away.

She swam to shore, her legs feeling heavy as she emerged from the water. She dropped onto the lounger next to Daphne's, shaded from the intense sun by the umbrella. She laced her fingers behind her head and looked at the glowing nylon fabric.

Instead of swimming nearer to home, they had driven down to Manhattan Beach. The beach was far cleaner and less crowded than the beaches around Santa Monica and Venice. Plus, Daphne had a friend who owned a large home right on the water, and he let Daphne park in his gated driveway whenever she wanted.

Daphne had no problem accepting gifts that men offered her—mattresses, meals, parking spaces. Why couldn't Greta do the same with Timmy? It was irrational.

Irrational or not, Timmy's affection scared Greta. The cell phone. The business cards. The words of love.

Why could Daphne accept gifts without care, and Greta could not? How come everything felt like a debt? She asked Daphne, "Why does Marco give you things when he knows you'll never go out with him? Does he still hold out hope?"

"Hope's part of it, maybe."

"Aren't you worried he might want something in return?"

"He does get something in return," Daphne said firmly. "But you should never think about relationships as transactions. Things never come out even."

"I worry about what Timmy wants," Greta said. "If I love him, and he loves me, what happens then?"

Instead of giving her advice, Daphne posed a question. "Do you want to be in love right now?"

"I've heard a person doesn't have a choice about such things."

"You always have a choice." Daphne's voice was deadly serious.

"In that case," she said, "I don't know."

Daphne replied, "Then you do nothing. You wait until you're certain."

"And if I'm certain?"

Daphne's brows raised behind her sunglasses. "Really?"

Greta nodded.

Daphne leaned back in her chair. "Wow. That's amazing."

Greta's hackles rose. "That someone might love me?"

"No, you goose. The other way around."

Greta contemplated Daphne's words, that she might have a choice about love. And that, perhaps, she was choosing wrongly.

She thought about her mother's notebooks and how she described the love her father felt. She still thought he was an asshole. But he loved her. She believed that now. She was grieving her mother, yes, but she was also grieving a grudge she'd held for nearly two decades.

How wrong had she been about the people who love her?

"I need to make a phone call," she told Daphne.

Digging her phone from her bag, she strolled down the beach. When she heard Timmy's voice, she knew she was doing the right thing.

"I'm sorry for pushing you away. You wanted to be there for me."

There was a long pause. "I did want that. But you were grieving, and my feelings are secondary, baby."

"They're not secondary to me."

Another long pause. "I'm glad to hear it." She could hear the smile in his voice, and she knew she was making the right choice.

Choosing love.

———

LATER THAT AFTERNOON, DAPHNE DROVE THEM HOME, SLOW GOING because they caught the beginning of rush hour. When they arrived back at their apartment, Daphne served up the two dozen pork-stuffed pot-stickers she'd picked up on their way home from her favorite take-out, and they sat on the lifeboat and ate them all.

Tomorrow, she would return to work and to Timmy.

Chapter Twenty-Three

TIMMY

Two weeks later, in early October, Timmy sat at his office table drawing a plan for a show for the following weekend —the annual Halloween party for Hilton Worldwide, his favorite event to produce. The budget was anything-goes, and the International Ballroom at the Beverly Hilton, the same spot where they host the Golden Globes, was epic in both proportion and history. Of course, a big show like the Hilton Halloween bash can also be a nightmare. He needed to cross-rent a bunch of gear from other production companies and hire a shit-ton of extra crew. But this year it would be easier, because he had Greta.

Before they finalized the crew lists, pack lists, and all the other lists a big show required, he had something important to ask her.

They'd come in together that morning. Greta spent three or four nights a week at his place these days. Daphne didn't seem as resentful about it anymore, or at least Greta didn't act like she felt she was letting down her friend. He hated when he played any part in making her feel torn, even if he didn't mean to do it. It was his job to make her happy.

As Timmy made a small adjustment to the ballroom's design, he waited for Greta to return to the office from the shop. She'd run out into the workshop to check on their supply of Rosco 49 gel, a magenta that Timmy dubbed *electric sex*—it was a hot, deep pink, but also corny, like the interior of a strip club. Clients loved it. And for the Hilton party, they'd need a bunch. Greta liked to have extra supplies on hand, so she wanted to place an overnight order with Rosco that morning.

She came back in, the cordless phone tucked to her ear. She ordered fifteen sheets, enough to gel every par light in his shop if they wanted to. Which they wouldn't. Timmy smiled. He loved his Greta—she was responsible and a good planner—qualities rare for production crew, who tended to work by the seat of their pants.

She hung up and dropped into the seat across the table from him, a spot he'd begun to think of as hers. She held a clipboard with what she called her drop-dead list. These were the supplies she believed they needed, or else the show would go to shit. She crossed R49 off the list, then scanned the next items.

"Babe?"

"Hmm?" She didn't look up.

"Wanna move in?" He decided to go casual with the offer. He expected her to accept, but he also knew she'd be more likely to say yes if he seemed not to care either way. She didn't like to feel pressured.

Greta was a strange bird, but she was his bird.

"Move in what?" she asked, meeting his eyes, as though he were referring to some large gear shipment.

"Do you want to move in with me?"

Greta sat up straighter, taking in his words. She blinked quickly. "I don't know."

Timmy smiled. Uncertainty was a good sign. It meant she could be persuaded. And lately, he'd been able to persuade her more and more. The cell phone. The Pac Lighting business cards with her name on them. The promotion.

She just needed to keep saying *yes*, and he'd have them married, running the best production lighting company in town, with a baby gate at the entrance to the conference room, and two green-eyed kids playing in there.

He'd keep that particular vision to himself for now.

"You're already spending so many nights at my place, and your lease is almost up. I figured we'd just go ahead and find a new place together. Maybe something in Santa Monica so our commute would be shorter."

"Santa Monica rents are much higher."

Typical Greta—hiding behind calculations. He tried not to smile.

"We can afford it together." He kept his voice reassuring. He definitely didn't tell her that he could afford the rent on his own. Even now, offering to buy her something expensive was a sure way to send her running.

But she always came back.

She crossed her arms over her chest. "What about Daphne?"

Here was the Rubicon. He knew that if he could get Greta to take this one small step—to sign her next lease with him rather than with Daphne—she would finally be his. He wouldn't have to share her anymore. But he also knew he couldn't push her into turning her back on Daphne. And he didn't want to, really. Daphne was Greta's friend, her sister. He understood that now.

So he said, "I guess you'll need to figure that out with her." He kept his voice casual, but he didn't feel casual. Why couldn't she fully accept that their future was together? Why was every step a battle, a hesitation, a rejection?

He took her hand from across the table and squeezed. "I love you. I want us to build a life together."

"I...I know you do." As usual, Greta didn't say the words back to him. Instead, she nodded, looking thoughtful. "I'll talk to Daphne about it tonight and see how she feels."

He tried to ignore the sting of her rejections, but it was getting harder.

Then she said, "Can we please focus on the show?" She tapped her drop-dead list with her pen. "I don't know where you get off saying we have enough stage-pin cable."

He contained his resentment. God, he didn't want to feel resentful toward Greta. But sometimes, she made it hard. So he gave her another easy-going smile and said, "Whatever you think."

Chapter Twenty-Four

GRETA

For nearly a week, Greta agonized over Timmy's offer to move in with him. Daphne was part of the problem, sure. But if Greta were honest with herself, and she tried to always be honest with herself, she was afraid.

Timmy was her boss and her boyfriend. And if she agreed to this arrangement, he would become so much more; they'd be tied together in a way she couldn't easily escape from. An image of her father's house flashed in her mind. A home that was also a trap.

Timmy didn't bring up his request again. She knew he was being patient with her, and she felt guilty for not being able to give him an answer. How could she explain her fear in a way that would make sense to him? The task was impossible. He would insist he wasn't trapping her. He would take offense at being compared to her father.

Which was exactly what she was doing, but she didn't know how to break the cycle. And why should she? He should love her as she is, fears and all.

Tonight, though, she would take it over with Daphne. When she entered their apartment, Daphne was sitting on the lifeboat drinking coffee, waiting for her and their plans to go to Iguana.

Daphne hopped up and dumped her half-empty mug in the sink. "Do you want to change first?"

Greta shook her head. No need to dress up for Iguana. It was one of the things she loved most about the place. "As long as my hands are clean, I'm fine as I am."

As they walked to Iguana, Daphne seemed delighted to be going out together. As Daphne chattered about her day, guilt ate at Greta. An outing they used to take for granted now was a special occasion.

And she was about to make things even worse.

At Iguana's bar, the bartender Jorge prepared to pour their usual drinks, a tequila sunrise for Daphne and a rum and Coke for Greta.

"Hola, Jorge!" Daphne chirped.

"Hola, Daphne," he replied, and spoke to her in Spanish. Greta was able to catch a few words now after listening to them speak over the past few months.

Greta rocked on her barstool, a missing horizontal dowel making it unstable. Tonight, for once, the rickety furniture at Iguana didn't irk her.

Turning to her, Daphne said, "You wouldn't believe what crap Marco pulled this week," and proceeded to tell a story about her boss firing the entire production crew for a pilot they already had underway. "Sometimes he gets in these snits, and then I have to smooth things over. So I spent all week calling every person on the crew and begging them to come back. Fucking Marco. Are men congenitally unable to apologize?"

Greta laughed. "Some men, yes." Jorge slid their drinks to them, and Greta took a sip. "How are your screenplays going?"

Greta knew Daphne's dream had nothing to do with staying on with Marco. Every day, she put in hours of work on her own, determined to make a career in screenwriting.

"Marco has promised to get me a meeting with the higher-ups, but he hasn't so far. I'm about to make the call myself as his assistant. They don't have to know this hot new writer is the person making the appointment."

"I'm actually surprised you haven't done that yet." Daphne knew how to get what she wanted, and she didn't like to wait around for it.

Greta took another sip, a big one, to help build her courage. "I have something important to talk to you about, but please don't freak out."

"Remember—"

"You never freak out, I know." But this time, Greta wasn't so sure. "So what is it?"

"Timmy asked me to move in with him when our lease is up."

Daphne's eyes widened in shock. "What did you tell him?"

"I think I want to."

"But what about our place?"

"Our lease is almost up, right? And I would keep paying my half until it is."

The hurt on Daphne's face almost made Greta cave.

Daphne said, "You're just going to leave me in the cold?" She looked like she was about to cry. Either cry or throw her drink. "What happened to us, G? What happened to sisters forever?"

This conversation was going far worse than Greta could have imagined. She didn't want a fight. She wanted to discuss the decision with Daphne, get Daphne's advice about such a difficult choice—putting her fate in Timmy's hands.

But Daphne, as usual, was thinking only about Daphne. Or, at least, that's what it felt like.

Greta felt her own anger rise. She wasn't moving away. They would still see each other. And if Daphne came home and said she was moving in with the man she loved, Greta would support her.

Daphne's voice was bitter. "What have you decided to do?"

"I wanted to discuss it with you first. I haven't decided."

"Don't move in with him." Daphne's voice was laced with urgency. "What will you do if you decide you don't want to be with him anymore?"

Greta had already thought about this possibility. It was, after all, her biggest fear: feeling trapped in a home that wasn't her home at all. Again.

Daphne pressed on. "And what if he breaks up with you? If you come home and your stuff is sitting by the curb? That happens a lot in L.A.," Daphne laughed. "The unintended yard sale."

"I don't think Timmy would do that."

A long moment passed.

"Me neither." Daphne sighed. "But I can't help but feel like this is the wrong decision."

"I don't think your feeling is driven by concern for me."

"What?" Daphne screeched.

Greta tried to explain. "Come on, Daph. We don't lie to ourselves. Don't act like this is about concern for me."

Daphne's eyes narrowed. The hurt was gone, but the anger remained.

Daphne's voice rose in pitch. "You don't think it's possible that I just care about you, Greta?"

"I know you do. But ever since I started dating Timmy, you've been trying to drive us apart. Tell me I'm wrong."

At Greta's words, Daphne dropped her head into her hands. "I do care about you, G. I *love* you." Daphne looked at her, red-eyed, spine stiff. "Are you going to move in with him or not?"

Greta recognized an ultimatum when she heard one. *It's either him or me.* She never thought she'd hear one from Daphne.

"I can't decide yet."

Daphne stood, shoulders back, nose high. "Then you have already decided." She pulled a ten-dollar bill from her purse and dropped it on the bar. "I can't believe you chose a wanker from the Valley over me." She stalked out.

Greta sipped her drink slowly, replaying the conversation in her head. She was usually so good at predicting outcomes, whether scientific hypotheses or interactions with people. She'd spent her whole life studying people as an outsider so that she could fit in better. Even people who seemed unpredictable weren't unpredictable to Greta.

For example, Marco Bertucci seemed unpredictable. He was a bully who was also generous, a narcissist who was also loyal. But she'd spotted the patterns in his actions months ago. All the warnings were hidden in plain sight. Those copper doors of his office. The bed he'd bought for Daphne. The beautiful servers at Rivet, whom he ordered about like personal servants, but who wouldn't quit because Rivet allowed them access to directors, producers, and other animators of dreams. Based on her observations, she knew Marco's actions tracked a dangerous pattern of behavior. A man who liked to own people. Who believed he should own whatever he wanted.

Tonight, Greta knew Daphne would be upset when she mentioned moving in with Timmy. Daphne's reaction had been extreme, but it was still within the pattern.

This thought did not comfort her at all.

She pulled out her cell phone and called Timmy. "Can you come and pick me up?"

Chapter Twenty-Five

TIMMY

Later that night, Timmy wrapped his hands around Greta's waist as she straddled his bare hips, her pale nakedness dappled by the stained glass above his bed. She wore a look of intense concentration on her face, like she always did when she was close to coming. Her abdominal muscles moved beneath his hands. Then, some of her other muscles moved too, and he was lost. His last coherent thought was a hope that he'd kept going long enough for her to find her pleasure, too.

She collapsed on him, and he stroked her back with his fingertips. Her face nestled in the crook of his neck.

This was what heaven felt like.

"I love you, baby."

She murmured something in reply, but not the words he wanted to hear more than anything.

He often told her he loved her. Before Greta, he'd never said the words to a woman. It wasn't that he was afraid to speak them; he'd just never wanted to.

But Greta never said the words to him. He'd brought up the issue a week ago, one evening when they were driving home. But the conversation had gone nowhere.

"I don't understand why people have to give verbal existence to such an abstract feeling," Greta had said. "Either we love, or we don't. Saying it changes nothing."

He hadn't argued with her, but in his mind, he disagreed. Saying it, he thought, changed everything.

So, he said it all the time. And every time he did, he swore Greta's smile got a little bigger. He figured she was hiding behind her words, and so he tried to be patient.

But his patience was wearing thin.

Her bent knees hugged the sides of his torso, holding their bodies together. Timmy never wanted her to move. After a few minutes, she stirred, sliding off of him and padding to the bathroom.

After her mother's death, Greta threw herself into work and her relationship with Timmy. He couldn't say he wasn't glad. He'd emptied the top drawer of his dresser for her, and she brought some clothes over. She kept three pairs of underwear, one pair of jeans, one bra, and one pair of sneakers at his apartment. If she needed socks, she borrowed his.

The drawer, then, was nearly empty. Timmy bided his time, waiting for it to fill. Earlier, she'd told him about the fight with Daphne and Daphne's ultimatum. He'd resisted agreeing with Daphne, even though he did.

Greta needed to make a choice.

He reached up and flipped the switch on the stained glass. The room fell into darkness except for the glow of the streetlights through the windows. Greta would have plenty to see by when she returned to bed.

THE NEXT DAY AT PAC LIGHTING, TIMMY MET WITH GRETA TO DISCUSS their upcoming schedule. They did this at least once a week. It was Greta's job to get the crew lined up for smaller shows, so she needed to know exactly what was going on and when. He really enjoyed these morning meetings with her, as though they were the model for the rest of their lives together.

Sometimes, as she made notes, he pictured a ring on her finger.

All of this imagining was inspired by her gold-green eyes, by the crinkles at their corners when she smiled for real—not the stiff fake smile she gave when she was nervous or shy. The real smile that she only gave to him.

Well, to him and Daphne.

"Halloween is Wednesday," Timmy said. "We need to stay late to prep for the Hilton Worldwide Halloween party on Saturday. Load-in starts on Friday."

"I can't work Wednesday night. I told you a while back."

Timmy vaguely remembered Greta telling him this. She'd been getting dressed one morning, her long legs lit by the early sun shining through the windows, the lean muscles of her thighs glowing.

Obviously, he hadn't been paying much attention to her words.

"Right," he said. "Why's that?"

"I'm going to a party with Daphne. Halloween is Rivet's big annual bash, apparently."

"So you're leaving me hanging with an eleventh-hour, eight-hundred-seat banquet because of some Hollywood party?"

Her voice retreated into a cold, precise tone that told him he'd overstepped. "Rivet is located in Pacific Palisades."

He sighed. "It's a Hollywood party, Greta. Don't hide behind details."

He picked up Greta's hand. "Please, baby," he said. "I need you."

"I can't. I promised Daphne." She squeezed his hand, then let go. "I really want to be there," she said. "I do."

He relaxed. He could tell from her voice that she really did wish she could be there with him. "How can you have fun knowing I'll be slaving away packing gear while you're partying with movie stars?"

"B-list and has-been movie stars," she said.

"And some up-and-comers. There are always up-and-comers."

"Point conceded," she said. "But the up-and-comers never talk to me."

And like that, the tension between them was gone completely.

"I love you," he told her.

She smiled. "I know."

That smile soothed the ache in his gut, but not completely. Timmy knew that soon, Greta would have to choose between him and Daphne, even if Greta herself couldn't see it. He was terrified she would choose to stay with Daphne.

He didn't know what he'd do if she rejected him like that. He glanced up at her over the top of his laptop, watching her study the list on her clipboard.

He couldn't imagine her gone from his life. But he couldn't keep going on like this, in limbo.

Chapter Twenty-Six

GRETA

On Halloween night, Daphne strutted into the living room. Greta couldn't help but admire her costume. She was wearing tall black Manolo boots she'd found on sale at Saks, fishnet hose, stretch-leather hot pants, and a black corset. She wore a wig with thick, wavy black hair and deep-cut bangs. Confidence rolled off of her in waves. Greta was rarely jealous of Daphne, but she wished she felt one-tenth of her confidence.

Greta finished buttoning the jacket to the pin-striped suit she'd donned, one with wide lapels and a cinched waist. They'd found it at a vintage store on Melrose. Beneath the suit, Greta wore a corset just like Daphne's.

That surprise would be revealed later, once they were at Rivet. Greta swallowed down the urge to cancel everything and hide in her room for the rest of the night.

But Daphne, as always, had a plan. "You look to-die for, G," she said.

"I feel like an impostor, dressed like this."

"But you're wrong. You are beautiful, and it's time you see that. It's time for everyone to see it."

Greta looked in the mirror to add the finishing touch to her costume. Her slicked-back hair gleamed like copper, held in place by a combination of old-school pomade, hair spray, and a hair band tied at the nape of her neck. She then set a black fedora upon her head. She swallowed hard, trying to build her courage.

"Ready?" Daphne asked.

"For this?" Greta laughed. "Never."

"So," Daphne said. "I have a plan."

Greta snorted. "Of course you do."

"Once Marco invites us over to his *throne room*, I mean his booth, you take off the jacket, and we'll match."

Greta laughed. "We will never match, Daphne."

Daphne poked her in the arm. "Stop being so literal for one second and try to picture the scene in your head. I'm Bettie Page, but there will probably be four or five Bettie Pages, so my costume is kind of boring. But you're the twist! My photographer and lover, but then suddenly, we flip the script. Amazing!"

"Yeah, totally amazing," Greta deadpanned.

"So you'll do it?"

"Striptease for Marco?" Greta was beyond skeptical.

"Um, that makes it sound awful. You're just taking off your jacket." She paused. "And you're doing it for us, not for him."

Greta pondered her words for a minute. "Okay. I'll do it for us."

Daphne clapped her hands in excitement. "Great! Now, how do you feel about kissing?"

"What?" Greta's mind spun.

"So, kissing is when two people—"

"Kissing Marco?" Greta screeched.

"Christ Jesus, no. Kissing me."

"Daphne…" Had Daphne's brain fallen out of her ear?

"You are my date, after all. Just a peck on the lips."

The thought made her gut churn with nerves. She told herself to stop being a chickenshit. It was Halloween. Plus, she didn't care what the people at Rivet thought of her. "Um, maybe?"

"How about this. Just trust me, okay? It's all in good fun. It's a party."

Greta still felt uncertain.

"I would never hurt you, Greta," Daphne said. "You know that."

Greta believed that Daphne would never hurt her.

Not on purpose, at least.

Greta nodded. "Okay. I trust you."

Daphne squealed with excitement.

———

THEY TOOK SUNSET BOULEVARD TO RIVET, WHERE TRAFFIC WAS HEAVY but steady. Daphne zipped through the cars with ease. While she rode along, Greta seriously considered selling her truck to get a smaller car with better gas mileage and acceleration.

Daphne's cell phone rang. "Grab that, will you? Tell me who it is?"

Greta looked at the caller ID. "Federico."

"Ugh," Daphne said.

Greta knew this pattern of Daphne's. Federico had been calling a lot lately because he sensed Daphne was pulling away. Daphne chose men she wouldn't get attached to. But, as she explained to Greta, it was important never to burn bridges, especially in Los Angeles, where your connections could make or break a career.

Fortunately, gentle break-ups were Daphne's specialty. Another thing Greta envied—how to hand out disappointment in a way that felt like a gift.

"Hand it to me," Daphne said. After Greta passed her the phone, she put it on speaker. "Freddy?"

"*Hola mija,*" he said. "I thought I'd pick you up and we could go to the House of Blues Halloween party. I just happen to have two tickets."

Daphne rolled her eyes at Greta. Greta knew Daphne had expressly told Federico about the Rivet party tonight. He could pretend that happenstance had handed him the tickets, but even Greta saw through the lie.

It was a move driven by desperation.

Daphne replied, "That sounds like a blast, sweetie, but I'm busy tonight. Didn't I tell you?"

"Dr. Dre is hosting the party this year."

Somehow, Federico managed to befriend people who seemed out of his league. Greta suspected his father owned a lot more land—and perhaps more politicians—back home in Colombia than Federico let on.

"You should go," Daphne told him. "Have fun without me."

"Last chance, love."

"Kiss Dre for me." Daphne hung up and handed the phone back to Greta. "Are you sure you don't want some lipstick?" she asked. "A dark red would create the perfect irony with that outfit."

"I hate irony," Greta said. And lipstick, which Daphne knew already.

Daphne hooted with laughter. "Oh, Greta. Never change."

"People don't change," Greta said. It was one of her most fundamental beliefs.

A short while later, they pulled up to the valet stand at Rivet. The line of cars was three deep. After handing the keys to Mario, one of the regular valets, Daphne threaded her arm through Greta's, and they walked through the door.

Once inside, Greta leaned back against the bar, surveying the room. Daphne stood next to her, cloaked in perfection if not in much actual clothing, tapping her dark red fingernails on the lacquered wood. The bartender filled two glasses with Champagne. As was usual for her and Daphne, he didn't request any payment.

Rivet had been transformed for the evening. At the far end of the bar stood rows of martini glasses, each filled with a cocktail chosen just for the occasion, glowing greens, purples, and reds. A young woman dressed as a cat—what a cliché, Greta thought—collected the flat-rate fee for the drinks in a black leather apron.

The dining tables were gone, the lights dimmed. Tall black candles stood in clusters on the high-top tables placed around the room. Around these tables, people clustered. The booths were reserved for special guests, like Emmy and Oscar nominees. In the far corner, Marco sat at his regular booth. His *throne room*, Daphne had called it earlier, and Greta chuckled at the accurate description.

People stopped by to greet him while he held court. Outside on the back patio, a band was playing to a packed dance floor. Around the fringes, onlookers smoked cigars. Timmy had been right, Greta admitted to herself. This was the quintessential Hollywood party.

Greta wondered when Daphne would ask her to perform their little play. Now that she was here, she didn't think she could go through with it. It was one thing to joke about corsets and kisses in their apartment. Here, among all of these perfect-looking people, Greta felt like there was no way she could pull off something so brash.

She would get laughed out of the building.

"Nice suit," a familiar voice said from Greta's left.

Sandy Martin leaned back against the bar next to her. He wore no costume, just jeans, cowboy boots, and a fitted button-down shirt. His physique was lean and muscular, his shoulders broad. If it weren't for the few wrinkles on his face and the silver threaded in his hair, he would still be the film idol from decades before.

Since their very first dinner, she and Sandy had become friends. He was often here at Rivet when she was, and he always made sure they had a drink together. He was one of the few people at Rivet she could count on to be kind to her.

"Are you being serious?" she asked him.

Sandy gave a half smile. "Yeah. You look great."

Greta couldn't make herself answer, so she nodded her thanks, feeling her cheeks flush.

"Having fun?" he asked.

She exhaled, grateful that he broke her spiral of embarrassment. "I guess so," she said. "Mostly I'm conducting observations."

"Any interesting findings?"

"A few. For example, the ratio of women to men—two to one—appears to be identical to the inverse ratio of the average ages of each group." She nodded at one particularly egregious example, a woman whose narrow hips and smooth, pale skin led Greta to estimate she was, at the very most, sixteen, on the arm of a man at least a decade older than Sandy.

"Touché," Sandy said. "I'm lucky if I'm only twice as old as you."

"Once again, you are excluded from the general observation."

"Why is that?"

"Because you aren't, to use Daphne's term, a total sleazeball."

Sandy laughed deeply and sipped some of the dark liquor from his glass. "What am I then?"

"An ally?" she suggested, her voice hopeful.

"Cheers," he said, and they clinked glasses.

Greta clung to the comfort of Sandy's friendship in this otherwise hostile environment.

"Have you greeted Marco?" he asked.

"Not yet. Daphne's waiting for something." Thinking of their plan, Greta shuddered.

At the mention of her name, Daphne turned to Greta. "Come on. It's time." She nodded at Marco's booth, where a crowd still surrounded him.

To Sandy, Greta whispered, "I have to go. Please rescue me if things get ugly." She was kidding, but part of her was afraid.

Before she turned away, Sandy slipped a small white card into her suit pocket. "In case you need a knight in shining armor," he said.

He'd given her his phone number. Wow. "Um, thanks."

Tapping her foot, Daphne waited impatiently. "Will you be so kind as to escort me to yonder table, sir?"

"Sure thing." Greta held out her elbow, and Daphne slipped her fingers through.

"Showtime," Daphne whispered.

Greta winced.

As they sidled over to Marco's booth, Daphne whispered, "Marco's been pretending to ignore me all night. I think he wants me to grovel a little bit."

Greta snorted. "Like that will ever happen." Like Greta, Daphne never, ever groveled.

As she and Daphne came to a halt at his table, the people gathered around stepped aside.

"Daphne, babe!" Marco said, but he didn't bother to stand. "And Miss Greta. How are you this evening? Everyone, this is my assistant and her roommate."

Everyone turned their eyes on them both. Assessing. Judging. Daphne rested her free hand on her hip and jutted it out to the side. Greta stood even straighter, pretending to ignore everyone around them. This was just a regular night, she told herself. Just her and Daphne with Daphne's creepy boss.

"My name is not Daphne," Daphne said. "You must have me confused with someone else. My name, sir, is Bettie."

"Is it, now?" Marco said, his eyes running up and down Daphne's body so obscenely that Greta wanted to step between them to protect her friend.

"And this is Giorgio." Daphne pointed at Greta. "He's my photographer. And my lover."

Greta tipped her hat at him, willing to support Daphne if only to protect her from this awful man.

The club was as packed as Marco would allow. Patrons stood in small groups with little space between them, most of them stealing peeks at Marco's table. She and Daphne were in the spotlight. The back of Greta's neck itched.

"I didn't realize you had a—" Marco paused, looking at Greta, "man."

"There's a lot that people don't know about me," she said, winking. They had his full attention now, and that of everyone at his table. People from neighboring tables were turning to look as well.

Greta could see what Daphne was doing—asserting her power. Her control. Like Greta, she'd spent her whole childhood under the thumb of a man who treated her like trash, or worse. This little scene was Daphne's declaration of independence. Marco might not like it, though, and Greta worried about getting caught in the crossfire.

Daphne turned to face Greta. "Trust me," she whispered in Greta's ear.

Daphne slipped her fingers down the opening of Greta's jacket, and Greta resisted the urge to step back.

Daphne slowly opened the top button of her suit. Her fingers slid lower. Suddenly, in one quick motion, Daphne ripped open her suit jacket, scattering buttons on the floor. Daphne threw the jacket off her shoulders, revealing the black corset beneath.

Greta gasped in shock.

Before she could move back, Daphne pulled her face to her own and kissed her fully on the lips.

Furious, Greta jerked away. This wasn't what they'd planned.

When Greta pulled back, Daphne stumbled. Marco, on his feet now, grabbed Daphne's elbow to steady her. "Color me surprised," he said. "Greta, you look fabulous. You must be some kind of wizard, Daphne."

Greta, still in shock, glared at Marco, then at Daphne.

He whispered in Daphne's ear, loud enough for Greta to hear. "I want to fuck you tonight, Daphne. To hell with your excuses."

Daphne turned to Marco. "There will be no fucking."

"There certainly will be. Eventually."

She tapped her lip. "Let's start with a date. A woman likes to be romanced."

Marco raised his brows in surprise. "When?"

"Friday?"

Greta couldn't believe that Daphne was actually considering going out with Marco.

She was done.

"I'm leaving," Greta spat at Daphne. "Don't follow me."

Daphne reached out to her, but Greta backed away. Escape. She needed to escape. Leaving her jacket on the floor, she stalked through the passageway that led to the patio.

She elbowed aside the revelers who blocked her way and earned dirty looks from two women whose drinks she spilled. The last time Greta had felt this angry, she'd smashed an antique desk drawer.

She made her way to the patio bar and wiped her mouth with a white napkin, leaving a smear of Daphne's red lipstick on the fabric. Her hands shook, so she crumpled the napkin in her fist. *Trust me*, Daphne had said, and then she'd ripped her clothes off in front of Marco Bertucci and his crowd of hangers-on.

That wasn't at all what they'd planned. Daphne had stripped her naked, literally and figuratively.

Greta's heart sank. Sandy had seen her. Hell, everyone inside Rivet had seen her. It seemed that being the center of attention had been Daphne's plan all along. Sandy was the nicest person, and now even he would think she was an attention-seeking floozy.

Suddenly, as if conjured by her thoughts, Sandy appeared next to her, flagging down the bartender.

Greta gritted her teeth, preparing for more hurt.

But Sandy's voice was kind when he spoke. "I guess that was a surprise."

She immediately relaxed. An ally, she'd called him, and here he was, being just that. "It was for me, at least. We'd talked about doing something else, but not that." Shivering, she wished she had her jacket. She was cold despite the propane heaters and the crush of people around her.

She crossed her arms over her chest, still horrified by Daphne's actions. She'd expect such a thing from the cruel starlets lining the walls of Rivet who were trying to make themselves look better.

But not her Daphne.

Her soul was dying, leaving her an empty physical shell.

"I don't think she meant to make you angry," Sandy said.

"Daphne is very good at predicting results. She should have known how I would react."

"I saw her face as you were running away. She looked surprised."

"I didn't run." No. But she'd wanted to.

Sandy rocked back on his heels. "Would you like something to drink?"

"Yes," she said. She wanted to dilute these feelings of embarrassment, betrayal, and horror. "Some whiskey."

"What kind?"

"Does it matter?"

Sandy chuckled and ordered a drink with *turkey* in the name. The bartender returned with two glasses of brown liquid over a single large ice cube. Greta lifted hers to her mouth and poured it down the back of her throat. The drink was cold and scalding at the same time.

When she set the glass down, the bartender promptly poured another.

Greta lifted the glass and looked at the sparkling ice and caramel-colored liquid.

"Oh, boy." Sandy nodded toward the patio entrance. He stepped in front of her, back straight, hands loose at his sides, like he was preparing for a fight.

Daphne was approaching fast, precariously trotting in her boots. "There you are," she said to Greta, smiling, her voice pitched too loudly. Daphne held out Greta's jacket.

For the first time since she'd met Daphne, Greta had no words for her. Daphne had never betrayed her. But now, for a flash of limelight, she'd humiliated Greta in front of a crowd that was not only unfriendly, but one that questioned the validity of her very presence.

An overgrown, awkward, and unattractive woman had no business trying to exist in Los Angeles, let alone at Rivet.

Greta started to cry, turning before Sandy or Daphne could see her. But she was too late.

Daphne looked stricken, and Sandy looked protective. "I'll take the jacket," he said. "You should go. Return to your party."

Leaving Daphne alone in the middle of the patio, Sandy handed Greta her jacket. "Come this way."

He led Greta out the back door of the club, the one reserved for slick escapes by men cheating on their wives. Standing on the sidewalk, she felt unsure of what to do.

"Do you have a ride home?" Sandy asked.

"Um, maybe." She could call Timmy. He would be annoyed with her, but he loved her. He would come. She pulled her cell phone from her pocket and dialed. When she heard Timmy's voice, she broke into tears.

"Babe," he said. "What's wrong?"

"Can you please pick me up? I'm at Rivet."

"I'm still at the shop. I'll be right there." He paused. "Are you hurt?"

"Not physically."

"So that's a yes. I'll be there as fast as I can."

Pocketing her phone, she said, "My ride is on the way. You don't have to wait out here with me."

He led her to a bench near the valet stand. "I don't mind. It's a lovely night."

Greta wrapped her arms around herself, wondering how she would ever forgive Daphne. Tonight, she'd chosen Daphne over Timmy, and she'd chosen wrong.

Chapter Twenty-Seven

TIMMY

Within ten minutes of receiving Greta's tearful phone call, Timmy pulled into the drive at Rivet. She strode over to his car as soon as she spotted him, quickly hopping into the passenger seat.

"What happened?" Timmy asked as they pulled away, heart racing when he saw Greta's tear-streaked face.

When Greta told him what had happened with Daphne, he wanted to turn the car around and throttle her, Marco, and everyone who had made Greta feel so small. Only some guy named Sandy seemed remotely cool. She'd mentioned him before, but assured Timmy that he was just a friend. Tonight, Sandy had put himself between Greta and Daphne and helped Greta call him. Timmy wanted to buy the man a beer for saving his girl.

"You hungry?" he asked her. "We could get takeout and eat it at my place."

She nodded. "Noodles. I want warm noodles."

"Anything, babe."

He called ahead to their favorite Thai restaurant and ordered everything on the menu that might appeal to Greta. By the time they made it back to Hollywood, it would be ready.

Once they were in his apartment, he spread the food on the coffee table. Greta put on one of his t-shirts and a pair of his socks, leaving her panties on but nothing else from her outfit. She wrapped herself in his extra blanket and cuddled next to him on the couch.

They ate in silence, one of the peaceful silences she enjoyed as much as he did.

Eventually, she told him she had spoken with Daphne about moving in together and that Daphne had given her an ultimatum.

"What did you tell her?"

"I told her I don't know what I want to do."

Timmy tried to figure out how to convey his frustration without pushing Greta away even more. Finally, he said, "I agree with Daphne. You need to stop waffling."

"I'm not waffling," she said. "I'm considering. You just asked me." Then she muttered, "I've never waffled in my life."

"I asked you three weeks ago." As soon as the words left his mouth, Timmy wanted to kick himself. He didn't want to pick a fight, especially while Greta was still hurting from earlier in the night.

"I do not waffle," she said, louder now. "I might withhold judgment because of inadequate evidence. I might refuse to be bound by an ultimatum—I received enough of those from my father. I turned down a top-notch physics program because I stick by my decisions." She sounded furious. "Why can't you see how significant this decision is for me? If I choose to move in with you, I'll hurt Daphne."

"It seems like she hurt you plenty tonight. Maybe you shouldn't worry so much about her feelings." Timmy was all in now. This was their first fight, and it felt awful. "What is there to consider?" he asked, his voice tight.

"For years, Daphne was all I had. I can't just turn my back on our history. She's my family." She pressed her fingers against her temples. "My only family."

Timmy tensed, lips pressed together as frustration surged through him. "Can't you see, Greta? I want to be your family."

She met his eyes, her gaze serious and mournful. "I do see. I just need some time to think."

"Damn it, Greta," Timmy snapped. "You have all the data and evidence and whatever else that even your crazy brain needs to make a decision."

Timmy watched as his words hit her hard. Greta froze under the blow of the words that he couldn't seem to stop.

"It would seem so," she said.

"What does that mean?"

She shook her head. "Let's not talk about this anymore tonight."

In silence, Timmy cleared the dishes. Then he went into the bathroom, shutting the door behind him. He rested his hands on the sink and looked at his reflection, drawing deep breaths.

Was this it? Had he found the love of his life, and now it was over? He'd had friends go through breakups, but he didn't understand why they moped around until now.

When he emerged from the bathroom, Greta was crawling under the covers. Her mouth was set in a tight line, and she wouldn't look at him.

"Good night," she eventually said. She reached over and grabbed his hand, tugging him to her.

He wrapped an arm around her middle and pulled her back to his chest.

"What's the matter?" she asked.

"Nothing." Of course, Greta could sense that something was off with him. She was way more observant than anyone gave her credit for.

She waited for him to give a more truthful answer.

He continued. "I'm just tired of feeling like at any moment I'm going to lose you."

"But why do you feel that way? I'm not going anywhere."

Timmy sighed. He wished he could get through to her, but he was beginning to lose hope.

She said, "Is it because I'm unsure if I want to move in with you?"

"That's part of it. But there are other things."

Greta waited for him to speak, but he remained silent, frustrated.

"Is it because I won't say I love you? If that's so important, I'll say it."

Timmy tensed in frustration. "It's not any one thing. It's a gestalt. It's like how we can transform an ugly warehouse downtown into a chic event space using two hundred lights. One light by itself is nothing. But the total effect is transformative."

She rolled over to face him, switching on the stained glass. "Saying I love you is an uplight?"

"Exactly," Timmy said. "I think."

"Why didn't you say something sooner?"

"I didn't want to drive you away."

"But you're not scared of driving me away now?"

He laughed, but he sounded bitter to his own ears. "You're going to stay, or you're going to go. It doesn't matter what I do."

She placed her hand on his cheek. "What you do does matter," she said and kissed him. "I love you. Very much."

Despite her words, he turned away. He couldn't bear to look at her, the woman he loved, whose words he couldn't let himself believe.

Chapter Twenty-Eight

GRETA

Early Thursday morning, after lying awake for hours, Greta quietly slipped out of bed. Timmy was sleeping soundly, like a hibernating bear. Grabbing the spare pair of jeans she kept at his place, she got dressed in the bathroom as silently as possible, putting on her spare bra under Timmy's t-shirt. The rest of her costume she stuffed in her bag. Then she snuck from the apartment, closing the door behind her with a soft click.

Greta sat on the bottom step of the exterior staircase to his apartment, careful of the splintery wood. She had never felt so alone in her life.

She pulled the cell phone from her bag and wondered if she should call Daphne. But the thought of seeing Daphne after what happened at Rivet last night made her sick.

A memory triggered, and she dug in her bag for the suit jacket from her costume. From one of the pockets, she extracted a small white business card. On it was printed a name and a phone number. When Sandy had tucked the card into the pocket of her coat, she never thought she'd need to call him.

Well, she needed something now.

She hesitated. It was still early in the morning—seven-thirty—but she decided to risk it. He'd once mentioned something about morning yoga, so maybe he was an early riser.

He answered after two rings, sounding alert and genuinely pleased to hear from her. She felt intense relief.

"You okay?" he asked. "Got home safe?"

She paused. "Sort of. I mean, I'm safe. Just not at home."

"Sounds like there's a story to tell."

"Probably," she said. Nervous, she continued, "So…I finally have a day off. I thought you might, too."

"The best thing about being my age is that every day can be a day off."

"I don't think your freedom from employment is a function of your age," she replied.

Sandy laughed. "Your honesty is going to kill me one day. Shall I pick you up?"

"I'll be in the parking lot at Pink's Hot Dogs."

"Trouble at home?" He sounded concerned.

Greta said, "I am currently without a home."

As she waited for Sandy, she leaned against the old restaurant building, the scent of cooking oil lingering in the air. Timmy would be disappointed, probably angry, to wake and find her gone. He'd sounded so hopeless the night before. She had no idea he felt that way about their relationship—constantly worried she'd leave him.

And now here she was, doing just what he was afraid of. Sort of.

She knew she could solve this problem with Timmy and probably the one with Daphne. But she needed time and space to figure out the best path forward.

For as long as she could remember, other people had muddled her ability to reason well. She hated having lab partners in school and treated them the way her father treated his assistants—ignoring them while she did the work, then reciting findings for them to write down. They never seemed to mind because most were pre-med students, delighted to find an easier path to a good grade.

So now she was calling Sandy to whisk her away from the two people who clouded her thinking the most.

She knew a few things for sure. She loved Daphne. She also loved Timmy. She realized just how much that morning, as she stood over him while he slept, the muscles in his face relaxed, his dark lashes brushing against the bluish skin under his eyes, his lips curling slightly into a smile. He was even happy while sleeping.

She was fairly certain that she wanted to move in with Timmy in that Santa Monica apartment he'd proposed. But she needed Daphne to support her decision.

She had no idea how that calculus would work.

A short while later, Sandy pulled into the empty parking lot, his famous face visible through the rolled-down window of his coupe. At first, she took the car for a Jaguar, but then spotted the winged logo. An Aston Martin, in a classic dark pewter.

She sighed. She loved a well-designed machine.

She hopped in, and Sandy headed north on La Brea. He turned onto Hollywood Boulevard, then merged onto the 101, heading north at about ninety. And on those leather seats, atop those twelve cylinders, it felt like a leisurely Sunday cruise.

She gave him a summary of her roommate dilemma and her current feeling of homelessness.

"You really can't decide who to live with?"

"At the moment I'm considering living alone in a studio in Silver Lake."

"You don't mean that."

Greta harrumphed. After a few minutes gazing out the window, she asked, "Where are we going?"

"You said you needed to get out of town. So we're going to Santa Maria. I grew up there."

They sped through the hills, then entered the Valley. After about forty minutes, Greta saw an exit for Woodland Hills and thought of Timmy, growing up under these sweet blue skies, with parents, aunts, uncles—a bevy of people who loved him freely, if imperfectly.

They drove up the coast. Rather than worrying about direction, Greta let Sandy take charge. He put the Eagles on the stereo and asked her questions about her life. She deflected most of them, saying, "Your life is way more interesting."

"Then you don't know what I find interesting," he replied.

"Conceded," she replied.

At first, as they headed out of Los Angeles, Greta felt bad about abandoning Timmy so soon before a big show. Then she reasoned that she'd already lined up the gear, as well as the crew who would come today to pack the cases. He wouldn't really need her until tomorrow for the show, and she'd be back by then.

After about three hours of driving, Greta saw signs for Santa Maria. The town emerged from the farmlands along the side of the freeway. Sandy sped past the exit.

"We're headed to a small town just north of here," he explained, "called Nipomo. They have the best barbecue in the state."

Sandy exited the freeway and drove into town. At the eastern horizon, brown hills rose above miles of vineyards.

Sandy pulled into a large restaurant. It looked like a humble warehouse, with a shallow-pitched roof and flat exterior walls painted a dull beige.

They stepped through the double glass doors. Even though it was only midday, the place was packed, with a crowd huddled around the hostess stand.

"It's popular with tourists," Sandy said. "But I don't think we'll have to wait long."

And indeed they didn't. When the hostess saw Sandy, she recognized him immediately and greeted him by name. But she didn't sound starstruck, no. She sounded genuinely happy to see him. Interesting.

She led them to a table near the back wall of the immense dining room, where they had a view of the entire place.

"You're from the South," Sandy said. "So I know you grew up with barbecue. I wanted to show you some California barbecue. They don't usually fire up the big smoker at lunch, but I think they might make an exception for us. I worked here when I was in college."

At that point, Greta recalled a conversation she'd had with him a few weeks back. Sandy had told her he'd attended theater school for a couple of years before landing his first role, and that the school was located in Santa Maria.

It was hard to imagine Sandy as a poor college student, waiting tables to get by.

She picked up a menu. "California barbecue," she said, shaking her head. "Although skeptical that such a thing actually exists, I shall withhold judgment until I gather more evidence."

"That's all I can ask," he said, laughing. "Plus, the wine will dull your taste buds."

A deferential server brought two bottles of wine to the table, and Sandy selected one. The glasses were large globes, ten centimeters in diameter. She wondered whether the size of one's wine glass was meant to correlate to some other quality, like fame or income.

She lifted her glass to Sandy. "I think I'd rather drink from a tumbler," she said. "This thing is ridiculous."

He smiled, and Greta remembered a movie poster from the 1980s, his smile and hard jaw the primary features as he looked over a desert horizon from the back of a horse.

For a moment, she forgot where she was.

Who she was.

Sandy said, "What a great idea. No more pretentious glasses." He directed the server to bring them two lowball glasses, then poured and handed one to Greta.

When their meal came, she saw that California barbecue was unlike the vinegary pulled pork from back home. She laughed when her plate was served.

"This is just a steak," she said.

"But it was roasted on a spit. Over a raging fire."

Greta forked some into her mouth. It was spicy and tender. "Your argument is irrelevant," she said. "Because I'm going to eat all the evidence."

They drank a bottle of wine and half of a second. Two hours passed. The restaurant traffic slowed during the lull between lunch and dinner. The hostess kept the tables nearest to theirs empty. Greta figured this was a courtesy for Sandy.

Greta felt full and a little drunk. She leaned back against the plush vinyl of the booth and smiled. Sandy smiled back, raising his tumbler of wine to her in a salute.

Feeling brave, and remembering that old movie poster, she said, "Why would a man like you want to hang out with a girl like me?"

"We've already established you're not fishing for compliments. I'm pretty sure you're not coy either."

Greta made a rude noise. "I'm talking about the basic principles of attraction and repulsion. Ordinarily, a powerful, handsome celebrity would have little interest in me." She paused. "I could understand you wanting to be around Daphne. Everyone wants to be around Daphne."

"Your friend from Rivet? Marco's girl?"

"I don't think she'd want to be called Marco's girl." Greta remembered that Sandy had once thought she herself was one of Marco's girls.

"Nevertheless." He sipped from his tumbler. "Why would I want to hang out with her?"

"Because she's beautiful."

"Beauty's cheap." He laughed. "Or, in the case of my ex-wife and her plastic surgeon, very, very expensive."

"I don't understand why people choose to remodel their faces. It's gruesome." Greta frowned.

Sandy considered her question once more. "Since I don't think you'll believe me if I tell you the whole truth, let's just say I like to hang out with you because you never say something just because you think I want to hear it."

This was an explanation Greta could accept. But she wondered what the whole truth was. She really liked Sandy, in part because he seemed honest, too. She recognized, though, the differences between her honesty and his. Unlike her own, which was driven by a desire for empirical fact, his was a privilege of wealth and power.

Sandy could speak the truth because people had to listen. She spoke the truth because she couldn't bear to lie.

"I don't want to go home," she said suddenly, surprising herself. She pushed aside her feelings of responsibility—toward Pac Lighting, Timmy, and Daphne. And it felt good. "What else is there to do in Santa Maria besides get tipsy?"

"We should go to a spa. They're all over the place up here."

"I've never been to a spa," she said. "I'm not sure what a spa even entails."

Sandy laughed. "You'll love it," he said. "Just not for the reasons that other people do."

———

After he paid the lunch bill, Greta waited while Sandy called his assistant Marlon on his cell phone, who booked them two rooms at a spa near the coast. The drive was about an hour from the restaurant.

Once they were in the car again, Greta asked, "If I hadn't called, what were you going to do today?"

"After yoga, I would have taken my dogs for a walk up in Zuma Canyon. I had a few business meetings, but I had Marlon push those to Monday."

"You dropped everything to pick me up?"

He glanced at her. "Yes."

"But why?"

"Look. At my age, I've seen it all. I've done it all, too, which maybe isn't something to be proud of. The seventies were fun. The eighties, to be frank, were outstanding. Even though my hair had gained some gray and I grew a scruffy beard that is embarrassing today, I had endless adoration." He paused. "You know, Hollywood keeps women unnaturally young, but admires some age on a man." He paused again. "But then the nineties came, and I was suddenly old. The calls stopped coming. My wife left me."

"Are you saying you're a hermit up in your mansion in the hills? Because I see the way people look at you. You're wrong if you think they don't admire you anymore."

He shrugged. "I think I just stopped caring. After the divorce, I bought a run-down house up in Laurel Canyon and fixed it up myself. I immersed myself in the physical work. The deck alone took him three months to build, even with Marlon's help."

"Marlon, he's your personal assistant?"

Sandy laughed. "Something like that. He lives in the apartment over my garage. To me, he's more like an adoptive son. But he's also a lot like you."

"How's that?"

"Maybe a little too much pride to accept a person's help?"

Greta's mouth fell open. "What?"

"I've tried more than once to buy you a drink. You've said no every time. When I paid for lunch back there, I could tell you wanted to say something. You don't like owing people. Marlon's a lot like that."

Frowning, Greta crossed her arms. "You don't have to be so direct about it."

Sandy cracked up laughing. "Pot, kettle, my girl."

Greta smiled. "That's fair." After a moment, she asked, "Can I ask you a super personal question?"

Sandy said, "You can ask it."

"Why haven't you made any movies in so long?"

Sandy shook his head, a wry smile on his face. "It's not that my phone stopped ringing, I guess. It's just one day I realized I hadn't set foot on a set in years. I missed it. But I didn't miss it enough."

"Ah," Greta said. "You like being the hermit on the mountain."

Sandy laughed again. "Maybe I do."

Greta knew some things about Sandy, of course. Stuff that any person could find out, especially if that person were Daphne Saito. He didn't need the money from making movies, even after his ugly divorce. His residuals alone, Daphne told her, brought in close to twenty million each year. But more importantly, he'd made some real estate investments too, buying property all over the area. He was one of the richest men in Los Angeles County.

But to Greta, he sounded lonely. No wonder he dropped everything to pick up a stranded kid by a hot dog stand.

He steered into the circular drive of the spa. The main hotel, an old, three-story, timber-frame building, stood flanked by contemporary outbuildings. He pointed at one of the buildings. "That one has an indoor lap pool and various soaking tubs." He pointed at another. "That one has the gym, yoga studios, and massage and Reiki therapy rooms."

"What is Reiki?" Greta asked, unsure even how to spell the word.

"Oh, man. I can't wait to hear what you have to say about Reiki."

After pulling to a stop and handing his keys to a valet, Sandy offered her his arm.

"Thank you," she said, slipping her hand around his elbow. He placed his hand over hers and led her through the sliding glass doors.

For a moment, she felt disoriented, strolling into an obviously expensive resort with one of the most famous and wealthy men on the planet.

While she tried to regain her bearings, he checked them in. After a second glance of recognition, the concierge greeted him by name. They waited while the man extended the resort's sincerest welcome to Mr. Martin and his guest.

Greta stood, spine stiff, unaccustomed to such fawning being directed at her. She didn't like it. She could feel eyes on her from all around. She wondered if someone had a camera, if she would be in a tabloid tomorrow.

What am I doing here? She asked herself.

And then she remembered. Daphne, Timmy—forcing a choice she wasn't ready to make.

Sandy was still speaking to the concierge. "We'd like massages before dinner," he said. "Private, please. In our rooms."

"Of course," said the concierge, and tapped rapidly on his keyboard. "Your luggage?"

"We don't have any," Sandy said.

At this, Greta chuckled. She wasn't even wearing a bra.

When they reached their floor, Sandy handed Greta the keycard for her room. "Our massage therapists are on their way," he said. "You might want to get ready. See you in an hour or so, and we'll have dinner."

"Thanks, Sandy," and she meant it sincerely.

He winked at her, then entered his room.

Chapter Twenty-Nine

TIMMY

On Thursday morning, when Timmy awoke to find Greta gone, his first instinct was fear, because he was the kind of guy who was protective of the things he loved. And he was really protective of Greta.

When he realized her shoes, bag, and jacket were also gone, he felt aggravated. He didn't bother trying to reach her. He figured she had walked home, and he'd see her in a few hours at work.

By noon, when she didn't show up at work, he was really pissed off. He tried calling her cell phone, but she didn't answer. That's when he started feeling regret, tinged with desperation. He left her two messages over two hours, while his instincts told him she was ignoring him on purpose.

Because he was certain he'd be able to feel it if she were actually in trouble.

Around two in the afternoon, he called Daphne. He hated to bother her at work. Shit, he hated to talk to her at all. He still wanted to strangle her for hurting Greta the night before.

And he was still angry that Daphne was trying to drive a wedge between him and Greta. Why couldn't Daphne let her friend be happy? What the fuck was her problem?

But he never said these thoughts aloud—not to Greta, not to Daphne, not to anyone. The surest way to drive Greta away was to attack Daphne.

It was making him absolutely nuts.

But even more than he resented Daphne, he needed to know that Greta was safe. So he sucked it up and dialed.

"Bertucci Productions," Daphne chirped.

"Daphne. It's Timmy."

Her tone immediately changed. "What do you want?" she snapped.

"Have you heard from Greta this morning? She was gone when I woke up, and she hasn't shown up for work." He heard the desperation in his voice and felt embarrassed that Daphne could hear it too.

"Interesting," Daphne said, as though she were actually saying *wonderful*.

"She didn't go home?"

"No," Daphne said, "I haven't seen her."

"Will you try to call her? I just want to know she's okay."

"She probably went up to Griffith Observatory to read her mother's diaries. That's what she does when you're annoying her."

Timmy's heart shattered at the idea of a solitary Greta reading her dead mother's diaries on the famous overlook. He didn't want her to be alone ever again.

"Just call her, okay? Let me know what happens." He drew a breath. "If you don't want to talk to me, that's fine. You can send me a text."

"Fine," Daphne said, her tone resigned. "I'll call her."

Ten minutes later, Timmy's phone rang. It was Daphne.

"I can't reach her either," Daphne said, her voice tight. "I called three times. And she never ignores my calls."

Fear writhed in his chest. "I'm worried."

"Me too," said Daphne. "I'll let you know if I hear from her." She paused. "Will you do the same?"

Timmy sighed. "Yeah. Of course."

He leaned back in his desk chair and knotted his fingers in his hair, willing himself not to worry. Greta didn't make dumb decisions. She'd probably walked down to Melrose or headed up to the Observatory like Daphne had said.

He turned back to his laptop. He had a show to plan.

But his concentration was shit, and he kept making mistakes.

So he headed out into the workshop to get his hands dirty, but even that was unsatisfying. One of their most expensive moving lights had conked out at a recent event, and he'd dismantled it to repair it.

This is what I do, he thought. I fix things.

But he couldn't figure out how to fix things with Greta.

Chapter Thirty

GRETA

Greta slipped her keycard into the reader and opened the door to her hotel room. Her mouth fell open in surprise.

This was not a room. A room implied a rectangular space with a bed and perhaps other furniture, such as a table and chairs. A lamp. A window, maybe two.

Not this.

This suite of rooms, on the top floor of the hotel, had a lofted ceiling with exposed timber beams and a sitting room with an array of tall windows overlooking the valley below. To the right was a small kitchen. To the left was a passageway to the bedroom.

As she stood there, she wondered how one was supposed to get ready for a massage.

A knock sounded behind her. When she opened the door, a woman entered, pushing what looked like a stripped-down gurney.

Greta greeted her nervously.

"I'm Patricia," the woman said. "Your massage therapist."

Patricia draped crisp white sheets on the massage table, then stepped into the hall while Greta undressed and climbed between the sheets.

For an hour, Patricia's hands pressed and pulled Greta's muscles, revealing to her just how tense she'd been. She kneaded away the last of Greta's thoughts of Timmy and Daphne.

When I get back, Greta thought, things will be different.

After Patricia left, Greta showered and dressed. She sat near the tallest window and pulled out her cell phone. She powered it on, and it beeped over and over, each sound indicating a new voicemail message, twelve in total. Timmy and Daphne had each called multiple times, their voices growing more frantic as the day passed.

Greta felt guilty for causing them to worry. She immediately dialed Daphne.

"Where the hell have you been?" Daphne said. "Timmy and I are flipping out."

Greta was surprised to hear that Daphne and Timmy were doing anything in unison at all.

"I'm in Santa Maria at a spa."

"But your truck is in the carport."

"I'm with Sandy."

The line went quiet for a moment, and Greta wondered if the cell phone had dropped the signal.

Daphne said, "You're at a spa in Santa Maria with Sandy Martin?" Daphne sounded annoyed. "I'm impressed. That's a big fish."

"Sandy is not a fish," she said testily.

"Sure."

"I would never cheat on Timmy."

"That's true," Daphne said.

"You sound disappointed."

Daphne snorted. "When are you coming back?"

"Sometime tomorrow. Whenever we feel like it, I guess." She liked how her words sounded. Acting without a plan was new for her, and it felt good.

But she also wanted to make amends for worrying her friend. She wanted Daphne to understand that, even as she dashed out of town without a word, Daphne still mattered. "I am sorry, Daph."

"What for?" Daphne's voice managed to sound coy and aggravated at the same time.

"I'm sorry that I took off without telling you where I was going." She inhaled deeply before speaking words that might break her and Daphne forever. "And I'm sorry that I'm moving in with Timmy."

"So you've decided."

"Yeah." Greta was as surprised by her certainty as Daphne was.

"I know I should be happy for you." Daphne sounded put out, but not hurt.

Greta smiled, feeling hope in her chest. "Yes, you should."

Daphne sighed. "I'll try to manage it."

"I love you. You'll always be my family, even if we aren't sharing an apartment."

"I love you, too. And I'm so, so sorry about Rivet."

Greta remembered the stricken expression on Daphne's face as she came running after Greta. "I know you are. I knew it that night, but I was too upset to see it."

"You know I only want what's best for you."

"I do. But sometimes you have to let me lead the way, okay? I've been following your lead for so long it's become a habit."

Daphne paused. "You're right. You're so right."

"I should call Timmy now."

"Oh, god. Yes, you should. He's out of his mind with worry."

"I still can't believe you two spoke voluntarily."

"He's not so bad."

Greta grinned. "No, he's not so bad."

After they hung up, Greta contemplated her next phone call. Directly below her window, a large, lagoon-shaped pool glistened under the arid sun. She wanted to sink to the bottom of the pool and rest.

Instead, she braced herself and dialed Timmy's number.

He answered after one ring. "Babe. Are you all right?" He sounded panicked.

"I'm fine. I'm sorry I made you worry."

"Jesus," Timmy said. "I've been trying to reach you since six this morning."

"I left at seven-thirty."

"Damn it. You know what I mean."

"I know what you mean." She never wanted to hurt Timmy. Getting out of town wasn't about Daphne and Timmy at all. It was about figuring out who she wanted to be.

"Why didn't you come into the shop?" he asked.

"A friend asked me to take a little road trip. I'll be back tomorrow." A gentle fib, and necessary.

Timmy was silent for a moment. "What friend? Another guy?" He sounded so angry and hurt.

She hated hurting him. "I'm sorry I left without saying goodbye. I was angry that you and Daphne were pulling me in different directions."

"You should have called."

"You're right."

Timmy sighed. "Where are you?"

She explained where she was. "I'm with my friend Sandy from Rivet. The one who helped me call you last night," she told him. When he didn't respond, she tried to reassure him. "We have separate rooms."

Still, he was silent.

"Timmy, I…" She paused, gathering her courage. "I love you."

He laughed, sounding bitter. Timmy never, ever sounded bitter. Her bones ached at the sound.

"Maybe it is just words with you."

His words struck her like a rock. "You don't believe that."

He was silent.

She waited.

Eventually, he asked. "Will you be back for load-in tomorrow?"

Because he'd hurt her, she wanted to say no. But because she'd hurt him too, she managed to say, "I guess so."

"Can you give me a straight answer?" he asked, his tone cutting. "I need to know if I should arrange more crew."

Greta tried to remind herself that Timmy was hurt and lashing out. She tried to remember that he loved her.

But she failed.

In a cold tone that matched his, she said, "You should call Romero and Dell—Dell knows how to operate a lift, but he needs Romero to keep him on track, otherwise he ends up smoking on the loading dock all night." She kept her tone precise and informative.

She didn't want to reveal what she was feeling. She'd given her love to him, finally, and he'd thrown it back in her face. Saying those words to him was the hardest thing she'd ever done, but it made no difference.

"So you're not coming back for the load-in?"

"No."

"Damn it, Greta." She could hear him drumming his fingers on a table, his desk most likely. "You'd rather be away with a stranger than let me take care of you. What am I supposed to think?"

"It's not just words to me, Timmy." She paused, trying to settle herself. "A few days apart will do us good. I'll be back for the show. I promise."

After a terse goodbye, Timmy hung up. For a long time, she stood by the window, staring at the pool. She and Timmy kept hurting each other despite their love. Sandy had said she had too much pride. She struggled to accept help from other people. Sandy was right.

All Timmy wanted to do was care for her. To take care of her. But because of her pride, she struggled to let him.

Tears fell.

An hour later, Sandy called to say he was in the lobby, on his way up to her room. She'd turned on the television to watch music videos. The music was fine, but mostly she enjoyed trying to name the fixtures that lit the stages and sets. It was a game she and Timmy played. Thoughts of Timmy made her hurt all over, and she was beginning to believe that she deserved the pain.

When Sandy knocked, she didn't answer at first, too wrapped up in her thoughts. When he let himself in, she realized he had a key to her room. For the first time, she wondered what she was doing up in Santa Maria when the man she loved was down in Hollywood.

"Ready for dinner?" he asked. He held a small shopping bag in his hand.

"Can't we just eat up here?"

"I got you something to wear."

He handed her the bag and sat next to her on the couch. She pulled the fancy tissue paper from the bag and tore it open. Inside was a black bathing suit.

"They have poolside dinner service. Steak and lobster and all manner of decadence. I promise you'll like it."

At first, Greta was appalled. Sandy, the bathing suit—a far too intimate gift—and Timmy back home. But then she studied the suit, seeing that it was not a slinky thing, but rather a sleek one-piece, with sensible straps.

She choked when she saw the price tag from the lobby store. It cost eight hundred dollars.

"I can't accept this," she said. "This is way too much money."

"Not to me," Sandy said. "Not at all."

He wasn't bragging, she knew. He was appealing to her common sense.

Too much pride to accept help. Or gifts. A flaw she never understood completely until today.

Sandy reasoned with her. "I dragged you to this overpriced wonderland," he said. "At least let me pay for everything."

"You did not drag me." Greta stood. "But I do accept your gift. I'll meet you in the hallway in five."

They walked down to the pool wearing the thick, brown robes the hotel provided. They sat under a tall cabana by the pool and watched the painted desert sunset, the rapidly cooling air warmed by gas heaters attached to the cabana poles. They ate a meal of sushi so fresh that Greta wished Daphne were there to try it.

After dinner, Greta took off her robe and approached the edge of the pool. She planted her feet on the brightly painted words that proclaimed No Diving. Rolling her head to loosen it, she appreciated the post-massage suppleness of her muscles. After calculating the water's depth, she dove in.

Chapter Thirty-One

TIMMY

Around six o'clock Friday night, Timmy finally accepted that Greta wasn't going to make it back in time for the Hilton load-in. His crew—which included Romero and Dell, as Greta suggested—was helping him finish up at the hotel. Tomorrow, show day, he'd be on site all day, focusing lights and programming the board, then running through the dress rehearsal with the client. And Greta had better be there with him.

She'd skipped out on him before one of the biggest shows of the year. She was worse than Julius.

No, she wasn't. She was gorgeous and good, and that was the fucking problem.

He knew he'd screwed things up Wednesday night. In fact, between him and Daphne, it was no wonder Greta let some strange guy—Sandy something? Who the hell was he?—take her out of town. And then she'd told him she loved him, but he threw it back in her face.

God, he was such an ass.

He needed her to come home, and he needed to know what to say to make things better. Fortunately, he knew whom to ask.

As he drove home from the shop, he dialed Daphne's number. She didn't sound surprised to hear from him.

"She's still not back?" Daphne asked.

"Nope. I was calling to see if you've heard from her today."

"I haven't."

To Timmy, Daphne had always seemed like an exotic creature, beautiful yet dangerous. A leopard who'd rip out your throat if you got too close. But he needed her help desperately. Over the past two days, she seemed to have warmed to him, their fear for Greta's safety —and their feelings of guilt—driving them together.

"This probably sounds crazy coming from me, but I was hoping you could give me some advice about Greta."

"Sure," she said.

"Should we meet at Stir Crazy?"

"Or I can just come to your place and avoid the left turn off Melrose."

"Okay," Timmy said, giving her his address. "I'll meet you there."

Arriving a few minutes before she did, he left the door open for her. When he heard her climbing the stairs, he pulled a beer from the fridge.

"Hey," he said.

Stepping inside, she said, "Can I have one of those?"

"Sure." He grabbed another.

Daphne, always so glamorous, made Timmy feel embarrassed by his ugly apartment. He wished he'd turned on the stained glass before she'd arrived. It was the only beautiful thing he owned.

"Have a seat if you want." Nodding at the couch, he handed her the beer.

To his surprise, Daphne tilted her head back and drank most of the bottle in one chug.

"Damn," he said.

"I was thirsty," she said, smiling.

For a moment, Timmy felt what all men must feel when they see Daphne's smile. She bowled him over, and he liked it.

When they sat on the couch, he put a few feet between them.

"I spoke with Greta after I spoke to you," Daphne said. "She said she'd be back around nine tonight."

"She didn't call me," Timmy said, hating how hurt he sounded.

"I know."

"She told me she loved me, and I told her to fuck off."

"I know that too."

Timmy rested his face in his hands. "It feels like I've lost her."

"You haven't lost her." Daphne touched his shoulder. "Greta's special. She might not have told you this, but you were the first guy she ever kissed."

"She did tell me." At least Timmy had enough sense to feel awed by that tidbit. "Is there anything else I should know?"

"Don't be mad at her for leaving. She does it sometimes. It's like the rest of the world clouds her brain. Even me, sometimes."

"I'm not mad," he said. "I'm just worn out." Then, following Daphne's lead, he chugged the rest of his beer.

Daphne ran her hand down Timmy's back, a sympathetic gesture. Greta had him twisted into knots.

He wondered if Greta even knew. He doubted it. Greta always seemed to underestimate her effect on others.

"I'm sorry, Timmy. I know it's hard." Daphne paused. "Greta and I met in college. My father, well, he thinks he's a good man. But when I was a freshman in high school, our family business, a motel by the beach, was going bankrupt after a hurricane. A guest of the hotel offered money." She paused. "For me."

"That's horrible," he said. "I'm so sorry." His own father was a terrible drunk, but selling a child's body to a stranger? What monster did something like that?

"I knew I could trust Greta almost immediately with even my darkest secrets."

"Yeah," Timmy said, thinking of what he'd told her about his own family. "Same here."

Timmy raised his face from his hands and looked at Daphne. She had a strange expression on her face, like she wasn't completely in the room with him, but stuck in the memory of the awful events of her childhood.

He realized Daphne wasn't his enemy. She never had been. She was broken just like he and Greta were.

"Let me get us another round," she said, gesturing at their empty beers. Her voice sounded odd, as though she were drunk, speaking just a bit too slowly. "You should turn on the stained-glass window. Greta told me all about it."

Daphne opened the fridge to grab the beers, popping the tops with the opener Timmy had left on the counter.

Timmy flipped on the stained glass, bathing the room in purples, reds, and greens, the jewel tones of religious belief. He stood with his hands in his pockets, his head hanging, his shoulders slumped.

"She doesn't need me like I need her, does she?" he asked.

"No." Daphne shook her head.

He felt the truth in her words, and it made him ache.

"But don't feel bad," Daphne said. "She doesn't need me, either."

She paced toward him slowly, reminding him of the big-cat metaphor he had imagined earlier. As he watched her, she locked her bottomless brown eyes with his. She slipped the beer into his hand, letting her momentum carry her body into him.

Time slowed.

She reached up and stroked his cheek with her dainty fingers. She tilted her face up while pulling his face toward hers, and he let himself be pulled. Their lips touched.

Time stopped.

His entire body rebelled at the wrongness. He shoved her away from him, and a loud crash ensued. She flew backward, stumbling, landing on her ass in a puddle of beer from his broken bottle.

"What the *fuck*, Daphne?" he roared. "I'm in love with Greta. Your best friend!"

Daphne scrambled to her feet, slipping on the wet floor, and ran out the door.

As Timmy locked the door behind her, he scrubbed his face with his hands, wondering what the hell just happened.

Chapter Thirty-Two

GRETA

Around nine-thirty Friday night, Greta headed down the pathway to her apartment. Sandy had offered to walk her inside, but she'd insisted she'd be fine. Plus, she didn't want Sandy to witness any possible confrontation with Daphne. She'd be mortified.

She listened as all twelve cylinders churned when Sandy pulled from the curb. Such a sweet automobile.

She never expected to return so late. The food the previous night had been delicious, and the after-dinner swim refreshing. Then, she and Sandy drank poolside martinis, a decadence she surprised herself by enjoying.

After another massage in her room that morning, and the most extravagant brunch she'd ever eaten, Sandy dragged her around the golf course with one of the resort's pros. The entire endeavor took five hours, but it was the most fun she'd had in weeks. She lost four balls in water hazards, bent one putter by accidentally running over it with the cart, and learned she could drive a tee shot 250 yards. The entire trip had been just what she needed to get her head straight again.

She fumbled for her keys as she crossed the courtyard to the door, then jumped back, startled. Someone was sitting in one of the blue lounge chairs. Standing, he stepped into the porch light. Marco Bertucci held a half-empty bottle of liquor in his hand.

"You're not Daphne," he said.

"What are you doing here?"

"Daphne and I had a date," he said, gesturing at his suit and tie. "But she stood me up."

On Halloween, Daphne had set up a date with Marco. Greta had forgotten.

And now Marco was ripping mad.

"I'm sorry," she said, stepping toward the door. "Would you like to use my cell phone to call her?"

"I have a fucking cell phone," Marco said. "She's not answering."

He was drunk, but not terribly so. Just enough to be dangerous. Worried, Greta wanted to appease him and then get inside quickly.

"You should probably call a cab," she said.

"I don't ride in cabs." His voice oozed distaste.

"Um, okay then. Good night, Marco," she said. "Be safe."

She opened the door. As she flipped on the light switch, the world flashed white.

Pain exploding from the back of her head. Kitchen lights burning her eyes.

A man standing above her.

Marco.

A shattering sound. He'd hit her with his liquor bottle when she turned her back.

Her cheek hurt. She must have landed on her face.

"Before you got here, Daphne belonged to me. Then you arrived and took my place. I fucking hate you."

He grabbed her arm and jerked her inside the apartment. She felt her shoulder explode, and she moaned.

"You should never have gotten in my way."

She could barely move.

With distant horror, she watched as he knelt between her legs and unbuttoned her jeans, pulling them down around her knees. He unbuttoned his own pants and lay on her. She shoved against him with her uninjured arm, but he restrained her easily. She tried to scream, but her voice came out weak, nearly silent.

But then Marco roared in frustration and pushed away from her.

Standing, he leaned against the doorway, looking down at her with disgust. She felt warm moisture against her cheek. Tilting her head, she saw a pool of blood forming around her face.

Marco's eyes widened. He buttoned his pants quickly and then pulled Greta's pants back up to her hips.

Then he disappeared.

She closed her eyes, and everything was dark.

———

MARCELLUS

A BOTTLE SHATTERING WOKE MARCELLUS. A MAN'S YELL BROUGHT HIM TO his porch. When he saw a strange man run past the porch, he threw on a shirt and hurried around to the back of the building, where he found Greta lying on the floor of her open apartment. He used her phone to dial 911.

"There's been an attack," he said. "My tenant. There is much blood. She's not moving."

He dropped to his knees next to her.

Her skin was too pale. Her left arm lay at an unnatural angle. He thought—no, he was certain—she was going to die.

"Greta. Can you hear me?" Marcellus held her right hand and rubbed it, willing warmth into her. "Please, wake up."

Her head moved slightly, and she moaned.

"That's it," he said. "Wake up."

Sirens screamed in the distance, coming closer and closer.

"Come faster," Marcellus begged.

He heard the vehicles stop. He ran to the pathway, yelling, "Back here!" Two paramedics came running down the path.

"Are the police coming? Where are the police?" He couldn't keep the panic from his voice.

"They're on the way, sir. Please step back." The two young men knelt at Greta's side.

Soon, a uniformed policewoman arrived. "Sir," she said to Marcellus. "How do you know the victim?"

"I live there," he said, pointing to the front of his house. "I heard a noise, then a man ran past. I came back here to check on things and found her."

"Your name?" she asked.

After the interview, the uniformed officer told him to wait for the detectives. He sat in one of the girls' lounge chairs and watched the officer photograph Greta as quickly as possible, while the paramedics prepared to carry her out on a stretcher. She had an oxygen mask on her face. Her eyes were closed, her hands limp.

The police detective who came was a young Black man. He said his name was Detective Sepulveda.

"Who do you think might have attacked her, sir?"

"I saw a man run past. I didn't recognize him."

"Could you give me a description?"

"It was very dark."

The detective looked at him, eyebrows raised.

"He was a white man. Dark hair. He wore a suit. Not very tall. Her boyfriend Timmy is very tall, and he has lighter hair. It was not Timmy." Marcellus liked Timmy. He didn't stay too many nights at the apartment.

"Did you notice that the victim's pants were unbuttoned when you came to her aid?"

Marcellus felt horribly sick. "Oh, Sweet Mary, no. I just saw so much blood."

Detective Sepulveda said, "Nothing appears to be missing from the apartment, nothing rifled through. Her keys are still in the door, so either she knew her attacker, or he surprised her."

"Okay," Marcellus said, since the detective seemed to want a reply.

"You said you heard the attack?"

"I heard something shatter, and then I heard a man yell. I came outside, and a man ran past."

"Could you describe his face to a sketch artist?"

"I don't think so. I'm so sorry," Marcellus said, and he realized he was crying. "Where are you taking her?"

The detective told him the name of the nearest hospital trauma center. "But sir, you can't leave until we've wrapped up the investigation of the scene."

"This is my home," Marcellus said, suddenly angry. "It is not a scene."

Marcellus watched the detective and his partner—a young Latina woman—examine every inch of Greta's home. The man had said he was with the L.A.P.D. Sex Crimes Division. Marcellus felt even sicker.

But from the detectives' conversation, he could tell that the scene gave them too little to go on.

The man who'd beaten Greta had destroyed his weapon—a liquor bottle—when he pitched it on the patio. All over the patio were shards of glass, the remnants of liquid, and the odor of alcohol. Inside the entry was more glass, the bits that broke when the attacker smashed the bottle on Greta's head.

"Whoever this guy is, he's a vicious bastard," the lady detective said.

The crime scene people gathered blood samples and bagged the larger shards of glass, hoping to find a fingerprint.

Detective Sepulveda came over to him. "The CSI folks will be working for another hour or so, but you don't need to wait for them to finish."

"You found nothing?"

The detective looked grim. "Witnesses will make or break this case."

"She has a roommate," Marcellus said. "I don't know where she is. Her car is gone. She might know something."

The detective placed his card on the kitchen counter with a note asking Daphne to call him when she got home.

"With luck, the victim will be well enough by morning for an interview."

"Greta," Marcellus said. "Her name is Greta."

He entered the apartment, looking at the puddle of blood. He knew it was wrong, but he couldn't help but think about how expensive it would be to clean.

He took a seat on the girls' hideous orange couch and tried to slow his racing heart.

When the door slowly opened, he started. Standing, he met Daphne in the doorway. "Watch your step," he told her.

When she noticed the blood on the floor, she screamed.

"Daphne, be quiet."

"What happened?" she said. "Where's Greta?"

"The detective asked me to tell you his card sits on the kitchen counter. You are to call him now."

"Is she okay?"

"She is not okay," he said. "But she is living."

Daphne stepped over the blood and lifted the card and the note. Her hands shook as she dialed the number.

Marcellus left without saying goodbye.

Chapter Thirty-Three

TIMMY

Timmy arrived at the hospital just after midnight and tossed his keys to the valet, running through the sliding glass doors without taking his claim ticket. Disoriented, he stood for a moment inside the tall, glass-walled atrium. An older woman wearing a pink cardigan sat at the information desk. He jogged over to her.

"Let me guess, young man," she said. "Is your wife in labor?"

Her words were a brick to the chest. "No." He willed himself not to scream at this woman. Her nametag said she was a volunteer. He gave her Greta's name, and she told him Greta was being moved from Emergency to the Intensive Care Unit.

Unwilling to wait for the elevator, he ran up the stairs to the second level. He hurried down the hallway until he reached Greta's room. When he found her, he nearly broke down. Greta lay unconscious on the other side of a glass wall with a bandage around her head and a huge bruise on the side of her face. A nurse stood next to the bed, adjusting something on an IV machine.

A police officer sat outside her room. He stood when Timmy approached.

"I'm her boyfriend. I need to see her." The cop looked at his ID, then wrote down his name.

Timmy shoved open the door. He ran up to Greta's bedside and kissed her, gingerly holding her face in his hands. "Greta, baby. Oh,

Greta." He tasted tears, his own. "Is she going to be okay?" he asked the nurse.

"She's stable now. The bleeding in her brain has stopped. She has a terrible concussion."

"Who did this to her?"

"We don't know." She nodded at the uniformed officer who'd questioned him outside Greta's room and now stood in the open doorway, watching his every move. The nurse continued, "The detective is coming in the morning to question her."

Timmy looked at his hands, wishing he could do something to make things better for Greta.

Seeing Greta's unmoving body nearly made him forget about what he'd done that evening. Nearly. He wished he could forget how Daphne had slipped into his arms as though they'd been planning a rendezvous all along. How he'd let her kiss him.

After Daphne left, he lay on his bed, feet toward the wall, head propped up on his pillows. He stared at the stained-glass lamb on the hill.

Then, three hours later, Daphne called him, screaming about Greta, the hospital, and the police.

And now he was here with his girl, his Greta, the most important person in his life. And yet he felt like he had no right to touch her at all, less of a right than the nurse did, and the nurse was a total stranger.

With Greta's life sitting on the scales, Timmy realized his complaints against her were so trivial. His ego was to blame for everything—for the interlude with Daphne and even for Greta's attack.

She should have been with me, he thought. But I drove her away.

When Daphne arrived a few minutes later, the detective did too. He brought them into the hallway to recheck their IDs, writing their names and their relationships to Greta in his black notebook.

"Where were you last night between the hours of nine and ten o'clock?"

Daphne said, "I was alone in Santa Monica, at the beach."

The detective said, "Can you be more specific?"

Daphne spoke in the most monotone voice Timmy had ever heard her use. She seemed empty. "I drove alone to Santa Monica around eight o'clock and arrived around eight-thirty. I parked illegally at the Merigot hotel on Ocean because my buddy is the head valet. If he sees my car, he doesn't have it towed. I didn't actually see him, though, and I don't know if he saw my car. I'd rather not give you his name if I don't have to because I don't want to get him in trouble. Then I walked out onto the beach and sat in the sand for three hours. Then I drove home. Got home around midnight." She paused. "Then I found…" She paused again. "Then I called you."

The detective made notes. "No one can confirm your whereabouts during the hours of nine and ten o'clock?"

"Not that I know of."

The detective turned to Timmy.

"I was alone in my apartment during that hour."

"You don't have any roommates?"

"No, sir."

"Timmy Eisenhart, right?"

"Yes, sir."

"Any relation to the city councilman?"

"Yes, sir. He's my uncle."

"No kidding."

"No, sir."

"He's a good man."

"I like him a lot, sir." Timmy choked out his final words, holding back tears. Daphne was weeping openly.

The detective flipped his notebook shut. He waved Timmy and Daphne into Greta's room and joined the officer who sat in the chair outside Greta's door.

Timmy walked to the other side of the bed, keeping his distance from Daphne while holding Greta's uninjured hand.

She felt incredibly still.

"We should take shifts here," he said. "I'll go first."

"I'll go home and clean up the…" she paused, "the mess." Daphne covered her face with her hands and sobbed.

Timmy almost felt sympathy for her. Almost.

"Get some sleep," he said. "Come back in the morning. Bring some things for her."

"I'll bring breakfast for us too," she said.

"Don't bother bringing anything for me," he snapped, looking down at Greta's still form. "Just go."

———

AROUND FIVE O'CLOCK IN THE MORNING, GRETA FINALLY OPENED HER eyes. Timmy leaned forward in the dark room.

When she tried to lift her head, she winced. "Don't move, babe," said a voice to her side. Timmy.

"My head feels so heavy. And my shoulder." She tried to move it and groaned.

"Just stay still, okay? I'm going to get the doctor."

"Wait," she croaked. "I was attacked."

"Yes." His voice broke over the word.

"How am I hurt?" she asked. "My shoulder?"

"A dislocated shoulder and a crack on the back of your head. A horrible bruise on your face."

"Anything...else?"

"No," he said quickly. "They did a rape exam. It was clean."

"I guess it wouldn't really matter, since I can't remember anything." She tried to smile, but it hurt.

"It would fucking matter," he said, choking on his words. He kissed her forehead. "Do you remember anything at all? Who did this to you?"

"I...I don't know."

Timmy had the strangest feeling that she was lying, but he couldn't figure out why. And honestly, who was he to get on her case about honesty right now?

"The detective asked me to call him when you woke up, but we'll just wait a while."

"Thank you." She looked around the room. "Where's Daphne?"

"She went home to clean your apartment," he said, perhaps a little too quickly. "She'll be back in a couple of hours. She's bringing you a bag, too."

"How did I get to the hospital? Did Daphne find me?"

"Your landlord did. He heard a loud noise and came around to your apartment. Do you remember riding in the ambulance?"

Greta shook her head and winced.

"Do you need more pain medicine?" Timmy felt so helpless.

She shook her head again, more gently this time.

"God, Greta. This feels like it's all my fault."

"That's ridiculous. Why?"

"If we hadn't been fighting, you would have been with me. You would have been safe."

Timmy knew he had to tell her the truth. She had a right to know everything that happened with Daphne the night before. For a moment, he thought about telling her right then. But fear got the better of him, and he decided to wait until she was healed up more. He tried to convince himself it was for Greta's own good, but he knew that he was lying to himself.

Damn it.

"What is it?" Greta asked, studying his face.

"Something happened with Daphne last night. I called her to talk about you."

"About me?"

"I didn't know what to think when you just disappeared like that."

"I shouldn't have left so close to the Hilton show. I'm really sorry."

"Forget about the Hilton show."

"But isn't it Saturday morning now? And the show's tonight?" She looked at the clock on the wall. "You're supposed to be on site in a couple of hours. You should be asleep."

He pulled his hair. "How can you even be thinking about the show?"

She appeared surprised by his angry tone. "Because I care about Pac Lighting. And you."

God, he wished he could just spit out his dirty secret.

He'd kissed Daphne.

He needed to know if Greta would be able to forgive him. But telling her now would be selfish.

"What did you talk to Daphne about?" Greta asked.

"You just ran off. We didn't know where you were. We didn't know if you were coming back at all."

"Of course I was coming back. My car is here, along with all of my things. I have a lease and, you know, this really great job." She smiled, a crooked smile because of the swelling on her cheek. "And I have Daphne. And you."

Timmy turned his head away, unable to look at what was so obviously love in her eyes. How had he never seen it before?

"Timmy," Greta said, lifting her hand, the one with the IV stuck in it, and grabbing his wrist. "Look at me."

He looked into Greta's eyes, their bright green lit by the dim fluorescent hospital lamp. From the stony expression on her face, he realized he didn't need to explain anything.

She pulled her hand from his and looked at the ceiling. "Tell me what happened."

He had a feeling she knew already.

"Daphne came over to my apartment. I needed to know how to win you back."

"But you didn't need to win me back." She pinned him with a withering glare. "You never lost me."

"I see that now. But I didn't know that yesterday."

"So you called Daphne instead of waiting to talk to me?"

"Well, yes. She knows you better than anyone."

"But you know me, Timmy."

"Do I?"

"When you spoke to Daphne last night, did she tell you I had decided to move in with you?"

Timmy frowned. "No. She did not."

"Did she tell you I was coming back to help you with the show?" Greta huffed. "Just how helpful was this conversation with Daphne?"

"Not very, it seems."

"Of course it wasn't!" she hissed, then shut her eyes, pain marking her face.

He was physically hurting the most important person in his life, and he didn't know how to make it stop.

"But something else happened, didn't it?" she said.

"Yes."

She waited.

"Daphne kissed me."

"She kissed you? Not the other way around?"

"Yes."

"I suppose she'll agree with that assessment of the event?"

"She'd fucking better."

Greta smiled, shutting her eyes. "You should go," she said. "We have a big show today."

For a long moment, Timmy didn't move. He watched her face, hoping she would look at him one more time. She looked pale, sure, and her bruises were terrible. But his Greta was still there, and she was still tough as nails. As he walked from the room, Timmy hung his hopes on one small word.

She'd said *we*.

Chapter Thirty-Four

GRETA

When Daphne arrived at Greta's hospital room in the morning, she was awake and ready for her.

Daphne sat by her bed, an unsteady smile on her face. "Good morning,"

Greta's voice was hard. "It was Marco. You no-showed, and he took it out on me."

Daphne sat back in her chair, her mouth a circle of surprise.

"He was drunk. He tried to rape me, but he couldn't."

"I'm going to kill him," Daphne said, with a fierceness she rarely showed anyone besides Greta herself.

Greta would have shrugged, but her shoulder was screaming at her. "I don't want anyone else to know. I'm not telling the police. The information is yours. I'm sure you'll find a good use for it."

When Daphne tried to interrupt, she held up her hand. "He said you stood him up," Greta said. "And I want you to tell me why."

"Oh my God," Daphne said, studying her face. Daphne could always read her well. "You know already." Daphne's eyes filled with tears. "Did Timmy tell you?"

"He told me some things that happened. But I want to hear your version." She needed to hear Daphne admit what she'd done. She needed to know that Timmy was telling the truth, even though she believed him in her heart. And she needed an apology so she could forgive her friend. Eventually.

Daphne leaned toward her as though to take her hand, but Greta held up her hand once more. "Please don't touch me. Everything hurts." And it did. God, it did. But she'd wanted a clear head for this conversation and had let her pain meds wear off.

"Okay," Daphne said, her voice small. "I tried to—" she paused, "but Timmy, he pushed me away. I fell, actually. Landed flat on my ass."

"Why did you kiss him?" Greta's voice broke. "Why, when you could have anyone?"

"I didn't think he was good enough for you."

"So you tested him?"

"It wasn't a test." Daphne shook her head. "I was trying to save you."

"Save me?" Greta asked, incredulous.

Daphne nodded, eyes shut, tears spilling down her face.

"From what?"

Daphne shook her head. "I didn't think he was worthy of you. It was the only way I could think of to keep him away. You're too perfect, too pure. I didn't think he deserved you."

"You sacrificed yourself to save me."

Daphne nodded, looking ashamed.

"In your own albeit fucked-up way, you were trying to keep me safe."

Daphne nodded again.

Greta knew Daphne was being truthful. Daphne believed, truly believed, that Timmy was no good for Greta. So she'd been ready to sacrifice her friendship with Greta—the most important thing to her —to keep Greta safe. Daphne knew that if Greta discovered that Daphne and Timmy had slept together, she would have hated not only Timmy, but Daphne as well.

Daphne would have given up Greta, Daphne's only family, to protect her.

But for Daphne, the sacrifice would have been worth it.

"I understand," Greta said.

"You do?"

"It's very you, actually."

Daphne gave her a watery smile.

Greta said, "I love Timmy, and I'm going to move in with him. I know I'm taking a chance that he might leave or whatever, but it's the right thing."

Daphne nodded, wiping her eyes.

"A person can have a boyfriend and a best friend at the same time. You have boyfriends all the time."

Daphne sniffled. "You're right."

"You don't have to sacrifice yourself for others. You're worth more than that."

Daphne looked up at her, eyes shiny.

"You heard me. You are worth more than that. Don't do it again, not for anyone. Not even me."

"Okay," she said, her voice shaky.

"You can't pick who I love the way you pick my shoes," Greta said.

"I see that now."

"And even if I wear nicer shoes, I'm still going to be me, Daphne. I'm never going to change into someone else. I'll never want to be the person in the spotlight. You either love me as I am, or you leave."

"I'll always love you, Greta," Daphne whispered.

"I believe you. But you should leave now anyway. I'm still really angry."

Turning her head away from Daphne, Greta faced the shaded window. The morning sun was creeping around the vinyl blinds.

———

ON MONDAY AFTERNOON, AN ORDERLY WHEELED GRETA OUT OF THE sliding glass doors of the hospital. Leaning against his car door, Sandy waited for her.

He gasped when he saw her injuries. She knew she looked awful. Her face was bruised, and her arm was in a sling. Her head was partially shaved, with a bandage wrapped around it. As she approached the curb, her duffle bag on her lap, her bright eyes spilled over with tears.

"Oh, Greta. I'm so sorry."

He opened the door for her, and the orderly helped her in. Sandy tossed her bag in the trunk.

Once he was settled into his seat, she spoke. "Thank you for coming to get me." Her voice choked. "I don't have anyone else. Not right now, at least."

"I'm glad you called."

She told him about her predicament as they headed to his house in Laurel Canyon.

"Your roommate—and sister equivalent—tried to seduce your boyfriend, who is also your boss. Now you're homeless and perhaps unemployed. And pretty beat up to boot."

"Correct."

"But this boyfriend-boss-person. Timmy, right?"

She nodded.

"From what you've been telling me, Timmy didn't seem very interested in being seduced by Daphne."

"Apparently, he pushed her on the floor, and she spilled her beer on herself." Greta smiled.

"So why are you upset with him?"

"Why did he invite Daphne over for a heart-to-heart about me in the first place? Why couldn't he talk to me about me? If I'm the person he…" She choked on another sob. "That he loves, then why is he having secret conferences with someone else?"

"He broke your trust."

"He did."

"But that's a redeemable wrong, Greta. I should know."

"If you say so." She felt doubtful. "Doesn't make me any less homeless, though. Also…" She paused.

He waited.

"I'm scared, Sandy." Her voice shook slightly. She couldn't let go of the fear eating her up inside. "That the guy who did this might come after me again."

"Of course you're afraid. Some bastard nearly killed you in your own home." He patted her knee. "But the solution to that problem is simple. You'll stay in my hermit castle until you're back on your feet." He pulled through tall iron gates into a driveway.

"Here?" She stared at the house as he turned off the engine. It was a magnificent mid-century affair of glass, wood, and steel.

Sandy came around to open her car door. "You make the idea sound preposterous," he said.

"Why would you invite a person—who is at best an acquaintance—to move in with you? That is objectively preposterous."

They entered his house, Sandy carrying her bag, setting it on a chair by the front door. She followed him to the kitchen.

"One old dude living alone in a ten-thousand-square-foot house is preposterous." He rubbed the back of his neck and glanced around his kitchen and dining area, which overlooked the canyon below.

"Your house has ten thousand square feet?"

He nodded.

"You're right. We could probably live here together and never see each other."

"And if you count the deck I built…"

"It really is a nice-looking deck," she said, tapping her lip, glancing out of the floor-to-ceiling windows to the deck beyond. Outside, two medium-sized brownish dogs lounged in the sun.

"Come on." He held out a hand to her, and she took it. "You're safe here."

He hugged her gently, seemingly aware of the pain she was in. She rested her chin on his shoulder and relaxed into him.

Greta stepped back, still holding his hand. "I'll stay here, but only until I'm healed."

"Until you're healed."

She had a feeling that Sandy wasn't just talking about the wounds on her body.

"But I won't have you paying for everything."

Sandy shook his head, quirking a brow at her.

"Right. Too much pride." She sighed. "You can buy me whatever you want." Then she glared at him. "Within reason."

———

That evening, Greta watched the sun set beyond Sandy's deck. She sat in a zero-gravity lounger surrounded by freshly prepared food—soft foods, like smoothies, puddings, and now a lobster bisque. Sandy had locked the dogs inside so they wouldn't steal from the plates.

"Where is all this food coming from?" she demanded when Sandy brought out another dish.

"Here and there," he said with a wink.

"I'm not a baby," she grumbled.

"Of course not. You're just acting like one. Eat the bisque before it gets cold."

After handing her a spoon, he sat in the matching lounger next to her.

"At least you're not feeding me."

"I would never." He sipped his whiskey.

She ate. The soft foods were easy to consume, even with her bruised face. Sandy had known how to help her without her having to ask, and she was grateful.

After eating, she took her pain medicine—Sandy had filled her prescriptions. After a while, the medicine made her sleepy. "I need bed now," she said. "I bet you have great beds."

Sandy helped her to the bedroom where Marlon had put her things. Someone had even turned down the king-sized bed.

"Do you have invisible servants?" she mumbled.

"Yes," he said, chuckling. "I'm going to take off your shoes for you."

"Okay." She sat on the edge of the bed and let him lift her feet.

He removed her sneakers and set them on the floor, then helped her lie back against the bed without rustling her body too much.

After pulling the blankets up over her, he leaned close to her ear. "Greta."

"Hmm."

"Who did this to you?"

Her eyes shot open. "You tried to trick me." She rolled her eyes as the room spun. "I'm so stoned."

He sat down on the edge of the bed. "Just tell me. I think you know."

"How could you possibly know that?"

"Just a feeling."

"Hmm," Greta said woozily. "That's a lie. Try again."

"Jeez, girl. You're half-conscious and still busting my balls."

"Don't care. Spit it out."

"In the car, you said you were afraid. But you sounded like you were afraid of someone in particular."

"Oops." She grinned at him. These pain meds were spectacular. "I told Daphne," she said. "But I don't want to tell you. You might go to the police, and I don't want to involve the police. Statements, testifying, trials…" She sniffled. Oh no. She was about to cry again.

"Greta, no. I won't call the police. I promise." He sounded sincere.

"Good. Okay. I'll go to sleep now." She shut her eyes.

"Tell me so I can keep you safe."

She looked at him, this time a bit of clarity coming back to her gaze. "You won't believe me."

"Of course I will."

"Marco," she said. "It was Marco."

He inhaled sharply, taking in her words. Then he gently brushed her hair back from her forehead. "I'm so sorry."

"S'okay," she said. "Safe now." So safe, she fell right to sleep.

———

When Greta woke, it was dark outside, and her body ached something fierce. By her bed was an old-fashioned bell, the kind you tap the top of, and it dings to call a hotel clerk.

She tapped the bell, suppressing a giggle.

A few minutes later, Sandy strolled in, hands in his jeans pockets. "Pain wake you up?"

"Everything hurts. Ugh. Can you help me take more?"

"Sure. But I also need to talk to you about something."

"Help me up." She tried to scoot to a sitting position, but couldn't manage with one arm. He stacked pillows behind her and gently lifted her so she could see him better.

"I have a plan for how to handle Marco."

Greta's heart raced. "No police. You promised."

Sandy held out his hands, a placating gesture. "No police. But he can't get away with this. Until he's handled, you won't feel safe. You may not even be safe."

"What did you have in mind?"

He told her his plan. It was brilliant.

"I have one condition," she said. "I want you to call Timmy. Let him help you. It's like, a thing for him. He hates feeling helpless, and I know he feels helpless right now."

"Timmy Eisenhart? Brian's son?" Sandy grinned. "My girl, I was already planning to."

When Greta relaxed back into her pillow once more, she felt as though her world were finally reassembling itself as it should.

Chapter Thirty-Five

TIMMY

On Sunday, when the phone rang with Greta's number, Timmy answered immediately. He'd waited patiently for her to let him back in, but it took all of his energy to do so. He'd barely kept it together during the Hilton show that night. It was midnight now, and his crew was striking.

He would drop everything for her, and he didn't care one bit.

"Hello? Greta?" Timmy answered urgently.

"Not Greta," a strange man said. "But she's staying with me. You and I need to talk."

Later that night, Timmy pulled into the 1950s-era diner off Sunset that Greta's friend had described, then sat in a booth and waited.

"Timmy Eisenhart," a man's voice came from behind him. Then the mysterious Sandy sat across from him.

Timmy leaned back, his mouth falling open. "You're Sandy?"

The man nodded.

"I'm sorry, man. Give me a minute."

Greta had never said. She had talked about her friend Sandy a lot, "The only person at Rivet who doesn't give me brain cramps."

He was also the person she'd reached out to, twice, when she was desperate.

But Greta's Sandy was...He was Alexander Martin. The Alexander Martin. Timmy was in absolute shock. "But you're *you*." He finally found his voice.

"Is that a question?"

Timmy studied Sandy closely but couldn't get a read on the guy.

Sandy flagged down the waitress and ordered a couple of coffees. "Is coffee okay with you?" he asked Timmy.

Timmy nodded. Once the waitress moved on, Timmy continued. "Why would you be hanging out with Greta? What do you want with her?"

"As her boyfriend, I think you'd be the best person to describe her wonderful qualities."

"As her boyfriend, I am quite familiar with her magnificent qualities, yes."

"Are you saying I shouldn't want to hang out with Greta?"

"I'm saying I find it curious that a movie star…" Timmy frowned. "Correction. I find it curious that Oscar-winning, bazillionaire, movie-fucking-royalty wants to hang out with my Greta."

"Are you saying there's something wrong with Greta?"

Timmy was going to strangle the guy. "No. I'm saying there might be something wrong with you."

"Fair enough." Sandy actually laughed. "How about this: I find her enchanting. Brilliant. Brutally honest. Unique. I considered kissing her once, oh, maybe twice, but I didn't—because she deserves better than me. Even if I am Oscar-winning, movie-fucking-royalty."

"We're seeing eye-to-eye, then."

The waitress returned and set down their coffees. Her eyes lingered on Sandy, and it looked like she was going to either pass out or say something. Sandy gave her a kind smile. She pulled out a pen and her order pad, handing them to him.

"What's your name, love?" he asked.

"Rebecca." She fingered the hair of her brown ponytail, her darkly lined eyes disguising her youth.

Sandy wrote a short note and signed it, then handed the pad and pen back to her. He picked up his coffee and looked at Timmy.

Timmy supposed even movie-fucking-royalty could be decent.

"Now that we're seeing eye-to-eye," Sandy said, "I have a proposition for you."

"Is Greta safe?"

"She's safe. But I want to make sure she stays that way."

Timmy gasped. "She told you who hurt her."

Sandy nodded.

"I want to help." Timmy felt so fierce he thought his bones might rip from his skin.

Sandy smiled, a smile quite different from the one he'd shown Rebecca. "I thought you might."

———

THE NEXT MORNING, MONDAY, TIMMY FOLLOWED SANDY INTO CITY Hall. City Hall was a tall Art Deco building that shone brightly in downtown L.A. Timmy felt nervous, even though he knew he and Sandy were doing the right thing. He just wished the right thing didn't involve doing things that seemed a little wrong.

They took the elevator up to the floor where his uncle's office was located.

"This way, gentlemen," Brian Eisenhart's secretary said after they entered the office suite. The young man led Timmy and Sandy into a large office.

"Sandy!" Brian Eisenhart said, shaking Sandy's hand. "What's it been, a year?" His uncle, tall and fit, wore a tan-colored suit, a white shirt, and a light blue tie. He looked like the governor of a nearby state. Sandy, in jeans, cowboy boots, and a casual button-down, still managed to look put together. Timmy, in his khakis and polo shirt, felt scruffy.

"Since the fundraiser for the Tar Pits Museum, I think," Sandy said.

"Too long."

"I agree."

Timmy watched them, completely surprised.

"Did you know he was my uncle that night at the diner?" he asked Sandy.

"I did," Sandy said. "Greta told me. Plus, you favor each other."

"Timmy," his uncle said. "Come here." His uncle shook his hand, but then quickly dropped it and hugged him instead. "It's good to see you. You should come downtown more. Let me buy you lunch."

"Okay, sure." He loved his Uncle Brian more than his own father, he realized. He might have grown up with chaos, but Brian had been a safe person for him his entire life.

Brian gestured for them to sit at a collection of leather chairs gathered around a coffee service.

"Now," he said. "Tell me everything."

"There's a piece of land I want to buy," Sandy said. "The city's leasing it to someone else, though."

"If the city is willing to part with the land, it's easy enough to break the lease. But tell me," Brian Eisenhart said, leaning forward. "Which is more important: getting your hands on the land or breaking that lease?"

Sandy placed his hand on Timmy's arm when Timmy would have spoken, saying, "I'm willing to overpay in the most absurd fashion for this piece of land, so long as the deal happens quickly and quietly."

Uncle Brian's real line of work was development—long before he was a Los Angeles city councilman, he built buildings, bridges, and roads, and all sorts of other large-scale structures in southern California. The stained-glass window in his apartment was a gift from him.

If land could be made to move quickly, Brian Eisenhart could do it.

"What about you, Timmy?" his uncle said. "What's your stake in this?"

"Sandy and I are going into business together. A side venture."

He and Sandy had planned this answer. They wanted to give his uncle some plausible deniability.

"I see," his uncle said, leaning back in his seat, placing his hands together in front of his lips.

Timmy wondered exactly what his uncle saw. The man was not stupid.

"I'm willing to take this on, of course. But I don't know how much I can do until I know what land we're talking about. Hang on." Standing, he opened his office door, calling in his secretary. "Sandy, could you please describe the location to Joel? He can pull up some maps for us to look at."

Sandy gave Joel the general location of Rivet, who nodded and went off to find the maps.

While they waited, Sandy asked Timmy's uncle about a board they used to sit on together and how Timmy's aunt was doing.

He was really good at this, Timmy thought. He's done it before.

Timmy shook his head. He didn't want to know.

A while later, Joel entered, carrying a large bound book of maps. He set the book on a console table and flipped to the proper page. Brian Eisenhart stood and motioned for Timmy and Sandy to join him.

"Is this the parcel?" he asked.

Sandy studied the map, then nodded.

"Your side venture wouldn't happen to be the restaurant business, would it?"

"Perhaps," Sandy said.

"Hmm," Brian Eisenhart said. "There isn't even water service out there, apart from that one building that's in use. The rest of those buildings were once used for storing street cleaners. They're empty now." He eyed Sandy closely. "If we do this deal, you won't be able to develop any other building on the property." He pointed to a spot just north of Rivet's location, "That spot serves as a watershed for flash floods off the Palisades. This—" he pointed at Rivet, "is the only building safe from flooding on the whole property."

"In other words, the land is pretty much worthless."

"Yep."

"What about a park?" Timmy asked. "Playground equipment? Couldn't that take some water now and then and be okay?"

"Brian," Sandy said. "Do you want a park?"

"Sandy, I would love a park."

Smiling, Timmy climbed into Sandy's car at the valet stand in front of City Hall. He liked the feeling of the plan coming together.

Sandy surprised him, saying, "Your park suggestion was a stroke of genius."

He flushed under the praise. "Thanks."

"It's obvious your uncle really loves you."

Timmy nodded. "He and my Aunt Sally couldn't have kids of their own. And my father, Brian's brother, wasn't around much. Brian stepped in."

"I'm guessing there's more to that story than you're telling me right now."

Timmy nodded. "Maybe another time." As they rode west on the freeway, Timmy asked, "Any word from the studio?"

Sandy pulled out his cell phone and checked for messages. "Not yet."

The second part of the plan involved getting word to the proper places at Universal about just how commingled Marco Bertucci's interests were. Timmy had no idea how much Marco was conning the studio. But Sandy did, and people listened to him.

Must be nice.

So now, the right people were going to learn how much the studio was paying for Marco's restaurant hobby. And if Sandy could get enough people angry, he and Timmy could shut him down entirely.

Timmy said, "It must be nice to be you. To have anything you want so easily." He sounded bitter to his own ears.

"Do you know why I called you that first night?"

"You wanted help getting back at Marco."

Sandy glanced Timmy's way. "Do you really think I needed your help getting back at Marco?"

Timmy snorted. "No."

"I called you because you and Greta—you're a good thing."

"How could you possibly know that?"

"I've seen enough bad things to know a good thing when it comes along."

Timmy rode quietly as Sandy drove west. As he merged onto the 101, Timmy asked, "When can I see her?"

"Did you really push Daphne down into a beer puddle?"

"It sounds extreme when you put it like that."

Sandy laughed.

"Could we stop by my place first, though? I want to get my car so I can bring her home."

"Feeling sure about yourself?"
Timmy scoffed. "Not in the slightest. But I like to be prepared."

Chapter Thirty-Six

GRETA

Standing in Sandy's kitchen, Greta tried to figure out his espresso machine. He'd made cappuccinos for her all weekend, but he left early that morning for a work meeting, and she was missing the buzz. The machine was light blue and tied into the house's water supply. The bean hoppers sat on top, one full of decaf and one full of regular. She had a gallon of milk sitting on the counter next to her, ready to pour into the frothing cup.

The problem was that the labels on the buttons were in Italian. Which one did the grinding? Which shot steam? And how much steam? Enough for one shot or two? If this machine were hers, she'd use a label maker and put English instructions on it, if only to help houseguests.

She held the portafilter in her right hand, wishing she could remove her left arm from its sling for this one task. But her left shoulder still hurt, even with the painkillers. Plus, she really wanted it to heal well. Anterior dislocations, according to the hospital's orthopedics team, were notoriously tricky.

She made her best guess as to the location of the grinder spout and placed the portafilter underneath. She pressed one button, but steam shot out of a different spout. She pressed another button. More steam. The third button, however, made a promising rumble, and ground coffee shot from the grinder spout and into the portafilter. When it looked full, she turned off the grinder.

But then she was stymied once again.

"Damn it!" she yelled.

"What's the matter?" a voice asked from behind.

Startled, she shrieked, throwing the portafilter as hard as she could at the person who'd snuck up behind her.

Sandy ducked, and the portafilter dinged the wall behind him before dropping to the floor, spraying ground coffee everywhere.

"Sandy!" she said, seeing his surprised face. "I'm so sorry."

"No, Greta. No. I'm sorry." His voice was pitched low. He didn't take a single step closer to her.

Her hands were shaking. Actually, her whole body was. "I need to sit down."

"Yep," he said, matter-of-factly. "Living room? Deck?"

"Deck."

Sandy led the way, still keeping his distance, opening the door and leaving it ajar for her to pass through.

"It's all right. I'm done being startled."

"I've had enough friends who fought in enough wars to know what traumatic stress looks like." As he helped her settle in her chair, he said, "You tell everyone who loves you that they're not allowed to sneak up on you, ever."

"Also, that I might accidentally knock off their heads if they do."

"Nice throw by the way. But why were you angry at my espresso machine?"

"I realized I couldn't tamp the coffee with one hand."

Sandy sighed, looking angry at himself. "I shouldn't have left you here alone all day."

"I wasn't alone. I had your dogs."

Sandy shook his head. "Jodie and Foster are not much help."

"Yeah, they didn't even bark when you came in."

"They never bark when it's me."

Greta tilted her head. "Does she know they're named after her?"

"She's the one who named them."

At that piece of news, Greta just shook her head. Sometimes the surreal world she now lived in evaded even her own ability to measure.

"Regardless," Sandy continued, "I should have had Marlon come sit with you."

It was Marlon who had gone to get Greta's stuff from her old apartment and bring it all up here. Right now, her truck was parked in Sandy's spacious garage. Her necessary things were unpacked in the room she was staying in—Marlon did that, too—even though she'd said she wouldn't be staying long.

It had been Daphne who'd packed her things. At the thought of Daphne, her chest ached. She missed her friend.

To Sandy, she said, "He can babysit me the next time you need to go out, okay?" She was getting good at this accepting help thing.

"Have a seat. I'll make you a coffee."

"Make it a decaf. I need a nap after all of that excitement." Although her body had stopped shaking, she felt like she'd swum five kilometers in open water.

"One more thing." Sandy's expression turned serious. "Someone wants to talk to you, and I think you should hear what he has to say."

"This someone is here?" Her heart started racing. Although she told Sandy to reach out to Timmy, she didn't expect him to show up so soon. She looked like crap, and their relationship was on shaky ground.

"Outside the house. I wouldn't let him in without your permission."

Greta lay back in her lounger, considering. Did she want to see Timmy? Yes, of course she did. She loved him. But how did he feel about her, after everything?

Sandy interrupted her thoughts. "It's so obvious he loves you, Greta. It comes off him."

"I suppose you can tell that I love him too."

"I suppose that's true."

"Send him out then."

SHE HEARD THE SLIDING DOOR OPEN, AND SANDY ENTERED THE HOUSE. The dogs barked—he must have opened the front door. When she heard footsteps on the deck boards behind her, her hand tightened on the deck chair.

When he dropped to his knees next to her, taking her hand, tears blurred her vision.

"Hey, babe," he said.

"Hey," she choked out, and the tears spilled over.

"No—oh no. What's wrong?"

"Nothing. I swear. I mean," she said, "except the obvious."

"Sandy said you know what we did today."

She nodded.

"He also said that you asked him to bring me in on it. To let me help make things right for you."

She nodded again. "I did."

He kissed the back of her hand. "Thank you for that. I hate feeling helpless."

"I know that now."

"And you hate feeling like you owe people."

"Yeah," she gave him a wry smile. "I know that now, too."

"When I was young," he said, "and my father was a constant source of chaos, I believed the best thing I could do was be useful. Fix things. Be the one who showed up for my mom because he wasn't going to." He blew out a breath. "I didn't even realize that I never stopped. I've been doing that with you. I think sometimes I did it because I needed to for myself, not because you needed me to. I've been trying to take care of you because I was afraid you'd leave if I couldn't."

"You weren't wrong—I kept pulling away every time you wanted to be closer to me. I was afraid of what it would cost me to let you take care of me. I knew you loved me—*love* me—but after a lifetime of my father using his power and money to jerk me around, when you gave me something I felt I hadn't earned, I ran. God." She was angry now. "I hate that he's still controlling my life from a distance. He almost ruined the best thing that's ever happened to me."

Timmy gazed at her, blue eyes twinkling. "Oh, you mean me?"

She rolled her eyes. "Oh my god. What else would I be talking about?"

Timmy grinned. "Just making sure."

Greta sobered. "I'm sorry I ran off before the Hilton show. It was wrong."

"I'm sorry I gave you an ultimatum."

She gazed into his eyes for a long time, letting the truth of his apology settle around her, along with his unconditional love, so unlike what she felt from her father. Timmy was nothing like Jim Donovan.

Finally, Timmy said, "I assumed I knew what you needed instead of asking. I won't do that again. We're a team, if you want to be."

"I've figured out how to let you do things for me. But I'm still going to make mistakes. Be patient with me, okay?"

"I can do that."

Leaning forward, he kissed her gently, careful of her bruised face.

As Timmy sat in the lounger next to her, she heard Sandy's phone ring inside the house, and his voice. She couldn't make out his words, but a few minutes later, he came out to join them.

Sandy said, "You two okay? Need anything?"

Greta smiled. "We're good."

Timmy said, "I'm fucking great, actually."

Greta chuckled. "Yeah, okay. Me too."

"Good news," Sandy said, holding his phone. "I just heard back from Brian. Marco's lease is done for. The city is calling it in for a future land transfer to some investment group."

Greta glanced from Timmy to Sandy. "You are the investment group, yeah?"

"Well…" Sandy said.

"Um…" said Timmy. "So, we three are the investment group."

"Wait," she said. "What?"

Sandy ignored her question. "The sale will take a little while longer to put together, but Rivet will be temporarily shuttered by the end of the month. "Faster, perhaps, than is strictly appropriate, but Marco won't be in a position to argue."

"Why not?" she asked. "Oh! The other part of the plan."

Sandy nodded. "That was Universal on the phone. Not only are they so very interested in Marco's side hustle to shut down his production operation, but they're also bringing in the State Bureau of Investigation to launch an embezzlement investigation." Sandy smiled. "Marco will either be in jail or out of the country within the week."

"He'll be gone? Are you sure?" Greta said.

"He is certainly never coming back to Los Angeles," Sandy said. "And if legal channels don't make it happen, I will."

"You're scary, dude," Greta said.

"Only when it comes to my friends."

At the word *friends*, Greta smiled.

"So you own a restaurant now," Greta said to Timmy. "That's two businesses. You'll be so busy I'll never see you."

"No, Greta. We—the three of us—own a restaurant now."

She shook her head, not understanding his words. "No, Sandy is the silent partner, right? And you're the day-to-day guy. That was what we planned."

Sandy said, "I'm going to head back in and let you sort this out."

"Traitor," Timmy said.

Sandy was still laughing as the sliding door closed, giving her and Timmy privacy.

She turned to him. "What do I have to do with Rivet? I'm just sitting around drinking smoothies all day."

"You're an equal partner on the paperwork."

"I'm what?" she said, her voice rising.

"I told Sandy that I wanted to give you half of my share in the restaurant. And then he thought it would be better if we split it three ways."

She blinked at him a few times in shock. "Do either of you understand math?"

Timmy laughed. "Not as well as you, no."

Greta dropped her face into her palm in frustration and then squawked when she hit her bruise. "Do you see what you just did? Your idiocy caused me actual physical pain."

"If you don't want it, I'll make him change it. But Greta, I want to share this with you. I want to build a life with you."

The tension left Greta's shoulders. She could accept this generosity, even if it chafed a little at first. "Help me up?" she asked.

Timmy helped her to her feet, supporting her whole body as though he knew just where she were hurting. They shuffled to the railing. The edge of the deck overlooked a twenty-meter drop into the canyon below, and farther off, the Pacific. As they leaned against the railing, Timmy's left arm wrapped around her waist, holding her close. She liked how it felt to be held by him.

She wanted him to hold her forever.

"Greta, babe." He tucked her good hand to his chest. "I'm going to want to share things with you. Not to control you or trap you, but because I love you. Do you think you could let me do that?"

At his words, warmth suffused her body, melting away some of the pain. She nodded. "In fact, I'll start now. I forgive you for making me a partner in the restaurant even though it was a terrible financial decision."

Timmy laughed. "That is a start, I guess."

"Speaking of forgiveness, I should call Daphne and let her know I'm okay."

Timmy hesitated. "What she did to us, Greta? It was wrong."

"You don't have to understand it, but I do. She thought she was doing the right thing."

"How was trying to seduce me the right thing?"

Greta paused, thinking of Daphne's awful secret. How that one nightmarish afternoon defined her. "You'll have to trust me."

Timmy took a deep breath. "It'll be hard to be around her for a while, but I can manage."

Greta rested her head on his shoulder. "I spent my whole life holding a grudge against my father for all of the things he did to hurt me and my mom—sleeping around, acting like an overbearing ass, bullying me. But my mom gave me a new perspective recently and helped me see his point of view. I need to work on forgiveness. And understanding other people's perspectives, especially when it comes to me. It's my blind spot."

Timmy opened his mouth to speak, but she held up her hand. She didn't want to hear his protestations about how she was perfect or some nonsense like that.

"I know it's true. It'll always be hard for me to see where other people are coming from. But part of it is me not wanting to. Before Daphne, no one ever interested me enough to try. I was content to be alone."

"But you don't want to be alone anymore, right?" When she didn't answer right away, he said, "Now is when you say, 'That's right, Timmy.'"

"That's right, Timmy," she parroted with a small smile, teasing him.

He laughed. "I just wanted to be clear, since I'm not letting you go." He pulled her closer, and even though it hurt some, it also felt really, really good.

"Daphne and I are a package deal. She is the only family I have. My mother is dead. My father is estranged. She's it. And I know, if we all try, we can strike a balance."

Timmy smiled down at her. "And if she and I start sniping at each other, you will not run off with a movie star to some exotic locale?"

Greta frowned, feeling guilty. "I didn't know it would hurt you so badly—see? That's what I mean. I couldn't see your point of view. About the running off. About telling you I love you. I hurt you without meaning to. I'm sorry."

"It's time you come clean about that trip," Timmy said, his face serious.

"Okay," Greta said, hating that Timmy was still worried. "But really, nothing happened with Sandy. I promise."

"You must be completely honest with me."

"I am," she said, as sincerely as she could.

"Good. I have one more question."

She nodded, nervous.

"Was it a total blast?" He grinned.

Relieved, Greta laughed, even though it hurt her bruised face. "It was! Completely over the top. I had my first massage. It was in my room, which was the size of an entire house. And you wouldn't believe the food, which we ate poolside, naturally. And I played golf. Golf!" She laughed again. "What a preposterous game. Such a waste of natural resources."

"We should go back there together."

"Someday," she said. "Maybe in a few years. It was outrageously expensive. We need to be conscientious about money for a while."

Timmy grinned maniacally.

"What is wrong with you?"

"Nothing."

Greta snorted. "Liar."

His eyes heated. "You just said 'in a few years.'"

Turning his back to the railing so that they faced each other, he rested his hands on her hips. The magnificent view became a backdrop to his handsome face.

"I did say that, didn't I?" She hadn't even thought about her words. They'd just tumbled out.

"No take-backs," Timmy whispered, then he kissed her, a brief brush of the lips, so gentle it didn't hurt at all.

"I don't want to take it back," she said, breathless.

He held her to him. "You are my brightest light."

As she leaned against his chest, her universe finally made perfect sense.

What's Next in the Hollywood Lights Series?

Daphne's story continues in *Chasing Chaos*.

Although Daphne and Greta have long since mended their friendship, Daphne hasn't reckoned with the guilt of the awful night Greta was attacked. Will she be able to forgive herself and find love?

And be sure to catch the rest of the award-winning Hollywood Lights series, now complete, at hollywoodlightsseries.com.

———

Are you a neurodivergent creative like me and looking for support? Do you want to keep up with my writing and get an inside peek at my process, including early pages? Subscribe to my letter at pryalnews.com.

Acknowledgments

This book could not have been written without support from many fronts.

First, thank you to my writing partner of twenty years, Lauren Faulkenberry, who pushed me through so many drafts of this book and of the entire Hollywood Lights series, holding my hand the entire way. May everyone find such a supportive friend one day. Go read her books. They're fantastic.

Thank you to my writer friends who have supported me as I worked on the Hollywood Lights Series and other books through the years: Camille Pagán, Kelly Harms, Ayla Samli, and Rachel del Grosso. Go read their books, too.

Thank you to the local coffee shop in Chapel Hill that keeps me fed and watered: La Vita Dolce in Southern Village. Thank you for never complaining about my sitting at a table all day. I need to step out of my writing cave sometimes, and you always welcome me.

Thank you to my writing friends who first read the early drafts of Entanglement: my Durham writing group, Todd Levins and Leslie Frost, and my long-distance writing friend, Rinku Patel.

Lastly, thank you to my inspiration, my whole entire life: my two backyard sprites, A. and E., and my tectonic plate, Michael.

About the Author

Katie Rose Pryal, J.D., Ph.D., tells stories about the outsiders, the misfits, and the beautifully complicated. She is a Bipolar-AuDHD author of many books of fiction, nonfiction, and memoir.

Her books include *Your Kid Belongs Here: An Insider's Guide to Parenting Neurodiverse Children* (Johns Hopkins, 2025), *Life of the Mind Interrupted: Essays on Mental Health and Disability in Higher Education* (Blue Osprey, 2017), the IPPY-Gold-winning *Even If You're Broken: Bodies, Boundaries, and Mental Health* (Blue Osprey, 2019), and the IPPY-Bronze-Winning *A Light in the Tower: A New Reckoning with Mental Health in Higher Education* (Kansas, 2024).

Her Hollywood Lights romance series includes *Entanglement* and the IPPY-Gold-winning *Take Your Charming Somewhere Else*. Like all of Katie Pryal's writing, the series centers neurodiversity, in addition to angsty romance, star-crossed lovers, sexy woodworkers, movie stars, and happily-ever-afters.

She lives in Chapel Hill, North Carolina, with her spouse, children, and many, many animals. Subscribe to her monthly letter at pryalnews.com.